THE STEGAN BREACH

THE STEGAN BREACH

Clive Eastman

PARTRIDGE
A Penguin Random House Company

To order additional copies of this book, contact
Toll Free 800 101 2657 (Singapore)
Toll Free 1 800 81 7340 (Malaysia)
orders.singapore@partridgepublishing.com

www.partridgepublishing.com/singapore

PROLOGUE

(TWO YEARS AFTER THE COMMENCEMENT OF THE STORY)

Ming had been shopping for a black "Eric Javits" Swinger Wide-Brim Hat to go with her "R29" black chic outfit. This would sort the men from the boys she mused.

She is a most beautiful and intelligent woman and is well trained as a spy with the US government. She is unpredictable, and she is dangerous. As she swayed down the road with her hips rolling, she was aware of the eyes that were following her. She scanned for any eyes, which seemed out of the ordinary and noticed she was being followed and coolly observed by two men dressed in dark suits, each with a single chest bulge showing from its size to her trained eye that they were packing "Glock 19s."

These men were not following her for her beauty; she thought, but to kill her as "payback" for the loss of the prototype that they believed she caused. She was not responsible for planting the bomb in the device that would revolutionize telecommunications and bring about a technological Renaissance in science. This was planted by another organization preventing any other from seizing it, the dog in a manger attitude held by many organizations today. Her own faction of four colleagues had died in the explosion while she was attending to matters elsewhere. The fact that she did not die made her the guilty party.

She did not return directly to her safe house, because it should be known to her and her colleagues alone, and she did not want any opposition agents learning of its location through her carelessness. She performed the nesting bird's tactic and led the agents in the opposite direction for about one and one-half kilometer from her apartment. From this position, she twisted and turned until she managed to evade them before returning home.

However, all her efforts were wasted as the opposition agents already knew of her safe house and location.

Ming being a very experienced operative realized that there was a high likelihood that they already knew where she lived and wanted to put her off guard by pretending to lose her trail.

She would wait for them to come to her tonight and then move to a different safe house. She rang her control to let her know the situation and to arrange for a new safe house for that evening onwards.

Ming did not have to wait long for her unwelcome visitors to arrive. She could feel them entering her apartment. She sensed and then saw their shadows furtively opening the front door. She knew that they had come to kill her. She crouched down next to a large lounge chair in a half light coming in through the French window and waited for them to enter the room completely. Once in the room, she fired up at the first agent, mortally wounding him. Standing up, she aimed at the center of the forehead of the second agent, killing him instantly. Moving over to the first agent, kicking the gun from his hand, she says, "What country are you from?" When he did not answer, but only groaned, she left him and made her way over to the dead agent and rifled his pockets for any identification. As expected, there was nothing in his pockets except his hotel/motel key, for room fifteen, Salamander Bay Resort. As she pocketed the key, she thought she can probably find the rest of his compatriots at this address and get rid of them before they come looking for her. She left the apartment and walked down a flight of stairs. The dead agents were two of the five foreign agents who initially suspected that her group planted the bomb into the prototype. But when only she survived the explosion because she went looking for Roger, suspicion immediately fell onto her.

At the bottom of her stairs, she could see into the street and could see a large Toyota Avensis Wagon with the remaining colleagues of the two dead men getting out of it and preparing to come up to her apartment.

She descended to the next floor below and waited for them to pass her. Once, they had gone upstairs Ming rushed out into the street and looked inside the Avensis to see if the driver had left his keys in the ignition. He had done so, so she now had wheels and without wasting a second more, she drove off before the remaining agents could give chase.

After a few minutes, she pulled off the main road and into a side road where she checked the glove compartment for any car rental agreement. Finding nothing, she then entered the name of the dead agent's hotel into the GPS that had come with the Avensis. When the address appeared, she drove there and on arrival checked her Sig Sauer M11 equipped with night sites. After walking around to ensure that she wasn't being watched, she entered room fifteen, and searched for anything that could tell her who these men were. She found in the waste paper bin under the desk a boarding pass stub, showing that this agent had originated in Belgrade and had flown on the Russian Airlines Aeroflot. She looked into his wardrobe and the drawers in the wardrobe and in the drawers of the side tables next to his bed and found nothing. This person was not planning to stay long.

She rang her control explaining that there were still agents in her apartment and asked her to send a cleanup squad and seal the apartment after ascertaining that it was no longer being occupied by anyone. Sealing would prohibit its use until sometime in the future when this safe house had cooled down.

In the afternoon, when the three agents eventually returned to their motel by taxi, she shot dead with a bullet to the head the first agent as, he was getting out of the taxi. This was followed by several bullets to the body of the second agent. The third agent was almost ready to fire back, but was not quick enough to prevent a bullet, one in the throat and another in the head. The taxi driver was in a state of panic and was screaming like it was he, being attacked. He put his foot on the accelerator and took off like he was the one being shot at. Ming sauntered over and got into the Avensis, driving off to get something to eat as she had not eaten all day. She drove to Roger's area to look for him to join her in an early evening meal.

Ming and her colleague, Roger, both held a PhD degree in particle physics. They met at an International Conference on particle physics and after talking, they found that they worked at nearby Universities and lived quite close to one another. This allowed them to meet and socialize together.

With her special lecturer's pass, thanks to Roger, she could drive into the University grounds and park next to Roger's offices.

She walked over to Roger's office and called to him from the main door connecting to the building corridor. A minute later, appearing in the corridor, she heard him reply with "Who is it?"

Ming asked gently, "Can we go and have something to eat? I am famished."

Roger answered, "Sure."

They drove in Ming's stolen Avensis. Roger asked, "Where did you get this car and where are we going?"

She answered, "From three guys I killed on my way here; they were loitering around my apartment, and we are going to Irondequoit to eat seafood."

Roger snapped back, "Can't you ever answer properly?"

That evening they dined well at the: Tavern58 at Gibbs, in University Avenue and returned to Roger's apartment. Ming had plenty of clothes at Roger's place as she stayed there often. She let her control know what had happened that evening and where she was sleeping. Ming was tasked by her control to report anything of interest that Roger was working on.

The next morning she called Roger to get up and have his coffee with her. She tried to tempt him by letting her dressing gown open, exposing herself to him. He was not interested at this time in the morning and as a result; he had to take a lot of verbal abuse from her. She showered and left the apartment to go to work.

Later, that morning Roger looked out of his office back window reflecting on his heavy workload, when he noticed five men dressed in three-hole balaclavas coming towards his offices, aggressively treading all over the neatly laid-out flower beds. What in the hell is this all about, he said under his breath. He thought it better to run rather be taken by these uninvited guests as they would be doing most of the talking. He ran out the front door just as Ming drove by calling him to get into her Avensis whilst it was still moving. Roger jumped into the front seat, closing the door that Ming had opened for him.

Roger bellowed, "What is all of this about?"

Ming replied that she was not sure, but it looked like they meant business. Why were they dressed up in ski clothes in the middle of a Rochester summer?

Roger protested, "What did they want with me?"

Ming said, "They were not looking for you; they were looking for me."

"Why are they looking for you?" Roger croaked.

Ming angrily replied, "I already told you yesterday afternoon when you asked me where I got the car, but you chose not to listen."

Roger incredulously replied you killed three people on your way here yesterday afternoon? You are nothing but a killer!

Ming laughed out loud, "You mean, assassin."

They must have more than one faction here. That means I have to be on my guard for five more killers and arrange for them to join their colleagues.

Roger asked her, "Seriously, how are you going to do that?" They will come looking for me, not I go looking for them.

She asked Roger, "Will you protect me?"

Roger looked at her as if she was mad. Roger replied, "There you go again."

They did not have to wait long before shots rang out and riddled her Avensis. Ming exclaimed, "It's about time we found ourselves a new vehicle." They drove into the next parking lot they found and parked the Avensis where it could easily be watched. She placed in the glove box a mobile phone bomb and left the keys in the ignition. Then they walked over to the edge of the parking lot and crossed the road and sat down in a quaint café where Ming ordered coffee and bruschetta with tomato and basil.

Ming said, "When we are served our lunch that will be the time our assassin friends reclaim their Avensis Wagon." When the meal arrived, they could see four of the foreign agents clambering into the vehicle. The fifth agent was nowhere to be seen. Perhaps, he was waiting in the car they had been using.

Ringing the mobile, Ming said, "bye." The Avensis exploded, leaving only one assassin to contend with in the future.

Roger exclaimed, "That's four human beings you have just snuffed out. Are you pleased with yourself?" Ming answered with irritation in her voice, "Better them than us. You can be such a Drake at times."

Roger said, "I need to get back to work."

Ming asked Roger, "What are you working on that is so interesting?"

Roger answered, "The usual particle interactions now. I hope something original will come out of it to allow me to move forward and discover something new. What are you doing these days?"

Ming responded, "Entropy. I am looking into the quantification of entropy in Hadron interactions, but I have nothing yet to report."

Roger hailed a taxi, and they went back to the University. Roger alighted from the taxi, and Ming went on.

Chapter 1

INITIAL SITUATION

Roger has his offices in the Physics Department of Rochester University, situated in a leafy tree-lined avenue. The office, where he normally worked doing his research contained; his desk with scattered papers all over it, two white boards, filing cabinets, a coffee making machine and various other pieces of furniture. Opening a door to an adjacent office allowed him to enter his laboratory furnished with his test and experimental equipment.

Roger and Peter once worked together for many years on projects that were of interest to them both. Peter was mainly working on mathematical modeling, solving problems associated with particle physics, namely, hadrons, quarks and strong forces. Whereas, Roger became more interested in what caused the strong forces and how they could be generated and harnessed. And so, they both, in their own inimitable ways progressed and moved forward, each understanding what the other was doing without duplicating his work. Both men parted when Peter moved to a different University, being offered a better position and higher salary. The relationship between the two men always remained close and each felt as if they were working in adjacent offices. Their usual communication was via email due to their commitments outside of their offices.

That morning as Roger manipulated his equations trying to isolate the reoccurring stable blocks that represented the strong forces, he noticed the same lines of mathematics in his equations appearing as groups at different places when he read down the page. He became highly excited because he could observe in each group the lines of mathematics indicating an oscillation was occurring. This signified to him, that a strong force was being generated at a constant intensity and was being propagated through space.

He knew that it was not any form of electromagnetic wave propagation as his equations dealt only with hadrons. In particle physics, a Hadron is a composite particle made of quarks held together by the strong force. If it was molecules that were being considered, then these would be held together by an electromagnetic force, and the oscillation would be electromagnetic.

Roger's heart raced as he saw the implications of what he discovered: A new milestone of understanding reached along the road to enlightenment.

"A new form of telecommunications is born, not requiring waves set up by electromagnetic fields to propagate, but something unknown set up by some other type of fields arising from the strong force."

Roger walked over to his office and lab. He was quite eager to continue and expand his work. He really needed to think through, in detail, what he had just discovered in case he had made a mistake that would set the whole world laughing.

When he arrived, he met Vivian sitting in his chair. She has to be the most beautiful creature he ever set his eyes on. He felt his blood rushing through his veins, and he was awash with lust for her. He contained himself and instead he asked her if she wanted to do anything she should normally not be doing at this time in the morning as he locked his office door. He saw her expression change, and her eyes become like those of a fox fixing onto his, and her thighs move in the chair like she was no longer comfortable. He knew he had roused her interest. When their ardor had been quenched Vivian asked Roger what he was working on. Roger did not want to give Vivian too many details as he had no reason to trust her. She was his plaything as he was hers.

What she did, when she was not with him, was her business, and she never let him know what she did for a living. They met in a bar called Hot Shots Volleyball on University Avenue and from their first encounter, they made arrangements to meet again. They met several times after that and Roger wined and dined her to her liking, and after a while he could satisfy her appetite. Each time they met, she always wanted to know the details of his work and Roger's natural reticence prohibited him from discussing it in any detail. Unbeknown to Roger, she would seek and supply information to any agency that would pay her a reasonable retainer. Roger, in her mind, was a sleeper who may be useful in the days to come.

On the average, she would turn up at his office three times a week, and he would wine and dine her at different restaurants and then take her back to his apartment. Her demands never subsided, although they were not excessive. In this way, they enjoyed each other's company. He wondered if the guy who eventually married her could tolerate her disappearing three days out of each week.

Once Vivian had left, Roger walked back to his office as it was only mid-afternoon and the day was still young. He started to think this new discovery through, line-by-line. He didn't miss having Peter or Ming with him at the moment because his problem was at this stage a personal one.

Colleagues and students often called on him in his offices and discussed various matters concerning particle physics, no one having any idea about what he was working on in his present research project.

He thought about all the work he had to organize, the theory, the hardware, the experiments, the testing and how he was to arrange it.

First, he was to find a place on the Internet that only he knew, and that could be used to store his theory and revisions. The University campus servers would not be secure enough.

For little cost, he rented an inconspicuous host computer that could be accessed from anywhere in the world at any time, and had sufficient storage and capacity to suit the present and future projected requirements as well as operating with software installed by himself. This permitted him to build into his network a higher level of security. Roger designed the security software, installed it and tested it.

Next, he thought about the hardware that he would need to set up his experiments and test his theory. Once done, he prepared a list of his hardware requirements and the test equipment over what he had already. He submitted his requirements to the University administration for them to action. The administration was prompt and once satisfied that the project was bona-fide, wasted no time procuring the items required.

The testing would be done with Peter with a minimum of additional hardware required by him.

Roger sent off an email to Peter explaining that he would be ready for testing a new project in the months to come, and how he wanted to design a Stegan code they could use for secure communications between them. He would explain his project via the Stegan code.

After writing notes on what was required to be done after the initial effort was complete, Roger noted that the day had finished, and it was now evening. He drooled over thoughts of a few wines and Cheesy

Brussels Sprouts Gratin, followed by Creamy Scalloped Potatoes with Artichokes. That would go down well, he thought.

He drove his car to Il cucchiaio d'argento in Rochester Hills and ate and drank well.

The next morning at eight o'clock he awoke to a ringing of his front door chime. It was Ming, who wanted to know why he had not waited for her. He showered and dressed, and they both left for breakfast and coffee at a nearby café. She had an uncanny knack of knowing that something new was afoot. She asked Roger how his project was progressing. Roger looked at her and wanted to know why she was always so interested. She replied that she knew when he was lying, and he was lying now. Roger said why don't you mind your own business and stop prying into what I am doing. She looked deeply hurt by his rebuff and said it's because what you are doing is also my field, and maybe I can catch errors if you make any. Roger accepted this and apologized to her. He explained briefly that he had found some strange behavior in his equations that required further investigation, and that was about it for the moment. She asked if she could help in any way. Roger shook his head, thanking her for her offer and said she would be the first; he would call if help was required. She asked him to keep her posted on how he was progressing. He said that he most definitely would.

Roger walked over to administration from his offices to ensure that his request was being progressed. The clerk ensured him that there were no problems at this stage and if all went well, orders would be placed in three working days from today.

Roger started working on his Stegan code and continued on it for the rest of the afternoon and into the night. Feeling hungry, he got into his car and drove to the nearest pizza place and ordered a thin-crust pepperoni, large size and two diet Pepsi. He waited until he returned to his office before starting to eat. After eating, he felt sleepy and then drove back to his apartment. When he arrived, he found Ming waiting for him. Why didn't you wait for me to come with you? She said. Roger answered, "There was no need for you to wait like this. Why didn't you ring me?" She looked thankfully at him, "I am not fussed." She took the rest of the pizza and the second can of diet Pepsi from him and sat down at the dining room table and supped the remaining food. He didn't know what it was with her. Was she falling in love with him and always wanted to be by his side or what? He suspected it was because of his project that she could understand in all its detail and could see its potential more clearly than he. Roger did not want to discuss his project now as he was very tired. He showered and afterwards put on some soft music and went to bed. He was drifting in, and out of consciousness when he felt Ming snuggle into his back and put her arms around him.

The next thing he knew, looking out of his window from his bed, was that it was a morning with clear July azure skies and a singing wren. What a beautiful morning it is, he thought.

He rose from bed, showered and sat down with Ming to drink a freshly brewed coffee, toast and bacon with a fried egg that she had prepared.

What are you doing today? Ming asked him. Roger replied; I want to finish off the Stegan code this morning, so I can send details to Peter without having prying eyes reading what I am up to. Ming asked casually, "Will I be privy to this code?"

Yes, answered Roger.

She said ok, I will go to work, and she left.

Ming reported to her control that Roger had a devised a Stegan code for communicating between himself and Peter and would commence to use it from today. She also reported that Roger had progressed significantly on his project, but what it was he was progressing, was unknown at this time.

Roger sent Peter an email written in the new Stegan code for his use, explaining all that had happened so far.

In addition, a different email was sent containing the key to this new Stegan code. This separate email was written in a familiar Stegan code, one that they both knew and had used together in the past. They agreed to use this old Stegan code if they didn't have a more recent code to use.

Roger received a phone call from his Dean, who asked him to come over to his office as soon as he could, to discuss an important matter. Full of trepidation, Roger knocked on the door and on hearing, "Enter," he opened the door and walked into the Dean's office. The dean walked over to him and shook his hand and thanked him for coming, offering him a chair to sit on. Roger took the offer and sat directly opposite the dean. The dean said, "I have asked you to come here today because one of our sister universities requires your services immediately and for a short while." Roger asked, "Where do you want me to go and for how long?"

The dean answered, "Cadi Ayyad University, Marrakesh in Morocco." You are requested to set up a Particle Physics department as part of the National School of Applied Sciences in Safi. You will be there as long as it takes to complete this task. You will be given a Berber assistant, who will meet you on your arrival. He is a senior University staff member who is an articulate, amusing, educated man who speaks many languages and who speaks English fluently. He will assist you in your requirements for accommodation, transport, and equipment for the brand-new department, etc. Your new project will be funded by the Morocco University. If you accept this assignment, you will leave the day-after tomorrow.

Roger said, "I will give you my answer tomorrow morning." With that, Roger left the dean's office and returned home. It was early afternoon, and he wanted to work. He was sure that he did not leave any project design or Stegan Code details here or in his office, they were secreted away on his rented hosting site. He will not give Ming any information at this time, but will leave it until she needed to know. He downloaded his project and started working on his mathematics once more. This time he wanted to check its iterations at various points in his design. Three or more hours later he saved his work and closed down.

The next morning again he awoke to the smell of bacon and eggs and thought he was dreaming. There it was; he thought, the azure skies and singing birds. Ming called him for breakfast.

Roger spoke to her as kindly as he could through his slurs, "I have something to discuss with you." She looked at him, and he hoped she didn't bring her Sig Sauer M11 with him. She mimicked his kind voice with a slur, "Yesh, whaaat ish itch, you want to discushh wishhh me?" Roger ignored her mocking and came straight to the point, "Tomorrow I will leave for Morocco on a jet plane, and it may be some time before I'm back again." She looked at him in disbelief. Finally, she blurted, "How could you do this to me?" Roger did not know if she was playing or not, so again he chose to ignore her remarks. Perhaps you could get Sabbatical and come and join me. Her eyes lit up and she said, "What a super idea. I will go and ask my dean after breakfast. What are we going to do there and for how long?" Roger gave her all the details and suggested her dean could talk with his dean.

Roger rang his dean and said that he accepted his offer. Furthermore, he mentioned that his colleague was also interested and would discuss this matter with her dean this morning.

That afternoon it was all arranged that she would fly to Morocco with him and help set up the particle physics department at the National School of Applied Sciences in Safi.

They flew out the next day and met with Afulay, Roger's assistant, when they arrived in Casablanca.

On the 200km drive from Casablanca to Safi; Afulay gave details of his country's background:

He explained that in 1975, Spain surrendered control of the Western Sahara to Morocco and Mauritania, but then a war broke out between these two countries and the Polisario Front. Mauritania withdrew in 1979, and Morocco eventually secured effective control of most of the territory, including all the major cities and natural resources.

The Polisario Front was recognized by many countries as the legitimate representative of the Sahrawi people. It had been seeking the independence of Western Sahara since 1975.

There has been a cease-fire between Morocco and Polisario since 1991 but outbreaks of fighting in Moroccan-held territories as well as the continuing dispute over the legal status of the territory, ensured continued United Nations involvement.

Roger and Ming thanked Afulay for the background information.

Once they arrived at the National School of Applied Sciences in Safi, they were introduced to their administration and colleagues whilst Afulay organized a hotel for the night. The dean explained how fortunate the University was by asking for one particle Physicist and ended up by getting two. He added, It bade well. Over the next couple of days, we will discuss your requirements in more detail, but meanwhile, you should now go to your hotel to relax after your long journey.

They both settled in and got on well with the staff. Over the next three days, they would put in all the main orders required to launch their new department, make copious notes on where certain equipment was to be placed when it arrived and outline a course of action on what additional orders were required to be placed and what tests should be performed on the ordered lab equipment.

Ming asked Roger, "Aren't you worried about the politics here?"

Roger quietly answered, "Only if they get wind of what I am working on, and no one will know because I am not telling."

Ming said, "You have never told me, and I tell you everything."

Roger said, "If it was suspected by either of these groups that you knew, you would be tortured for the full story, so it's better you do not know for your own safety."

Ming retorted, "You think it's better than I get tortured for nothing, eh? You Drake!"

Roger said, "It is important that we do not discuss our projects between ourselves, so we can never be overheard."

He continued, "We have a job to do, so let's finish it and get the hell out of here."

However, they did not realize that every word they said, when in the laboratory that morning, was being monitored. This was mainly due to their field being highly specialized and not being understandable to many scientists. Where ignorance abounds, suspicion is rife and these two individuals were sitting right on top of the suspect tree.

Well, after Roger made his comments, the cat was out of the bag and Ming for once was not to blame.

Roger said as normally as he could, "Let's go outside and get a breath of fresh air."

As they strolled in the University grounds, Roger said to Ming that he was convinced that they were being overheard when he had mentioned about his project. I think we should buy a couple of pistols, and I sleep with you tonight for protection, in a different hotel, because I am certain that there would be an abduction this night if we stayed in our present quarters.

Ming replied, "I am OK. I am retiring to my usual bed, and you can sleep elsewhere. I will go to the souk to try to find a gun."

When she was out of earshot of Roger, she rang her control and informed her of what was happening. Her control said she would arrange for her to pick up a gun from a contact in Safi as soon as she could arrange for it to be done.

Roger stood alone in the University grounds, for a few more moments before returning to his laboratories. Once back into his laboratory he took these moments by himself to download, using WiFi, his mathematics onto his laptop and continue to check it through. Three hours later and well satisfied with how he had progressed; he closed down and replaced his files.

He went back to his hotel and ordered room service as he felt like eating in his room. After eating, he lay on his bed dozing when three men looking like Arabs, burst into his room, seized him and frog marched him out of his room into a Ford Expedition SUV. They tie-wrapped his wrists behind his back and drove the SUV for a couple of hours. When they stopped, they parked the vehicle in the garage of a private mansion. They beckoned him to follow the lead of the first Arab with the other two close behind. After climbing sumptuous decorated stairs, they entered a foyer that led to a lavishly furnished sitting room, lined with fully laden bookshelves interspersed with oil paintings of the Gainsborough variety. Roger thought, What is this guy up to? It was not long before his question was answered.

Good evening, Doctor Redman. I hope you are not too put out by my rude invitation. As you do not know me, nor do you know about me, I was really left no option but to force this invitation on you. Let me introduce myself. I am Karim Khalid. I and my family made most of our money from slave trading. As you can observe from our affluence, we were successful.

Roger was not the least bit interested in Karim, nor his family, nor his wealth. He was starting to get annoyed, and maybe his expression reflected his impatience. Karim sensed Roger's impatience, and his expression changed from kind benevolence to calculating executioner as he asked Roger what was the meaning of his words "Only if they get wind of what I am working on, and no one will know because I am not telling."

Roger expected that he would be asked what these words meant by all who heard them, so he had been thinking hard and long about how to answer this.

Roger answered that he was working on basic particles that make up matter and, which can be converted more easily into energy in practical fuel cells.

He knew that his words would be sent to Universities throughout the world for verification as a worthwhile project.

Karim asked, "Why didn't you want Dr. Lovelace to know what you are working on?"

Roger answered, "Because she would start competing and try to show how much better and clever she is."

Karim asked, "How long have you known Dr. Lovelace?"

Roger answered, "About three and one-half years. We met at an International Conference on Particle Physics."

They discussed the project, Roger's Department at Rochester University, funding, and Dr. Lovelace abilities for a couple of hours more.

Roger was then shown to his bedroom where a King-Size bed awaited him.

In the morning, he was met by Karim, who accompanied him to breakfast and outlined his plan.

He said:

I have been looking for a project that can enhance the international standing of the National School of Applied Sciences (NSAS), Cadi Ayyad University in Safi. I know that you, and your colleague is setting up a Particle Physics Laboratory in NSAS, here in Safi. I wish you to continue this until it is finished. As a patron, I will give a grant to each of your Universities to permit funding of your fuel-cell project. Both you and Dr. Lovelace can independently work on this project back at your individual universities. Once the project is successfully finished, I will arrange for its production, and as I will hold the patents, I will be able to reclaim my costs and make a profit.

Roger agreed, in principle, and Karim, and he signed a letter of intent for taking back to each of their Universities. He hoped Ming would agree with him on everything to do with this new project. However, like everything else to do with her, he wasn't holding his breath.

He left Karim's mansion and returned to his University to get back by two in the afternoon. He looked for Ming and found her in the laboratory. She had been crying and when she saw him, she bursts out crying again. In between her sobs, she explained that people saw him being abducted from his hotel room and feared the worst. They walked to a restaurant where they could eat and once seated and orders placed, Roger explained everything that happened since he last spoke with her.

Ming said, "That's a lot to take in! It will take me a few more hours of thinking and listening to you before I can say that I am comfortable with what happened."

Over the next three days, they put in all the orders required to launch their new department.

During the period of order placement to equipment arrival, Roger was able to complete the design of his main project and inform Peter that he should be ready for building a prototype when he arrived back in Rochester.

After three weeks, the equipment started arriving and from their notes, the post-graduate students together with Afulay could place it correctly in the laboratories and start testing according to the test plan.

All equipment placements and testing were completed after two months of Roger and Ming arriving. The University administration was satisfied as the post-grad students were familiar with it and its operation.

Ming returned her gun to her control's contact and informed her control that she would be flying back to Rochester tomorrow and would she arrange accommodation for her.

A going-away party was held for them both and there was much gaiety and fine speeches. Roger, also on behalf of Ming, gave a special speech of gratitude to the Dean, Afulay and the post-grad students for their assistance and cooperation.

On the flight back Roger asked Ming if she was interested in Karim's fuel-cell project. She asked, if she would be working with him. He replied, "Yes, whenever you wish to compare notes, or we can make it a joint project if you prefer. I am easy any which way." Ming fell silent and Roger did not ask again.

Both Roger and Ming returned to Rochester, and to a hero's welcome by their respective universities for a job completed and well done.

Chapter 2

ROGER

Roger met with his dean and informed him of his discussions with Karim. Roger explained, Karim was not directly connected to the National School of Applied Sciences (NSAS) in Safi, and how he proposed a project to him, which used the basic particles making up matter to be converted more easily into energy in practical fuel cells. Karim stated he would be honored to become Roger's patron by giving a grant to our University and also to Ming's University for this project. Karim continued to say that I, and Dr. Lovelace could independently work on this project back at our individual universities. However, Dr. Lovelace was still thinking about Karim's proposal and had not yet made up her mind.

Once the project was successfully finished, Karim would arrange for its production, and as he would hold the patents, he would reclaim his costs and make a profit.

Roger's dean was most enthusiastic about this new project and when Roger passed to him the signed letter of intent, he said he would take action on it immediately.

However, Roger would put this fuel-cell project (FCP) on a lower-priority list of projects to be completed, as he was already committed to the higher-priority Telecom project. Nevertheless, he thought it prudent to place orders for the parts and the test equipment as soon as possible, and so he made up his lists whilst it was in the forefront of his mind.

Roger was being secretive, as he suspected that there was going to be a lot happening over the next couple of weeks, and it all hinged on what he had just discovered in his Telecom project. This was the emergence of a changing characteristic variable with periodic oscillations that occurred in his equations. This oscillation concerned the basic structure that a new form of telecommunications would take. This encouraged him to rethink the work that he had been doing. He revised his work and after coming to the same technical conclusion, he decided that it really was something brand new and worthy of further investigation. Fired by his discovery, he considered its ramifications and consequently, didn't wish to convey it openly to Peter and Ming. In all of his life, there was only one person, he found, that he could trust and that was Peter. He would be placing a lot of trust with him from this day forwards. Roger always could see outside of the box, and so it was with this new form of non-electromagnetic radiation. He could see a major change in the fabric of science as we know it and the direction that it may take in the future. There would be a technological Renaissance.

He was thankful for Karim's fuel-cell project (FCP) as it gave him a chance to order equipment without arousing suspicion within and outside of the university and allow him to work on the Telecom prototype without Ming being suspicious. He constantly sent emails to Karim that kept him informed about the progress of the FCP. This was advancing well, much to the delight of his University, Karim and himself, because proportionally, he had not expended as much effort as he had spent on his Telecom project. Through his university's dean, Karim wanted to know why Roger chose the Alkaline Fuel Cell (AFC) type, otherwise known as the Bacon fuel cell after its British inventor, to launch his project. Roger answered that NASA had been using them since 1965 or so. They consume hydrogen and oxygen producing drinking water, heat, and electricity, and they can reach an electrical efficiency of around 60%. Roger wanted to surpass this 60% figure (not including waste heat expended)

Roger checked with his administration on the status of the orders; he placed two or more months back. They told him all the items had been received and stored in his laboratory. He thanked them for being so diligent and gave them the orders for the FCP.

Roger had thought a lot about Vivian and wondered if she still came to his apartment. He hoped she would come soon, as he missed her.

He had not seen Ming since his return and thought maybe she harbored some grudge against him, but she was her own person and probably went off somewhere to kill a few agents.

He went to one of his Italian restaurants for a meal and a few wines. He met Igor, a university security guard, in the restaurant. He was dining alone, so Roger asked him if he could join him. Of course, Dr. Redman, I am most happy to have your company. Igor had more to him than meets the eye and on previous occasions, Roger had many fine discussions on Russian history and its characters. Igor asked Roger, "What shall we discuss tonight?" Roger replied, "White Russians, Red Russians and Cossacks."

Igor chortled, "A subject very close to my heart, not that I am a Cossack, but like most Russians, we respect and revere them." Roger asked him to continue, which he did:

In the 16th century Cossack communities sprang up in the southern areas, the Moscow area, and to the West; Belarus and the Ukraine. From the second, half of the 16th century on, along the river Don, the community of the Don Cossacks developed, whereas during the very same period, Ukrainian Cossacks formed a similar community far out in the steppe.

In the 18th century, the Ukrainian Cossacks, who did not belong to Poland anymore, were obligated to become subordinates of the Russian Tsar.

Cossack communities accepted Tartars, Germans, Turks and other nationalities into their communities to become Cossacks if they believed in Christ.

Cossacks had their own elected headman, called Ataman, who had executive powers and was supreme commander during the war. The Cossacks were named by their geographical locations, such as; the Zaporozhian, Don and Kuban Cossacks.

Cossack military traditions are strong and boys were trained as warriors from a very young age. At the age of three, the child could already mount a horse and by five, he was a confident rider. His father would also teach his sons the art of war from a very young age.

In the 18th century, their main responsibilities were to guard the country's borders, and they were given special privileges and autonomy.

During the Romanov Dynasty and up until the October Revolution of 1917, Cossacks were the most vigorous defenders of Russia.

During the Russian Civil War, the Cossacks fought mainly in the White Army. Therefore, after the victory of the Red Army, they were heavily persecuted. During the Second World War, the Cossacks were split; some fought for the Soviet Union and some supported Nazi Germany."

Roger expressed his admiration with a clap of his hands and asked Igor to explain White and Red Russians.

Igor responded with, "The white army came from the southern Russia, whereas the red army came from western Russia.

White Russians, is the name given to the counter revolutionaries, that fought against the Bolshevik Red Army in the Russian Civil War (1918-1921).

After the October Revolution it was decided by Vladimir Lenin that the old Russian Army would have to be turned into an instrument of the Communist Party.

Fearful of the spread of Communism under Lenin, Britain, the United States, Italy, and Germany intervened on the White side, supplying military and financial support. Despite this combined force, the White forces lost to the Red Army.

After the October Revolution, it was decided by Vladimir Lenin that the old Russian Army would have to be turned into an instrument of the Communist Party. This army was then demobilized and in January 1918, the Soviet government ordered the formation of the Red Army of Workers and Peasants.

Leon Trotsky, the Commissar of War, was appointed the head of the Red Army on 13th March, 1918. The army had to be established quickly as it was needed to fight the White Army during the Civil War. Trotsky was forced to recruit a large number of officers from the old Russian Army. He was criticized for this, but he argued that it would be impossible to fight the war without the employment of experienced army officers."

Roger exclaimed, "Bravo!"

Igor said to Roger that a lovely looking lady had come to the university on several occasions looking for him.

Thanks, answered Roger.

They drank vodka and red wine and chatted until seven in the evening. Roger said, good night and thanked him for a very pleasant evening.

Roger returned to his apartment to find Vivian waiting for him. She threw her arms around his neck and kissed him all over his face repeatedly.

Roger said, "Do you want to eat last or play first?"

"You are provoking me again, you naughty boy!"

After they played, they went to their favorite Italian Restaurant and dined.

Over dinner, Roger explained briefly what had happened. Vivian was not that interested, so even relating a shortened version did not enliven the conversation. They returned home to Roger's apartment around ten-thirty that night. She was interested in his project, and she perked up when he told her how he set up a new Department in a different university that was located overseas, to work on special batteries. She carefully noted what he said when he was talking about his work. From her intense expression as she tried to understand and remember what said, he suspected she was working for some spy organization, so he was careful what he said to her. He didn't want to sow the seeds of a future industrial theft.

The next morning she left early to go and make her report to her employer. Roger knew that he wouldn't see her for a couple of days.

Roger went over to his offices and inspected all the equipment he had ordered. He met Igor and asked him if he would help him set up the new equipment. Igor was most happy to oblige. After three days, all the equipment was correctly placed, and the test equipment had been verified as working properly to Roger's satisfaction.

Roger was ready to start building his prototype. He didn't waste any more time and started the next morning. He locked the door of his office that opened into the hallway that serviced the other offices. He also locked the door to his laboratory that opened into his office. In his laboratory, he started on the base plate that would be used to support the following layer of his design and be used to support the succeeding layer, and so on. He worked day and night on his prototype and then ran into a snag. He went back to his design equations and started checking them from the beginning. He felt his frustration increasing, which to him was a danger sign because he would start correcting equations that did not require correcting. He thought to himself that it was better to put down the pen and tools and rest. After all, he still had his fuel-cell project (FCP) to return to. Roger replaced his Telecom project design to his secure place on the Internet and boxed his prototype, depositing it on a shelf in an inconspicuous place at the far end of his laboratory. He downloaded his fuel-cell design from this project's Internet secure place and unboxed his prototype and set it up on the lab bench, so he could start immediately with his work on this project. He was half expecting Ming to burst through his two doors, guns firing, and seize the FCP design and its prototype. However, on listening for a few moments, all was quiet.

He made good progress with this project and expected to have it completed in less than two months. He was using parts that had been purchased for the Telecom project, but was not worried as his FCP project orders would start coming in any day from today.

There are many different forms of Fuel Cells that have been developed these days with high efficiency and capacity, Basically, Hydrogen Fuel Cells efficiently convert the atmospheric gas; hydrogen into electricity using an electrolyzer. The only byproducts are heat and water.

Roger's fuel cell is a variation of the Alkaline Fuel Cell (AFC) that has a typical electrical efficiency up to 60% and capacity that is around 12kW. NASA has been using these types of fuel cells in Apollo-series missions and on the Space Shuttle. They are also used in submarines and for terrestrial transportation.

Roger had a choice of which type he would concentrate on. Some of the different fuel cells he could have improved upon are: Polymer-Electrolyte Fuel Cells (PEFCs) (up to 50% electrical efficiency), Molten Carbonate Fuel Cells (MCFC) (65%), Phosphoric Acid Fuel Cells (PAFC) (37-42%), Solid Oxide Fuel Cells (SOFC) (50-60%), Direct Methanol Fuel Cells (DMFC) (40%).

The next morning Ming came to his apartment looking for a fight. She said to Roger that he had been avoiding her since they had come back from Morocco. Roger did not answer her. Ming demanded that Roger answer her. Roger said that on the flight back he asked her if she was interested in Karim's fuel-cell project. Roger said, "You did not reply." He continued, "When I said we would be working together in a joint project, or if you wanted to work alone and compare notes when you wanted, that would be OK."

Ming said like she was doing Roger a favor, "I will work with you on a joint project."

Roger spoke angrily to her, "Sorry, that was more than a month and a half ago, too much time already has been spent on the design, ordering of parts and on the fabrication, for you to claim joint rights." He continued, "In the three and one-half years I have known you; I have not known you to do anything. I bet you have not discussed this project to date with your dean."

Ming burst out crying and stormed out of his apartment.

Roger thought; what a lame duck!

Roger showered, ate breakfast and walked over to his offices.

He met Igor and after passing the time of the day with him, asked him to make sure Ming did not enter his offices when he was not there. Igor said, "No problem Dr. Redman."

Roger continued with his design and construction. Now, his objective is to build an Alkaline Fuel Cell (AFC) that has a typical electrical efficiency up to 80% or more and a capacity that is as near to 12kW as possible. At the moment, his design indicated that he should be 73% with a capacity close to 12kW. He spent the next six weeks constructing, monitoring and testing until he reached an 80% efficiency and a capacity of 11. 76kW. He recorded his design and his practical results and uploaded them to his safe place on the Internet. He stored his properly labeled fuel cell and his inconspicuous tagged Telecom project in his dean's room after explaining that he would display in his laboratory an earlier and far less efficient version of the AFC that did not resemble the concluding design. This was because many people and companies would be very interested in the latest fuel cell, and he feared a break-in and theft of the device. He warned Igor to be on his guard and increase the number of security personnel watching his office and laboratory area. He asked the dean to relay to Karim his results and let him know that we are awaiting his further instructions before shipping the prototype and forwarding to him its design and test results.

Roger wanted to get his prototype Alkaline Fuel Cell and its design to Karim quickly before it became a monkey on his back. His University had received its grant, and all remained was to close the project.

The next day he had to face his ransacked office, a stolen obsolete Alkaline Fuel Cell prototype and its design documentation.

Igor was in Roger's office and said to him that five balaclavas clad men had broken into his office and laboratory at around ten last night and taken the prototype fuel cell and papers off of his desk. He said that the security guard on duty mentioned to him that one of the men had spoken English to the others. Roger thought, maybe these were Ming's people.

The dean informed Roger that Karim asked him to ship the AFC prototype out to him with the design documentation. Roger downloaded the documentation from the dean's office and printed it for placement with the prototype. The dean arranged to have it sent directly to Karim.

The dean asked Roger if he suspected that Ming was involved in last night's raid. Roger shrugged and answered that he didn't know, all he knew was that it was a relief seeing the last of that project.

The damage to his office and laboratory was minimal, and he was back working before lunch time. He retrieved his Telecom prototype from the dean's office and started working on it like he had never stopped.

The next morning he went to his offices and met the dean waiting for him.

Roger asked nervously, "Do we have a problem with the AFC project?"

The dean replied, "No, but Karim and the dean of the National School of Applied Sciences in Safi, want to discuss with you a new proposal. Would you please fly out there tomorrow? Afulay will meet you at the airport in Casablanca. I will look after your prototype whilst you have gone. What is it, by the way?"

Roger replied, "Thanks. It will take some time to explain so, let me discuss it with you over dinner when I return."

The dean agreed.

Roger arrived the next day in the afternoon, and Afulay was there to take him to his hotel in Safi. He showered and then dined before going to bed. The meeting with the dean and Karim in the dean's office was scheduled the next day at ten in the morning.

When he entered the dean's office, he noticed Ming sitting there. Roger said, "What are you doing here?" She replied, "Karim and the dean invited me to come because of my contributions." Roger trying to contain himself answered, "You made no contribution whatsoever, so you got here by cheating." She answered, "You may think that, but they do not see it that way." Roger continued, "If it is like that, then you do what you want because I will return to Rochester without entering into any negotiations with them." Ming smiled and said to him, "We will see about that." Roger was livid and got up to leave when Karim, and the dean entered. They welcomed him back and shook his hand.

Karim explained that although we know that Dr. Lovelace did not contribute to the AFC project, the dean and I, did not want to exclude her from this meeting due to her contribution to the establishment of the particle laboratory.

Ming looked triumphantly at Roger, who dropped his eyes in anger. Roger knew that he did not want to work with her any longer and wanted her to know that right now. However, out of courtesy to the dean and Karim, he felt he had to listen to what they proposed.

Karim opened the proposal discussion by stating all conditions would be the same as those of the AFC project. Roger stated he could not approve of this until he knew what they wanted. The dean took over and proposed that they design a propulsion system better than any presently available. Roger gasped. He thought, do they know what they are asking. Ming looked blank.

Roger asked, "How long do you expect us to take to complete this project?" Karim replied, "As long as you need." The meeting finished, to convene tomorrow at the same time. They all left the meeting, and Ming said to Roger when they were out of earshot from the others, "What do you think?"

Roger retorted, "It is important what you think. It is your project, because I am returning to Rochester."

Tears welled up in Ming's eyes. "I am not responsible for being here. They invited me. Not wanting to be churlish, I accepted and thought that I could change your attitude towards me by making a positive contribution."

Roger asked her if her agents had stolen the AFC prototype and design notes from his lab. She was surprised by his question. How did he know about her agents?

She answered, "No."

Roger softened, I suggest the following and stop me if you do not agree:
- We will ask for 10% royalties on delivery of the prototype and design,
- We work in Rochester at each of our Universities,
- Under no circumstances, any design notes are to be passed to any party other than the dean and Karim,
- Karim will fund the projects through the Rochester universities.
- No part of our research and development is to be used for weapons.

Ming said that she agreed, except she wanted to work with Roger at Rochester University.

The dean here can help by liaising with our deans on this matter, Roger commented.

That evening after they dined, they prepared a list of propulsion systems that could be used for selecting their project. These were different forms and variations of beam-powered systems that use energy beamed to the spacecraft from a remote power plant.

The beam would either be a beam of microwaves or a pulsed or continuous beamed laser. Roger said, "Take your choice, microwaves or laser."

We must ask what is the dean's involvement here. Maybe he could arrange for testing.

The next day they reconvened their meeting in the dean's office. Roger forgot that the university's and Karim's people had put microphones in their bedrooms, so Roger and Ming were only a little surprised when the dean didn't waste any time explaining that their recently installed particle laboratories would be used by their post grad students in verifying their project results.

Roger and Ming tabled their conditions. The weapons' clause caused some looks to be passed between the dean and Karim, but nothing was said. As everything was agreed upon, there was nothing further to discuss and as on the last occasion, a letter of intent was signed by all parties for taking back to their respective universities.

They all went off to lunch where they enjoyed themselves until night. Ming and Roger planned to return to Rochester the next day. On the flight back Roger and Ming discussed the looks that were passed between the dean and Karim when Roger's weapons clause was read out. Roger remarked, "We are heading for trouble with those two." Continuing he said, "Do you have any plans on what you want to work on when you get back?" Roger hoped she was going to pull herself together and do something worthwhile, but he was not holding his breath. She did not answer, which could mean that you can do it all again, like last time—sucker.

When they arrived in Rochester, Roger hailed a taxi to go directly to his apartment. Ming asked, "What are you doing now?"

Roger slowly answered that he was going home to shower and afterwards go out to dinner before arranging his work for the next working day and after that going to bed.

Ming replied, "Sounds good, can I come?"

They dined on Beef Stroganoff and a couple of bottles of Australian Cabernet Merlot and slept like babies when they finally got to bed.

The next morning Ming went her own way, and Roger went to give his letter of intent to his dean. The dean was most delighted having another grant for the university.

Roger started thinking about his latest project, wanting everything to stabilize between him and Ming before getting back into his Telecom project. Roger waited for Ming to come before starting on anything fresh, so that she would not think that he was creaming off the best project. Finally, she came in the afternoon and explained how her dean had berated her for not working on the AFC project. Ming was going to give him the letter of intent; however, instead she put in her resignation. Roger asked when her resignation was to take effect. She replied immediately as she had no students to teach or supervise at this time. Roger thought her dean would come here to talk to his dean in an effort to talk her into withdrawing her resignation. Roger said to Ming that it was a storm in a teacup and would pass. Let's get down to the project and get something started.

I suggest that our project is a better and more sophisticated light craft, using for each of our two vehicles, an external source of pulsed laser energy and an external source of pulsed maser energy. Each is focused to a high intensity by a parabolic reflector mounted on the underside of the vehicle to create a plasma that expands the air, violently producing thrust.

When a light craft is in the atmosphere, the propellant material or reaction mass is air. In space, the propellant material would need to be provided by on-board tanks or elsewhere.

Leaving the vehicle's power source on the ground and by using the atmosphere as the reaction mass for much of the vehicle's ascent, a light craft would be capable of delivering a very large payload to orbit.

At the moment, small hand-sized test specimens of the bottom-lasered type of light craft are attaining altitudes of a few hundred feet. In addition, a light craft's propulsion is dependent on the external laser's power and so is not limited to that contained by the rocket fuel.

Roger ended his monologue with, "What do you think?"

Ming said, give me a couple of hours and let me come up with something to present to you.

As she promised, she returned with her project details, namely an ion thruster.

Ion thrusters expel ions to create thrust and can provide higher spacecraft top speeds than any other rocket currently available. Modern ion thrusters are capable of propelling a spacecraft up to 90,000 meters per second (over 200,000 miles per hour (mph). To put that into perspective, the space shuttle can reach a maximum speed of around 18,000 mph. The tradeoff for this highest possible speed is low thrust (or low acceleration). Thrust is the force that the thruster applies to the spacecraft. Modern ion thrusters can deliver up to 0.5 Newtons (0.1 pounds) of thrust, which is equivalent to the force you would feel by holding a sheet of A4 paper in your hand. To compensate for low thrust, the ion thruster must be operated for a long time for the spacecraft to reach its maximum speed. Ion thrusters use inert gas for propellant, eliminating the risk of explosions associated with chemical propulsion. The usual propellant is xenon, but other gases such as krypton and argon may be used.

Ming continued by saying she proposed to build a prototype that would allow her to measure its thrust and then if this is successful, build within two years a high-power electric propulsion machine (HiPEP) that is a variation on her ion thruster prototype. Its use is for outer space travel, not for launching vehicles nor for terrestrial use.

Roger exclaimed, "Excellent! We will start on our designs tomorrow and if your dean does not try to get you to come back by tomorrow, we will attempt to transfer Karim's patronage for you to my University."

They closed down Roger's offices and went out to dine and have a few bottles of wine before retiring to bed in Roger's apartment.

Chapter 3

DESIGN OF THE STEGAN CODE

The next morning whilst Ming was preparing breakfast, Roger took a brisk walk over to the dean's office to inquire whether Ming's dean had come over to see him. He replied that he had not and asked why. Roger explained what Ming had told him and mentioned that she had intended to give him the letter of intent but instead had given him her resignation. Roger explained to his dean that yesterday, Ming, and he had planned their projects and would start working on them today. Roger said that if nothing happens this week to rescind her resignation, perhaps they should send a fax to Karim asking him to transfer his patronage to Ming, over to this university. Roger's dean remained silent. Roger returned to his apartment and an angry Ming over his spoilt breakfast. He said that she could put it in the microwave oven and warm it. Don't worry, it is easy to make another coffee. He explained what he had been doing, and she smiled warmly at him. She asked if it would end favorably for her. Roger said, I am sure it will. After breakfast, they walked over to Roger's laboratory and started working on their respective projects.

In steganography, the intended covert message does not attract attention to it and so becomes invisible to any unsuspecting person. It veils the fact that a clandestine message is being sent as well as concealing the contents of the message. It is the science of hiding information.

In this context, the cover medium is the file which will hide the hidden data, which may also be encrypted using the stego key. The resultant file is the stego medium (which will, of course, be the same type of file as the cover medium). The cover medium (and, thus the stego medium) is typically an image or audio file, which in Roger's case is an image file.

In contrast, cryptography doesn't try to disguise the fact that a message is being sent. It just makes the message unreadable. The bona-fide recipient of the file has the key, using it to decrypt the file.

Roger and Peter had been designing Stegan codes for military and commercial use for some years, and now this unused code was to be employed by them to communicate between each other over the Internet, using email. They each had the same key, in case they could not communicate a fresh key to each other.

Roger looked up to see his dean walking over to his offices. When he had made himself comfortable in Roger's office, he explained that he had spoken to Ming's dean.

Roger suspected that some of his initial equations in the Telecom project were not correct. This was because an internal calculation that should have converged and completed quickly was still iterating, indicating that it may be divergent and would never close to a closed-form expression. These early equations need to be checked, as soon as possible and revised where required. Any incorrect equations, if not corrected, would cause a snowballing effect on later theoretical calculations and at best, invalidate the integrity of the project. At worst, it would cause unknown events to occur when a final prototype was constructed and tested.

Ming's dean was an obstinate fool, who really should not be in the position of dean in Ming's university. Slowly, he realized that Ming was worth money for his university, and it didn't take much convincing after that for this buffoon to change his tack. He wanted Ming to come to his office, collect her resignation letter and give him the letter of intent from Karim and his cohorts. Ming arranged to meet Roger at his offices and go off to lunch with him when she finished with her dean. Whilst she was getting into her car after her meeting with her dean, a black SUV pulled along side her and three men jumped out and jostled her into the back seat. They proceeded to rip her clothes off, and even though they enjoyed her beauty, they did not interfere with her.

Roger received a phone call from Neville explaining that Ming had been abducted by Government agents.

Neville is extremely well-connected and is usually one of the first who knows what is going on. He gives Roger sanctuary when government agents want to arrest him. At the end of the day he saves the project and code from falling into the wrong hands by giving Roger a fully equipped laboratory to work in and suggesting to Roger that he should limit his project revision distribution to Peter and himself (Roger) and by changing to a new key code.

He is an extremely rich young man with an aptitude for understanding complex systems, making the people he interacts with, hold him in high respect. He is a stiff upper lip type of character who will keep trying until he wins and is thus, very reliable.

Ming noticed the bulge of the Sig Sauer P227 on the chest of the agent sitting beside her. She pulled out of her hair, a six-inch syringe-type hat pin charged with cyanide. She stuck it in the agent's eye and at the same time seized his Sig Sauer from his chest holster and shot the agent sitting on her other side through his temple. Then she shot the third agent, sitting in the passenger's side of the front seat, through the back of his head splattering his brains and bone fragments all over the windscreen. She told the driver to pull over to the side of the road. When he had done so, she told him to pull the deceased agents out of the SUV. She warned, "Don't do anything silly, or you will be dead meat also." She got into the driver's seat and drove to Roger's apartment and put some fresh clothes on. She drove to Roger's offices and met with him. She yelled, "Follow me!" When she was well and truly outside of the campus boundaries, she parked the car and got into Roger's vehicle, and they continued on for lunch.

Roger asked her, "What happened? Why are you late?" She explained that she was seized by three agents, thrown into a black SUV, and then had her clothes ripped off. After killing three of the four she returned to his apartment to get some clothes to wear, before driving here to meet him. Roger said, "Why didn't you keep the SUV?" She answered, "Because it was bloodied very badly, and it would attract the dogs after an hour or more." Roger was unconvinced, but he received a phone call from Neville explaining that a nude woman, he assumes is Ming, shot dead three agents and let one go to report the incident to his control. Roger went very silent, then thanked Neville, and he and Ming went to lunch.

Roger said with a touch of sarcasm in his voice, "You have been on a killing spree; I hear, but why did you have to kill them in the nude? It wouldn't have been good enough if you were clothed?"

After lunch, Ming rang her control and asked her why she was being treated so badly. Her control asked her for all the details, and after she had finished, she said to Ming that it was not her group, and she is going to look into the matter and report back to her on the outcome. Ming thanked her and hung up. Later, her control reported back to her that it was the Foreign Agent Control Group that tried to neutralize her, thinking she was a foreign spy out of Morocco. She said, they complained bitterly that they had lost three good men to that nude gun slinging bitch.

After lunch, they returned to Roger's offices to work. Roger arranged his office and lab for the best privacy it could offer them both. They both started working. Roger felt that he should bide his time with his Telecom project as he really wanted Ming to go back to her own university to work so he could get some privacy. Best thing, he thought was to test the Stegan code with Peter in readiness for sending details of the Telecom project.

Roger arranged for the following message to be encrypted with his photograph: I suggest as my project, a better and more sophisticated *light craft,* where an external source of pulsed maser energy, focused to a high intensity, by a parabolic reflector mounted on the underside of the vehicle, creates a plasma that expands the air, violently producing thrust.

Peter replied, "Received your message. Is this what you are doing now?" Roger replied that this project was for Morocco and was an additional project requested by a university there. Peter acknowledged Roger's reply.

Roger was careful not to let Ming see the six-digit key. He had to do something immediately about replacing the entered digits and numbers with asterisks, so anyone watching couldn't determine what was being entered. He started working on this, and three hours later it was finished, tested and stored in a safe place on the Internet.

Roger said, "I'm hungry, fancy a pizza?" Ming answered that she definitely would. They closed up shop and drove to the nearest pizza place.

For the next three months, they worked in Roger's offices, designing, building and testing their propulsion projects. Both scientists had something to show for their efforts, and they filmed their rudimentary efforts so far, for passing to Karim and his dean. Karim replied to Roger's dean with a request that Roger and Ming go to Rome to demonstrate their basic prototypes to one of Karim's company's there. Roger said to

Ming that it would be a welcome break, and they both agreed to leave the details to the deans of both universities to sort out the details.

When they arrived at Fiumicino-Leonardo da Vinci airport, Rome, they were met by two men in black suits sporting dark glasses, concealed weapons and very active walkie-talkies. They were taken to their hotel: Hotel Concordia, Trevi Fountain in Rome where they showered and changed their clothes before venturing out. It was early evening and very brisk with light rain falling. If they went for a stroll, they would get well and truly lost. If they tried walking North for approximately one kilometer, they would reach the Spanish Steps. However, they would not be able to walk in a straight line due to the way the roads and streets are laid out. These steps and the piazza at their base are, collectively, both an incredibly romantic spot to spend an evening with a loved one on your arm. As tempting as it was, they decided to eat at the hotel restaurant and do their exploring tomorrow. Where would they start? One can live in Rome for fifty years and still not visit all the piazzas and restaurants and cafés the city has to offer.

Italian food that they take in Rochester is among one of their favorite cuisines. So, here in Rome they didn't feel out of place reading through the menu. Local Italians do not need a menu as they know what they want and order accordingly.

There was a message at the front desk informing Ming and Roger that they had a meeting at eight-thirty tomorrow morning and would be picked up at eight. They cursed, but knew as soon as the meeting was finished, they would be free to walk around Rome.

When they arrived at their meeting, they were surprised by seeing Karim and his dean, who introduced them to the Directors of a company that went by the following name: Azienda di Transporto Rapido. Karim was the chairman and explained to the meeting that Drs. Lovelace and Redman came here to discuss their projects at my request. Please Dr. Lovelace, would you please explain to the meeting what your project is all about.

Ming explained every aspect of her project and how far she had progressed over the past three months. She produced the film of her lab tests for all to see and then opened the meeting to questions.

Roger did the same after Ming was finished.

Everyone at the meeting became more interested when they were told the two prototypes' test results had so far equaled those earlier developed by different organizations and that over the next three months, it is expected that they would exceed anything available today. The meeting was adjourned for coffee and there seemed to be a highly animated discussion going on in Italian among the Azienda di Transporto Rapido participants.

When the meeting was reconvened the chairman explained what had been discussed in Italian over coffee. He invited Roger and Ming to live in Rome at the company's expense until their project was passed over to their engineering personnel. They would be given an office each, a laboratory, an English-speaking technician and a generous daily per diem. Roger thanked the chairman and the meeting and after conferring with Ming, he replied that they would give their answer tomorrow.

The meeting closed, and Ming and Roger returned to their hotel in time for lunch. Ming said, "Are we eating in or looking elsewhere?"

Roger replied, "It all depends on whether or not we take up their offer."

Roger was thinking about his Telecom project and how working in Rome would give him some privacy. The problem would be the language. Italians who are capable of speaking English feign ignorance if there are other Italians within earshot, and it is difficult to befriend an Italian if you do not speak their language. It takes three to six months to attain a rudimentary fluency. If you can speak a second language that part of your brain is developed, making learning faster and easier.

Roger did not ask Ming what she wanted to do because, he knew, she would remain silent if she thought she could gain the upper hand. She will find out what he wanted to do at the meeting tomorrow morning.

He went back to his room to freshen up.

Roger was lying on his bed when his door chime sounded. He got up and let Ming in. She was all dressed to brave the drizzle, so they went out and lunched at Antica Birreria Peroni and drank Frascati Regillo Castelli Romani with pecorino pepato cheese, until late in the afternoon. She did not ask him how he was going to answer tomorrow.

They met a group of Americans in the restaurant. This was good for both of them as it cleared their minds with fresh feelings and much laughter. They drank on with them until the early hours of the morning, promising to meet them again tomorrow night. Ming and Roger stumbled back to their hotel after making many wrong turns.

They were picked up at eight in the morning, and the meeting reconvened. The chairman asked what their decision was to be.

Ming answered that she did not yet know. Roger answered that he would stay and work on here, after his university gave their acceptance.

After the meeting was finished Ming asked Roger why he had not discussed his decision with her first. He said when you dressed to go out it meant you would not be coming back here and would not be taking up their offer. So, in effect, I discussed it with you. You did not ask me what I wanted to do, so I did not say anything to you.

You keep playing these childish games and all you do is well and truly piss people off. If you want to stay, then say so, don't keep waiting for people to beg you, because they will not. I am not sure that Karim will ask you if you have made up your mind. If I were him, I wouldn't.

Check with the hotel to see if Karim has left you a message. If you want to go, then say it to him. Likewise, if you want to stay.

Ming asked Roger what he wanted her to do. I want you to produce something special. You can stay here and work with me, or you can go back and work in Rochester, but do something special. She bleated, "Wouldn't you be lonely without me?"

Roger said, "Quite honestly no, as I have so much work to do."

When they got back to the hotel, Ming checked at the front desk to see if there was a message left for her. There was a note asking her to attend an eight-thirty morning meeting tomorrow to give her decision. A car would be waiting for her at eight in the morning to take her there.

She showed it to Roger, who said, "Don't screw it up and apologize for your delay." He continued, state that everything is dependent on your university clearing this.

When your meeting is over, join me at Antica Birreria Peroni for lunch; the restaurant we had lunch at yesterday.

She met him at the restaurant as planned and over lunch explained to him that she was returning to Rochester tomorrow morning. Her reasons were: She would be lonely here with Roger working all the time. She missed her agency job and couldn't wait to get back to the covert operations. She preferred Americans who spoke English, and she preferred American food and the American way of life.

Roger was relieved by her decision as he could drop his guard and get back to his Telecom project. After lunch, Roger returned to his hotel for a nap, and Ming went walking. She returned two hours later and rang his door chime. She explained how she was going to miss him, but as she had a commitment with her project, she would see it through and make three monthly reports out to Karim and the various deans on her progress.

The next day, Ming returned to Rochester and Roger got back into his Telecom project, calculating and rechecking his mathematics. He couldn't see for the life of him where his mistake was hiding. If he needed parts, he would ask Tulio, his technician to get them for him.

Roger sent a message to Peter explaining all that had happened and forwarded to him his calculations for checking.

After feeling frustrated by the Telecom project he decided to get back into his propulsion project (PP). Furthermore, he was not happy that Ming had left as he knew that he would feel empty for a couple of days. He continued designing the magnetron using a unique ferrite, he sintered himself and an unusual shape for the cavities that interlinked with each other. These cavities alternated in position around the anode enhancing the rotating field, and the microwaves produced. He kept tweaking his design by changing the positioning, increasing each time the microwave power he produced, all the time thinking about new design configurations that could increase power without unduly increasing size.

He now had to design and build a klystron to amplify the power of the magnetron beam that was to be sent to the base of the rocket. A klystron's power extends over a vast range, from a few watts to many megawatts and are also very efficient, as high as 80% with a narrow bandwidth, that is, they amplify only over a small range of frequencies. This means the main application is for radar and in high-energy particle accelerators. Roger's initial design is for a 3.50GHz, 100 kW carrier wave klystron to match his magnetron frequency. Roger worked on this for three more months until he had designed the beam type of propulsion machine that was better than all available throughout the world.

He demonstrated it to his colleagues and Karim, who came over especially for the occasion and bade his farewell. They asked him to stay and work on another project, but after six or more months, Roger needed a break from Italy, Italian and spaghetti, even though they were in summer. He thanked them and stated how he regretted going as he had made many friends, and had learnt how to speak broken Italian. His farewell party was large and boisterous, and he drank copious amounts of wine without vomiting. When Karim was nearby, Roger took the opportunity to ask how Dr. Lovelace's project was progressing. Karim said, after she left Italy, they hadn't heard from her again.

After finishing working at the plant, he spent a month touring Italy: Going on boat tours. Bus tours and every other tour imaginable. Finally, he had enough and he returned to Rochester without getting himself involved with any other woman, no matter how pretty she was.

His dean was at the airport in the morning to meet him and to welcome him home. Over coffee, he told Roger, Dr. Lovelace had not been seen around his offices for the past six months or more. He also added that there was a royalty document waiting for him, and the university thanked him for a job well done.

When back at his university, Roger took from the dean, his Royalty document and his Telecom prototype for setting up in his laboratory. Peter had replied that he could not find anything wrong with his calculations. He knew the dean would be asking him to explain what this project was all about, hopefully later than sooner.

He thought he could be seeing Vivian soon, as her grapevine would have let her know he had returned.

Once back in his laboratory, that afternoon, Roger arranged his Telecom prototype in a safe place that was not easy to see. Still, he was not happy as it was easily seen by someone looking for it. He thought he must give more thought to having it properly hidden from view.

For the Stegan Code, Roger started thinking about a key generator based on the US date format; of the month of the year and the year since zero BC with the day of the month as an offset, added to each pair of digits. For example, for March 18 2014, the key would have an offset of 18 for the number of days and would be 03+18,20+18,14+18 or 213832, and the next day would be; 03+19,20+19,14+19 or 223933. This would mean that if the algorithm was known, the key could always be determined.

Roger sent this to Peter for his approval, and any comments that he may have. Within the hour, Peter responded with OK I like it.

Roger felt that he had achieved something, so he went over to one of his drinking bars and ordered a bottle of wine. A fat heavy hand placed itself on his shoulder from behind, and he heard the words, "Hi Dr. Redman. Where have you been hiding?" Roger turned around to see Igor's beaming face staring into his eyes, and he replied, "Italy." Igor asked, "I hope it was a successful trip?"

Roger replied, "Yes. Let's see if we can find a table to sit at." Once comfortably seated, Igor asked Roger what he had been doing there. Roger briefly explained. Roger asked, "What has been going on here?" Igor said, "Dr. Lovelace returned and caused a terrible row at her university. It caused her dean to be sacked due to Gross Incompetence because he did not respond to a letter of intent she gave him over a space propulsion project. Roger replied how he was sorry for her, but not for her dean. He said to Igor, "Where is she now?" Igor said, he thought she was still working at her university, but couldn't be sure. Roger said, I will go over to her university tomorrow and speak with her.

The next morning, Roger drove to Ming's university to try to find her. He went to the Physics School and asked some students where he could find Dr. Lovelace. They pointed to a building, and Roger walked over to it. He saw Ming through a window and navigated to where she was sitting. Roger said to her cheerfully, "Hi Ming, how's tricks?" She looked up and scowled at him. Immediately, he regretted looking for her. Roger said, "I just came over to let you know that I'm back, but if you are busy I can come back some other time." He turned to walk to his car. As there was no response, he kept walking until he reached his car. He got in and started the engine. He now had a response from Ming, who was running towards him. She said, "What do you want?" Roger quite peeved answered, "I don't want anything, just came to say Hi." He continued, "Now that I have said it. I will be going." She said that she would come around and see him. He gritted his teeth and answered, "OK."

Roger drove back to his offices and started working on his prototype. It fired up OK, but did nothing spectacular, just lifeless hardware. He heard a knocking on his office door. It was the dean wanting to know what he was doing with his prototype. After the morning greetings, the dean said to Roger that this project of his has been going on for some time now, what is it? Roger knowing the dean was no physicist replied it was a device that allowed him to study the interaction of particles in such a way that it opened unknown doors into the subject, showing new particles arising from their combinations. This satisfied the dean's curiosity that wanted to know if it could be used for anything. Roger replied by saying that it is purely academic at this stage and would remain so until he discovered something of practical use. The dean thanked him for the explanation and his time and went his own way. Roger wrote down the conversation and sent it to Peter, in case he faced questions about the project sometime in the future.

The Stegan code design was finished, and nobody should be able to crack the key as the algorithm existed only in the minds of Peter and himself. However, the key was not changed from the old to the new now, as there was no reason to change it.

It was already lunch time and Roger was hungry. He packed up his project and closed down his computer, locked his doors and walked towards his car. Ming had just arrived and was getting out of her car. She waved at him. He stopped the car engine and walked over to her car. Where are you going, she said? Roger, not wishing to pay for her meal, answered that he was just going to a supermarket to buy some provisions.

Ming asked with a highly aggravated voice, "Why have you been lying about me? Telling Karim and the rest of the Italians that I haven't finished any project since you met me."

Roger replied with a tone, showing his annoyance, "What are you carrying on about? I have never in my life discussed you in a negative way with anyone. Check your sources, before you come accusing me!"

With that, Roger walked back to his car got in, and drove off. Ming followed him to the steakhouse where he had pulled in. He ordered a twelve-ounce Filet Mignon and French Fries. When she sat down next to him, he told the waiter that she may place her order separately if she wanted to eat. She waved the waiter off and got up to leave.

"What do you say when you're asked questions about me?"

Roger answered, I always say, "I don't know."

She raised her voice and said, "You are a liar."

Roger answered, "Whatever you say."

As she left the restaurant, Ming turned her head to him and said, "I hope I never see you again."

CHAPTER 4

MING

After some time passed, Ming started to fall in love with Roger, but he did not reciprocate, as his work was his only consuming passion.

Ming's loyalties are not steadfast, which may be due to Roger not wishing to marry her, though she wants, very much, to marry him. A desirable, beautiful and intelligent woman, but who is unpredictable. She is dangerous and ruthless when it comes to her enemies and can jeopardize the overall project in a bout of jealousy. She is also a spy for the US government.

Although she said that she hoped never to see him again, she went to his apartment that afternoon, crying and sobbing. After Roger calmed her down and caressed her, until she was back to her normal self, he asked her, "What happened?"

She told him, her dean told her before he was sacked that Karim, and the Italians felt that she couldn't do the project, so they said to her dean not to submit the letter of intent because it was no longer valid.

Roger said that this was nonsense, because I asked Karim at my going-away party how you were doing. He answered that they heard nothing from you since you left Italy, and they were still waiting for an answer from your university.

She said that she took the matter up with her Vice-Chancellor and gave him the letter of intent, which started proceedings to have her dean fired. However, in the furore, the reply to Karim and the Italians was overlooked.

Roger said, do you still want to continue with your project? She answered that she did. Roger said, let's go and see my dean and ask him to help.

They walked over to the dean's office, and Roger asked his secretary to inquire if he could spare a couple of minutes.

Roger explained all that Ming had told him, and Ming gave him the letter of intent. The dean said to leave it with him, and he would contact her university, Karim and the Italians, and would get back to them once he had something definite to say.

Roger said, "Where is your prototype?" Ming answered, "In my laboratory." Roger asked, "Can you still work there, or would you prefer to work here?"

Ming answered, "I would prefer to work there as I am not disturbed, and I have all my parts there. Furthermore, my prototype, the ion thruster, is fairly large."

Roger asked, "Have you done any work on it since leaving Italy?" She replied that she had and was about one month away from completion. Her project was already more advanced than anything in the world, and she wanted to get the last mile out of it. She wanted to make a film about her test results to show Karim and the Italians before handing it over to them that her prototype exceeded by a long way anything available today.

Roger's dean walked over to Roger's offices and met them there. The dean explained that the vice-chancellor of her university apologized profusely for being remiss in following through to its conclusion the administrative duties of his ex-dean and would be appreciative if Roger's dean assisted. Roger's dean agreed to help. Ming explained to Roger's dean that she was one month away from finishing her project, and that it was already more advanced than anything in the world today. She would make a film of her test results to show to all when she handed over her prototype. The dean said he would contact Karim and the Italians and pass on her comments and ask Karim to prepare her royalty document.

It was already evening, and they went to a fish and chip restaurant to eat. After the meal, Ming paid the bill.

The next morning Ming returned to her laboratory to continue with her project. Roger was at a loss with his Telecom project as he had checked and rechecked it and still it was not working as it should. He dared not proceed with the prototype construction until its problem has been resolved because it may cause a large runaway explosion. He put it away for another time.

Roger walked over to the dean's office, and the dean explained that Karim and the Italians had replied and were very excited over Ming's work and were looking forward to meeting her again on completion of her project. The dean asked Roger how his project was progressing. Roger explained that he had come to a complete stop because there was something he did not understand. It would take time for his mind to sort through all the combinations and alternatives. He said, it's better to stand back, and return after a while with some fresh ideas.

That afternoon Roger was very busy trying to arrange his design and papers for sending to Peter, for checking, and then Ming walked in. She was the last person he wanted to see right at this time, and he regretted giving her a key. He didn't want her to know what was happening at the moment, mainly because it would distract him by having to explain to her all the details. However, as soon as she looked at Roger's computer screen, she could make out an email to Peter explaining the problem.

"Hey, hey, what's going on? She demanded whilst reading all the email to Peter. Why haven't you let me in on this? Her voice was rising. Roger knew that she would next go into her screaming, ranting and raving phase. She will do it again, no doubt when he changes the lock to his door, but she is more than likely going to shoot the new lock open. Her voice had now reached screaming pitch at a level three decibels below the threshold of pain. What a noisy bitch!

Roger bellowed, "Why don't you shut up?"

Her voice was still increasing in intensity.

"If you shut your mouth, I will tell you what it's all about," Roger yelled back to her at the top of his voice, much to the delight of the rest of the University campus. Finally, he flung her into the bedroom and locked the door.

After all had settled down, Roger explained to Ming his problem with his analysis, and he was sure that only Peter could find out where the problem was. He promised to inform her about any new developments. He reminded her of her promise not to feed information on any of his projects to her control. She looked at him as if to say; you are pussy.

He thought to himself, what you want and what really happens are two different things. Still, tell her the minimum, and if you can tell her nothing, that is even better.

Roger explained to Ming what his dean had told him about Karim and the Italian's response to her project. She beamed with happiness that everything had been restored to normality.

Ming demanded, "Well, are we going out to dinner or not?" Roger really hated her at times, and this was one of those times. He preferred to be drinking with Igor or with any of his other men friends than being with her. He told her to stop being so aggressive otherwise she could go by herself.

She quietened down and asked where he wanted to go. They went to one of their favorite Italian restaurants and ate and drank until they were very tipsy.

The next morning Ming went back to her university to continue working on her propulsion project.

Roger helped his graduate and undergraduates in their studies. They both worked like this for the next one and one-half months.

It was late summer, and Ming was finally finished. She informed Roger and his dean, who in turn informed Karim and the Italians. They invited her to return to Italy with her prototype and the film showing her tests and test results. She arranged with carpenters to box properly her prototype for air shipment. Roger took the details of the carpenter for later when he may need to box his own Telecom project. Roger informed her of the tours she could take as it was late January and still warm there.

Ming said, "Why don't you come with me"?

Roger answered, "I don't want it to look like I am stealing your thunder, also, I think Karim and his dean will be inviting us to take up another project soon, before you leave for Italy, probably this time more akin to weapon development." Roger continued, "If you remember they didn't like my clause that stated: No part of our research and development is to be used for weapons, so they may want to test if the wind is blowing from that direction or whether it has changed."

Ming, still pushing her point, said, "It would be really fantastic if we could go together on a wine tour. I wouldn't want to go on one by myself." Roger said we should see what happens over the next couple of days before we start making our own plans.

Roger watched as his dean was walking over to his offices. Roger said cheerfully, "Good afternoon dean." The dean returned the greeting and said Karim and the dean of the National School of Applied Sciences (NSAS) in Safi had sent you a message inviting you and Dr. Lovelace to attend a meeting in Singapore, the day-after tomorrow.

When they arrived at Changi airport, they were driven to the Royal Plaza on Scotts, where they checked in and freshened up. There was a message waiting for them stating that they would be met at eight in the morning and taken to the National University of Singapore. They went downstairs to the buffet, at the Carousel dining room, which was one of the best in the world for choices. After eating they really couldn't do much else, so they went upstairs and each sprawled over their beds and dropped off to sleep.

Orchard Road and neighboring Scotts Road form Singapore's shopping district. Orchard road has several kilometers of the road lined on both sides by shopping malls. These malls in many cases link in an underground complex of pathways. It was eight at night when they surfaced. Roger was the first and banged on Ming's door. She opened the door bleary eyed, and Roger asked if she wanted to go out. The shops close around nine-thirty at night. Fancy a walk. They walked around for an hour. Ming said, is it my imagination or are these Singaporians the rudest people in the world? They keep walking in front of my feet. Roger said, yes I have experienced the same thing, but they move so fast you can't kick them. Definitely, you can't find anything like it elsewhere. They should make a tourist attraction out of it: Come to Singapore and make a trip out of it.

The next morning they arrived on time at the National University of Singapore (NUS) for their meeting. In the meeting, Ming and Roger noticed Karim, and four asian men were already seated. Karim chaired the meeting and introduced Ming and Roger to the four Asians, who were directors of two prominent Research and Development companies. Karim explained to Ming and Roger that what was required was an antimatter generator for space craft propulsion and scientific research that confines the antimatter in a strong electromagnetic field until required. Roger looked at Ming.

Roger passed a note to her to see if he could go ahead and table proposals more stringent than for the propulsion project. She looked at him and nodded. Roger stated that Dr Lovelace, and myself will table our conditions for the development of this project later today or tomorrow morning.

One of the Asians said that this was unacceptable. You are not in the position to dictate to us your conditions. Roger answered, are these also the feelings of your colleagues?

The answer came back by same Asian, yes these are our feelings.

Roger said, I must apologize to the meeting, but we do not have any common ground to continue with this meeting.

Karim suggested that there should be a break for coffee to give everyone a chance to cool off.

Roger said to Ming, I have a lot of experience of Asian intransigence during contract negotiations. Better to close off now rather than have them screw us stupid.

Karim came over and said, these people will never change, and they always wonder what they have done to lose contracts.

Roger asked Ming if she agreed with the following contract points:
- We ask for 20% royalties on delivery of the prototype and design,
- We work in Rochester at each of our Universities,
- Under no circumstances, will there be any design notes passed to any party other than the dean and Karim,
- Karim will fund the projects through the Rochester universities.
- No part of our research and development is to be used for weapons or weapon's research.

She agreed, so Roger passed the contract points over to Karim.

Karim spent some time talking to the Asians and there were a lot of heads shaking going on. After some time, Karim said the meeting is closed, for the moment, and if there are any further developments, I will contact you. Roger said, you can let them know that the price has now risen to thirty percent royalties, and we will return to Rochester tomorrow evening. Karim said, I like your style.

It was still early when they left the university and asked the driver to take them to Sentosa to ride the flying fox. It is over 450 meters long and at 72 meters above sea level, the MegaZip flying fox lets you ride over the jungle canopy and Siloso Beach.

Sentosa offers a suspended rope course and a free-fall simulator. For a more strenuous adventure, ClimbMax is an aerial obstacle course set among the treetops. It allows those who choose to take the course, to navigate wobbly bridges, balance on swaying tightropes and scramble along cargo nets high in the sky. Ming and Roger were not interested in passing an army entrance exam, so they rode the MegaZip flying fox. They asked their driver to take them to Imbiah Lookout Car Park, where they caught the flying fox and to meet them at the Beach Station to pick them up when they had finished.

They returned to their hotel for lunch and looked at the Carousel restaurant spread and agreed to try something else. They booked and caught a taxi to Raffles. Raffles Hotel is a colonial-style hotel in Singapore. It was established by two Armenian brothers from Persia—Martin and Tigran Sarkies—in 1887. It was named after Stamford Raffles, the founder of modern Singapore, whose statue had been unveiled in 1887. Ming and Roger went to the Tiffin Room for a buffet and ate at one of the finest eating places in the world. Again, they excelled themselves and after they finished, they returned to their hotel for a nap. There was a message from Karim waiting for them at their hotel lobby, informing them the meeting would be resumed at eight-thirty tomorrow morning, and a driver would be waiting for them at their hotel tomorrow morning. Ming and Roger arranged for an early-morning reminder call, so they could get a cup of coffee before they left.

Roger asked Ming, "Are we sticking to the thirty percent royalties or what?"

Ming replied, "After an hour of hard negotiating we will drop to twenty-five percent, but no further. We work in Rochester and the clause stating that our work is not to be used for weapons or used in weapons research remains."

They went up for a nap that lasted the whole afternoon. When they did eventually surface, they decided to go to BluJaz Café. Strolling in along the narrow Haji Lane's standalone boutiques, you can feel something distinctive in the air. Blu Jaz's characteristic yellow frontage and the three floors of this jazz venue are different from any others in Singapore.

They got back to the hotel by midnight.

The next morning after their coffee, they were taken to their meeting.

Karim chaired the meeting and announced that an agreement would be reached by the Asian Directors if the American contingent agreed to waive the weapon's clause. Roger nodded to Ming to give an answer. Ming explained that this would not be possible because, first we do not wish to design instruments of war and secondly, our Government would prevent us from working on a project that could be used for war without their approval. Again, we have arrived at an impasse unless you have something further to say. The meeting went silent and the Asian contingent really did not know what to say. Roger said. I am sorry, but I have to force the issue. We have very pressing projects, back in the States, that need to be closed off, and if we cannot reach an agreement now, we wish to close this meeting without any further delay. One of the Asians called Karim over and chatted to him. Karim stated that he wished to call a coffee break. They all stood up, and they made their way to the toilets. Karim came over to Ming and Roger and stated that they had them by the short and curlies now.

Look at them, they have all gone to relieve themselves.

Ming asked Karim when she should be going to Italy to present her Ion Thruster to them. Karim said he would get back to her after the present negotiations were complete.

Karim addressed the meeting and stated that the Asian contingent agreed to Roger's and Ming's demands and asked if they would provide details on how they were going to design this device without a Hadron Collider.

Roger replied, these details together with; their three monthly progress reports would be sent to their deans for forwarding to Karim and then, in turn, to yourselves.

The meeting finished, and everybody left. Roger said to Ming, Now that we got our thirty percent royalties, I can eat, and I'm hungry. She agreed, and they went back to their hotel for a sumptuous buffet, starting with the King Prawns, Oysters, Crab and so on.

Before retiring to their rooms, they checked at the front desk for any messages. Karim booked a flight for them that left at five in the morning. Their flight went from Singapore to Tokyo, Detroit to Rochester and would take thirty hours or more. Karim also passed on his congratulations on a job well done and was looking forward to receiving his first report.

Ming said, we should be in bed by midnight.

The two days later Roger met with his dean who was overjoyed by the letter of intent and gave his hearty congratulations. He asked if Dr. Lovelace had the same for her new dean. Roger said yes. He said, "They gave you both a tough time I hear." Roger remained silent as he thought it a rhetorical question.

The dean asked, "How did you like Singapore?" Roger answered, "It's good if you like an overcrowded place full of rude people who believe the sidewalk is their property."

Over lunch, Roger and Ming discussed their project. They knew that a project of interest to them was reported, by Gianluca Sarri from The Queen's University of Belfast, Northern Ireland, and colleagues in their report in Physical Review Letters. It described, a new tabletop method for generating electron-positron streams using a very high-powered laser (petawatt) fired at helium gas. It would cause the creation of a stream of electrons that would move also at high speed. These electrons if fired at a very thin sheet of metal foil would cause them to collide into individual metal atoms, resulting in dense, narrow streams of high-energy electrons and positrons. These jets emerged in shorter duration, denser pulses than those generated in traditional large-scale (~km size) particle accelerators. These two streams could then be separated using magnets. They also knew that each blast of the laser would produce ten to the power of fifteen positrons, which is a density level comparable to that produced at the European Organization for Nuclear Research (CERN) Large Hadron Collider.

The laser-based system, which is less than a meter in size, can simultaneously generate jets and plasmas, something that cannot be done easily using other methods.

It was clear why the Asian contingent acquiesced to Roger's and Ming's demands when scientists claim that antimatter is the costliest material to make. In 1999, NASA gave a figure of $62.5 trillion per gram of anti hydrogen.

Roger and Ming agreed that the first thing to do would be to construct a larger power and smaller physical size laser than the petawatt laser used in the Sarri report. This laser was externally supplied and was not a part of the tabletop unit.

Maybe an improvement on the Trident design of Los Alamos using neodymium glass, giving a power around 200TW or more would be suitable. We could experiment with that and see.

They guess that chirped pulse amplification (CPA) short pulse mode would give on each blast of the laser, many positrons.

They decided that Ming would design the laser and Roger the positron gun, positron storage and other ancillary equipment.

They continued in their design and construction for the next three months and made good progress. They submitted their report to the dean for passing to Karim and a film of their test results. After six months, they completed their project, had it professionally boxed and handed it to Roger's dean for shipping to Karim with the design and test results. They each received their fifteen percent royalty certificate.

After one or more weeks, Roger's dean informed them both that Karim thanked them on another successfully completed project and that the customer was satisfied.

Both heaved a sigh of relief that all was finished and agreed that they both needed a rest lying somewhere in the sun sipping on gin and tonic.

Roger said, "I have a funny feeling, and so we should take this opportunity to arrange for our own security in the event we are forcibly separated."

Ming agreed. Ming said, "What do you suggest?"

Roger said, "You are the expert in this area, what do you suggest?" She suggested that a coded, email drop box somewhere in the US would be sufficient. Roger suggested the Stegan code with the key; Mingsplace, would be adequate and they would check it every day they were parted. When they got back to Roger's offices, Roger arranged through his hosting site all the details. They tested that it was operational. They left to go to lunch. As they walked towards Roger's car, a black 2013 Ford SUV pulled up and two men jumped out and grabbed Ming. She swung around and kneed one in the groin, who collapsed onto the ground in pain, and punched the other in the throat. Her mobile fell to the ground during the fracas. Another man jumped out and pointed a glock 19 directly at her head. She had no option but to surrender to him. He put her in the back of the SUV and after the other two got back into the back seat, they drove off leaving Roger standing by the road. The other two men punched her incessantly in the head until she was unconscious.

Roger went through her mobile looking at her contacts until she found one that could be her control. He rang the number and explained that the owner of this mobile had just been abducted by four men in a Ford SUV. The line went dead, but Roger was sure he had passed the information to the correct people.

Roger got into his car and drove off to have lunch, as there was nothing, he could do.

Neville rang Roger in the afternoon to let him know that a covert group well known to Ming is holding her for reasons unknown to him. Roger thanked him for this information and replied; God help them.

After lunch, Roger returned to his offices. Ming turned up very angry at three. Her face was badly swollen, bruised and cut. Roger didn't dare to ask her what happened, but suggested going to a medical clinic for treatment. She agreed, and she was treated. She looked worse after treatment than before. Ming asked why he was laughing. He replied that he had just thought of a funny joke, but had immediately forgotten it. She was not impressed.

Roger mentioned that he rang, who he thought, was her control. She said, he guessed correctly, and it was that telephone call that secured her release. It was the same incompetent group that lost three men last time, the Foreign Agent Control Group. Roger asked, how many men did they lose this time? She replied, "They will never learn. They lost another three men." Roger asked if they were the same three who beat you up. Ming replied, "Yes, the same three." They locked me in a cell. When I lifted my dress, one came over to start fondling me. I was able to take his glock 19 and shoot him between his eyes. The gun-fire attracted the other two who couldn't see where I had gone, but I could see them, and I shot one in the temple and the other in the ear-hole.

My control said their control was very angry indeed because they didn't clear it through her before they abducted Ming. Roger asked, "Why did they want to abduct her?" Ming replied, "Because they thought she was a spy out of Morocco." Roger shook his head over how inane these people really are. Roger said, "Didn't they rectify the mistake they made last time?"

Ming answered, "Evidently not."

Roger said, "Well, I suppose you must be very hungry after your activities today. Do you want to go and eat a late lunch or early dinner?"

Ming wanted to go and eat steak and crab, so they went to the Crab Shack and feasted on Steak & Snow Combo, and Ming drank copious amounts of Blackstone Merlot and Rex Goliath Merlot until she felt totally relaxed. Roger said to Ming, "Can I fondle you?" Ming answered, "If you do it here, I will shoot you where we will both regret it. If you do it at home you will have to work very hard before I let you have any rest."

Karim sent a message to Roger's dean asking Ming to present her final Ion Thruster to the Italians. He booked a plane for her to depart in two days time. When she arrived at the Italian meeting with her prototype and the film showing her tests and test results, she presented them to the Italians. She explained every aspect of her project and how far she had progressed over the past three months. Her film of her final lab tests showed how she had surpassed anything available in the world at the moment. After she finished her presentation, the meeting was opened to questions. After the questions subsided, she was met by tumultuous applause.

She returned to Rochester the following day and was met by Roger and his dean at the airport who congratulated her on her efforts. The Press were also at the airport to interview her on her achievements. She received the hero's welcome on returning home.

CHAPTER 5

VIVIAN'S APARTMENT

Neville appears not to have the qualities to guard the secrets of the Stegan Code and the project, but he does. He came to Roger's offices and informed him that Ming is a very competent and respected spy in the Government and has passed on to the Government details of his Stegan Code, giving Roger his Stegan Code key as proof of what he is saying. Roger, thanks Neville for giving him this information, but notices that this is not his latest algorithm, but the key used to send to Peter the message concerning the problem that he is having with his analysis.

However, it does indicate that Ming is still cheating by giving to her control, messages meant only for Peter.

Roger asks Neville if he knows why agents keep abducting her. Neville answers; it is because she is familiar with all the different agencies and knows what each of them is doing. What is the function of the Foreign Agent Control Group?

Neville answered; they are an illegal government hit squad that operates, ostensibly, under the auspices of the FBI and targets legitimate groups inside the USA. The FACG believes that she is a danger to them, and so they have targeted her and will continue to target her until she has been neutralized. Where are they located? Neville replied, Who knows? They're a bit like the Scarlet Pimpernel.

Roger said, "Thanks for the information," and thought that at the rate, Ming had been reducing their numbers, they will not be around for too much longer.

Roger sent a message to Peter explaining that the last code, not the algorithm, has been compromised and never should be used again. Peter acknowledges Rogers message.

Roger thought it better to say nothing to Ming so as not to be on his guard when he sends messages to Peter. She will, for the moment, believe that the old code is still valid.

Not that there was anything to send to Peter as the Telecom project had ground down to a halt and all other projects had been completed.

There was a knocking on his office door, and Roger saw; Ming, Igor and Neville standing there. Roger smiling, said, "Is it my birthday?" No! Ming exclaimed, you and I are celebrities. We are on National TV for our Space Shuttle propulsion projects. Roger said, "Don't be too pleased with yourself, you know we will probably be kidnapped for this by some space cadets." Ming said we should go out drinking to celebrate.

They started with wine, Igor, of course on vodka. As the evening wore on and everyone was getting quite tanked up, some loud-mouthed kid who had been watching the news started making rude comments about Ming. Igor wanted to step in, but Roger said, just let her handle this because he doesn't know who he is playing with. Ming told the kid to go back and suck his mother's milk as he couldn't take anything stronger. The kid came over to slap Ming, who slammed his arm with her elbow snapping both bones in his forearm. She then punched him on the base of his nose rendering him unconscious and very bloody. Igor said to Roger, I won't ever argue with her. Neville said sarcastically, I'm so pleased she is on our side, and we should go out like this more often. They moved over to another bar to continue drinking. They drank for a couple of hours more and then left. There was an ominous SUV prowling around outside of their drinking place. Ming was aware of the danger and took a mobile bomb from her handbag. She clutched it and waited for the occupants to try to abduct her. She punched the first guy who lurched at her and rammed the mobile down his throat, making him choke as he was not able to pull it out. She fired shots into the SUV and shouted to Roger, Igor and Neville to run for their lives. The car raced off and when it was far enough away, she triggered the mobile with her own, blowing up the SUV and killing all of its occupants.

Igor and Neville said good night to Ming and Roger stating that they would take a taxi home. When they were safely inside the taxi, they said they didn't want to go drinking again with those two. They play too rough.

Roger said to Ming, I think it would be wise to go somewhere else for a change and let things cool off here a little. Ming was not interested in going anywhere as she was quite happy getting rid of the Foreign Agent

Control Group. Her control told her to stop killing the agents from this group. Ming testily replied that they were the aggressors, and she was only defending herself.

The next morning Roger went to his offices and saw a note under his door requesting him to go and speak to his dean.

He went to his dean's office and saw Karim sitting, waiting for him. After the usual greetings, the dean introduced the subject of developing a high-power hand gun for neutralizing an aggressor.

Roger explained to his dean such a project is progressing all over the world at the moment and thousands of man-hours of development time have already been spent by governments and private industry. For example, in 2010, Kratos Defense & Security Solutions were awarded an 11-million-dollar contract to develop LaWS (Laser Weapon System) for the US Navy, which spent about $40 million on research, development, and testing of the laser weapon.

Roger continued, how could we compete against the number of man-hours of development already spent and the amount of money presently being expended?

The dean shrugged and said the four Asian Directors had put this to Karim to see if we were interested.

Let me take this up with Ming, and perhaps you can check with the Government to see if there are any restrictions on this sort of R&D being carried out by a university without prior approval. My feelings are you will get a negative answer from all quarters.

The Dean thanked Roger for his comments and said he would reply to him once he has more information.

Roger drove over to Ming's university to see if he could find her. She was not around so he went to a fish and chip restaurant for lunch. When he returned to his offices, he found Ming waiting for him. She asked him why he was looking for her. Roger explained the conversation that he, and the dean had just finished.

Ming was not overly keen on entering another contract with the four Asians, especially over weapons, even though they were handguns.

Both Roger and Ming decided not to pursue this project any further. They walked over to Roger's dean's office to let him know their decision. The dean thanked them and said that he would inform Karim that afternoon.

Two days later, Roger's dean said the Asian men would pay thirty percent royalty as well as a handsome weekly per diem deposited into their local account in advance. They would provide; in Singapore's East Jurong, a two-bedroom condominium with an en suite bathroom in each bedroom, on the premise's clubhouse, swimming pool, tennis courts and gym, for them to live in for the duration of the project. The condominium is five to ten minutes walk to Boon Lay MRT or Jurong East Shopping Center.

They would provide each person an office and a laboratory in their factory at Jurong West and a technician for purchasing any parts required, as well as a driver to drive them back and forth between their office and condominium and anywhere else they desire.

Roger and Ming looked at each other.

Ming said, "How long do you think it would take us to complete this project?"

Roger replied, "No longer than six months and a hand gun will sell very well."

They both agreed to go for it and informed Roger's dean to initiate the paperwork for the commencement of a new project once more.

They found themselves properly settled in Singapore within the month. Their condominium was most suitable; their offices and laboratory were like they had been designed by them, and their per diem payment allowed them to buy the items they would have purchased in Rochester.

Ming and Roger moved into their productive mode, then they were kidnapped by one of the remnant gangland secret societies in Singapore. These societies have been largely eradicated as a security issue in the city-state since the 1950s. Strong police action such as the 1956 Operation Dagger and the 1957 Operation Pereksa greatly disrupted the secret societies' economic activities, but they managed to survive by going underground in a much reduced capacity. However, they still exist.

It all happened so quickly. Ming didn't have a gun or mobile bombs. She did have her cyanide syringe hairpin that would come in handy once she had a chance to relieve one of her kidnappers of his firearm.

They were taken to a Chinese home, well furnished without being opulent. Their captors were not carrying firearms, but they probably were carrying long knives under their changshan.

The matriarch of this household was a thin, well-dressed woman who spoke impeccable English. Not knowing what power she wielded, Ming and Roger kept their mouths shut until they were asked to speak.

She spoke softly and with authority, "I am Madam Chi ko Hong. I have invited you to my house to explain something to you of the utmost importance. Your laser gun project is for four of the wealthiest men in South-East Asia, who have factories in most countries in this part of the world. These men are all personally known to me and were the dons of our families from the Triad in Thailand, Taiwan, Singapore and Hong-Kong. Once you have finished your project and handed it over to them, they will conduct their trials by killing you with your own design, not by paying you as you expect. This better be understood."

After a brief pause, she continued, "Keep working until you near completion, then return to the USA and to ensure your royalty, have the closing negotiations completed by your university and Karim, and have them hand over your concluding test results and design plans. The prototype should be held by someone in Singapore, preferably a European and only released once your university is satisfied all payments due have been completed." She paused again, "My people now will return you to your condominium."

Roger said when they were on their way home, "It was very good of her to give us that advice."

Ming said, "Yes. Do you remember the English guy, Tony Townsend, working in Jurong East, on miniature antenna design for mobiles and handheld computing devices? We could ask him if he could hold the prototype until we are ready to give it over."

Roger replied, "Yes; that's a good idea."

They had dinner and had an early night. The next morning they were picked up and taken to their offices.

Roger suggested that Ming completed the laser design as she had a lot of experience in the design of the laser for the antimatter generator. Roger would design the gun mechanisms and anything else.

They worked without incident for the next three months and submitted their report to Roger's dean, who passed it onto Karim. They contacted Tony in Jurong East and arranged with him to take the prototype when they were ready. They continued working for the next three months or more and passed the prototype to Tony and caught their plane to Rochester without any problems. When they arrived back, Roger passed the final report to his dean who asked where the prototype was being kept. Roger explained that they needed to know where to send it. The dean passed the final report and design plans to Karim and asked him where the prototype should be sent. The dean asked Roger why the cloak-and-dagger stuff? Roger explained, without mentioning names, what Madam Chi ko Hong had told them. The dean understood.

Karim replied later that day with a Singapore address. Roger SMS'd Tony with the address and asked him to go to the Post Office and mail the packaged prototype to the Singapore address. He asked Tony not to write his address on the package, but a false one as it may cause him to have a problem later.

After he had completed what he was asked to do, Tony SMS'd Roger stating all was done as he requested.

Roger informed his dean that the prototype had been sent to the address given.

Tony rang Roger informing him that the false address he put on the package he posted had just been blown up. Fortunately, he added, the flat was unoccupied so nobody was hurt. Roger thanked Tony for all of his help and told him that these were criminals who wanted Ming, and himself put down. Probably best to keep the matter to himself rather than tell his friends about it.

A couple of days later, Roger's dean gave each Ming and Roger their fifteen percent royalty certificate.

Ming said to Roger, "That closes that chapter."

Roger replied, "I don't think that we want to be dealing with those people again, not even to give them an updated version.

We really should open our private factory, like Mr. Glock, and manufacture and sell our individual guns. We would do well."

"Yes," Ming answered, "but it would be quite boring sitting in a factory all day, each day doing the same thing."

Roger continued, "We could employ workers to do the assembly work."

Ming responded with, "Salaries, benefits, pension, and so on. Are you going to that or do we employ someone to do that? How do we cover ourselves against theft, accident, etc.?"

"I would rather keep doing what we have been doing." Ming said.

Roger replied, "Yes; you're correct. It starts to get boring when you take all of these things into consideration."

Roger returned to his apartment before going out to eat and met Vivian waiting for him. She said that she had heard that he was back and thought she would come over for some fun. After having their fun, they went out for dinner and happened to meet Neville at their favorite Italian restaurant. He invited them to join him. They did so and had a very good time, drinking wine and more wine. The next morning Vivian did her early morning, disappearing trick and Roger knew he wouldn't see her for a couple of days. He wondered how much longer he would be able to live this charmed existence where Ming and Vivian come to his apartment on different nights. Maybe he should say something, but not to Ming as she would probably shoot him. He had very vivid thoughts about what terrible things she would do if she caught them in bed. He shook his head, trying to banish the thought.

Roger went to his laboratory and thought about his stalled Telecom project. The lack of progression with this project was causing him some concern. He knew that it was only a matter of time that again, he would see his way forward.

He received an SMS from Tony, who informed him that the criminals who bombed the apartment near his were going through their ex-apartment with a fine-toothed comb, looking for something that could give them an indication of where they were now living. Roger answered, thanks for the information and make sure you keep your distance from these people and don't let them see you looking at them. If they think, you can give them information, you will die a slow, painful death even if you have nothing to give. We will not be able to help you. Please clear all messages to and from us on your mobile immediately.

Tony answered, "Really, cloak-and-dagger stuff eh? OK, I'm clearing all messages off of my mobile right now."

Whilst Tony was using his mobile to converse with Roger, he was observed by one of the criminals inspecting Roger's ex-flat. The criminal walked over to him and asked him what he was doing. Tony answered that he has been trying to SMS his girl friend about going out tonight. Why do you ask? He asked. The criminal walked off. Tony caught the lift and exited the condominiums to ensure that they wouldn't know where he lived.

As he walked away from the condominiums, three thugs grabbed hold of him and beat him senseless, leaving him bleeding on the pavement. On several occasions, passers by looked at him and walked around him, but offered no help. Eventually, he summoned enough strength to make it back to his condominium where he showered and patched himself up as well as he could. The following day, he went to the estate agency handling his condominium and asked for a new condominium on a higher floor and facing in a different direction. He moved in within three days. He rang Roger and informed him about his bad fortune. Roger said, I told you not to look at them. Think yourself lucky that you were beaten only.

Roger told Ming what had happened to Tony. She shrugged as she didn't care. She had bigger things to worry about. Her control told her that the Foreign Agent Control Group were out to kill her. Ming responded with, the morons. Her control told her that they had greater resources than she had, so she should be always on her guard. Ming said, she knows many groups like them and ours, and I will bring some of them into play, unless they assure me that they will cancel the contract out on me.

When her control told the FACG's control what she had said, they replied with, why should we be worried about that.

Ming started making phone calls to her contacts asking them for help. All replied that they would help her because the FACG had also been stepping on their toes and were looking for an excuse to put them back in line.

The next day, Ming's control got back to her stating that the FACG now has a hands-off policy concerning Ming and will no longer be trying to kill her.

Vivian came to Roger's apartment later that afternoon. Roger whisked her into his car and drove her for an early dinner. She objected as she wanted to have fun first. Roger said that he had a problem because his sister has come to stay after breaking up with her husband. He asked her if they could go to her place. She exclaimed, "No! What would my neighbors think of me, taking a man into my flat? They would start calling me a Brazen Hussy."

Roger responded by saying, "Ok, we should find a cheap hotel."

Vivian answered authoritatively, "There are no cheap hotels in Rochester."

Roger answered under his breath, "Yes, you would know."

He was very annoyed as he was going to lose this beautiful, satisfying woman, unless he could come up with an answer straight away. He decided to rent a one-bedroom furnished apartment near to where he was living. It would suit Vivian and give him some privacy from Ming's prying eyes. If he wanted, his royalties would allow him to purchase it. Not that he wanted to do that at this time. He made arrangements with his realtor and could move in straight away. Vivian was very pleased with it and asked if it was for her. Roger answered that it was not for her, but would be used like his other place that his sister is now living.

They had their fun and early the next morning she was off as was her usual habit and Roger went back to his old apartment to take his project and hardware for the Telecom project and set it up in Vivian's apartment. Ming was there, and Roger thought how clever and proactive he was to forestall a major disruption in his life. Ming asked him where he slept last night. He didn't answer her, so she shouted and screamed and ranted and raged at him until he answered, "At my Mother's place." She continued with her raging and added to it by blustering, "You lying son of a bitch; your mother has been dead already ten years!" She continued louder and louder, "Where have you been? Where have you been, you turkey? I'm going to get my gun and shoot you if you don't answer me RIGHT NOW!!!" Roger ran off and got into his car and drove off. He drove to Vivian's apartment, parking his car some distance away and settled himself down there. Again, he was thankful he had the good luck to have a back-up place to live and work. Ming tried to ring him, but he did not want to answer her. He knew that when she calmed down, she would be her usual purring self.

Roger drove to his usual drinking place, hoping to meet Neville and Igor. He met Neville and discussed the triad in Singapore, explaining how a very helpful lady advised them what to do. Neville said, "Ah yes, that would be Madam Chi ko Hong." Roger was aghast and said, "How do you know such things?" Neville replied by saying that it was his job to know these things. He continued, "I am very pleased that you both followed her advice to the letter. She will take it as your way of thanking her."

The hand guns will be useful to the US government. If these people didn't try to kill you both, I wouldn't entertain the idea of selling your invention to another organization. I can arrange a meeting with US army personnel to set up contracts, etc. I will set up the contracts and arrange for payments so that I can take my share. You and Ming can build the prototype and produce the final design test results.

I need to clear this with Ming, my dean and Karim first. Then we move forward from there.

OK said Neville.

Roger went back home and downloaded the plans for the gun, arranged them and uploaded them to his safe place in case Ming started getting silly again.

The next morning he awoke to the smell of freshly brewed coffee and bacon and eggs on toast and Ming's cat smiling face. He jumped out of bed and quaffed his coffee and greedily devoured his breakfast. Ming hadn't started eating hers. Roger poured himself another coffee.

He explained to her, his discussion with Neville and to his utmost surprise, she completely agreed. They put Neville's proposal to the dean and asked what he, and Karim thought about their plan. Karim thought it a little dangerous, but if Neville could get military or government backing, it would be quite safe. Neville said he would start scouting around for organizations that would be interested.

Within a week, Neville arranged and called a meeting between them and the military to be held in the dean's conference room at the university in two days time. Three days later, after the first meeting had concluded, another meeting was set up between them and the Government. Karim sent his apologies and hoped all went well with the meetings.

The first meeting was scheduled to begin at eight-thirty in the morning. Neville chaired the meeting. Attending the meeting from the military side were two Captains and two Lieutenants. All around the table were introduced.

Neville opened the meeting by explaining that a powerful handheld laser gun had been developed by Drs. Lovelace and Redman. This gun had one setting for kill and the other for stun, for operation at distances up to fifty, one-hundred, two hundred and one thousand meters.

The closer range kill setting permitted one-hundred shots to be fired, whereas the one-hundred meters setting permitted fifty shots, the two-hundred meters twenty-five and one thousand meters permitted five shots. The recharge time is negligible if portable battery packs were used. The remainders of the specifications are tabled for out of meeting reading.

I now open the meeting for discussion and any questions you may have for Drs. Lovelace and Redman.

I am Captain Kabour, and I am very angry that you haven't already handed over your designs and test results to us before this time. If you are true patriots and not pariahs on the state, you are to surrender your designs and test plans to us now, so that we can ensure that you complete the prototype under strict military supervision.

The meeting fell on a stony silence. Neville's face was very flushed, and he asked the meeting if there was anything else that needed to be discussed? After another stony silence, he closed the meeting and thanked everybody for their attendance. Roger and Ming heard Capt. Kabour ask Neville what was going to happen next, and they heard Neville answer, nothing we are all going home. Capt. Kabour asked, what about the designs and test plans. Neville answered there was nothing coming from this meeting.

Three days later the second meeting was held. Again, Neville opened the meeting by all round introductions and then by explaining that a powerful handheld laser gun had been developed by Drs. Lovelace and Redman. There was one setting to kill and the other for stun, for operation at distances up to fifty, one-hundred, two hundred and one thousand meters.

He continued to elucidate using the kill setting, the distinct number of shots available for the different range settings.

Once the gun's features were described, he opened the meeting for discussion and questions that the Government may have for Drs. Lovelace and Redman.

All Roger's people, including Roger's dean, were tense from their experience with the military contingent. However, this time it was a pleasant experience with intelligent and informed questions being asked. Ming and Roger could answer all questions put to them, to the satisfaction of the Government contingent.

The following contract points were asked to be ratified:
- We ask for 30% royalties on delivery of the prototype and its design,
- We work in Rochester at each of our Universities,
- Under no circumstances, are any design notes be passed to any party other than Roger's dean and Neville,
- The Government will fund the projects through Rochester university,
- The contact person for any further questions or negotiations for this project is Neville.

Neville responded with the Government's agreement with all the contract points, and the prototype commenced to be rebuilt at Roger's offices.

The doors to Roger's offices were to be locked at all times to stop prying eyes from seeing what was going on.

There was an aggressive knocking on his outside door. Roger answered the knocking and was met by a thin gnarled man who could have been one of the trees out of The Wizard of Oz.

Roger opened the door and noticed the man put his foot in the doorway to prevent the door from being closed.

Roger politely asked, "What can I do for you? Would you please take your foot out of the doorway."

The man rudely snapped back, "I am a Government representative, and I am here on official business."

Roger said, "I don't care who you are, get your foot out of my doorway." Ide complied, and Roger proceeded to ask him what was his name and what did he want.

"I ask the questions here." He said.

"Oh, no you don't," replied Roger, closing the door, and locking it from the inside.

Ide pounded on the door. Roger said to him to go away, or he would call the security guards forcibly to remove him.

The pounding stopped, and he disappeared. Ming asked what was going on. Roger explained to her that some guy claiming he was government came on official business, so he said.

CHAPTER 6

IDE

Ide failed to gain entrance to government service due to his limited abilities and having a suspect security clearance. His whole life has been marred by failure, and he is a psychotic. However, as a free-lance investigator his contacts extend into the government, and he arranges for his payments to be made into his account on completion of contracts he is awarded. A prototype and its design plans are lucrative contracts not only from his government, but from non-US governments. He informs the government of Roger's Stegan code, and his designs without checking the veracity of his sources.

Ming and Roger are still very busy on the laser gun project that they are nearing completion and do not need unwanted and unwarranted interference. However, nothing goes as planned and Ide's poison causes agents to come looking for prototypes and designs in his offices.

Neville rings Roger to let him know what is afoot and suggests that he leave his prototypes with him and work in his safe house completing the gun project. Roger thankfully agrees and arranges for the Telecom and the laser gun prototype to be left with him. The gun designs are updated on Roger's laptop and hidden in Roger's protected place and also in Neville's secure place on the Internet.

Governments (not all friendly) send out their agents to take the details and any designs. They go to Roger's laboratory first and take all the old, out of date design notes from his office. They start blaming a different overseas faction for taking the prime designs, and this turns into fighting and then to slaughter.

Roger with his laptop puts up at one of Neville's safe houses, not wishing to compromise Vivian's apartment.

Ming returns to her friendly Government's safe house undisturbed by the antics of foreign agents.

Ide has informed the Government that Peter is involved in the design, without knowing which design he is referring to. All he hopes to achieve from this is to disrupt Roger's work and destroy his credibility.

Roger continues to work alone on the laser gun project. He does not miss Ming's help as they both have completed the same work before. If Ming was with him, project completion would occur earlier.

Roger continues to work undisturbed like this for the next month, sleeping at Neville's safe house.

Finally, the project is complete and requires live target testing. Neville arranges this with the government who takes butcher's carcasses and spaces them as specified in Roger's test plan. The tests prove to be successful and Roger completes his final test report.

Roger hands over to Neville, his final test report, his designs and the prototype and thanks him for his hospitality before leaving to go back to his home and offices. Neville says to Roger that also he can take his Telecom project. Roger asks Neville if he can return at another time to collect his prototype, as he needs to check the security of his offices before he continues working on it.

Neville agrees.

Neville says to Roger that their fifteen percent royalty certificate will be given to him, and to Ming when the government has prepared them.

Roger thanks Neville once more and returns to his apartment. There was nobody there. He drives over to Vivian's flat, and meets a handsome young man lounging around and drinking coffee. Hi, said Roger. May I ask you who you are and what you are doing here. The man replied that he is Vivian's associate, and he is waiting for her. Roger said, please go and don't come back to this place. If you see Vivian before I do, tell her also not to return to this apartment.

Who are you? The man politely asked Roger.

I am the owner of this apartment.

"Oh, OK." The man answered. He continued, "You had better take the key then." Roger took the key, and the young man departed.

Roger returned to his apartment and met Ming.

Roger mimicked Ming, "Where did you sleep last night?"

She screamed at him, "Where did you sleep last night?"

As usual, Roger didn't answer, but walked out of his apartment to go to his usual drinking place anticipating he would meet Igor there. Ming came running after him yelling, "I'm only joking." He stopped and returned. After he went back inside the apartment, he told her that the gun project was finished, tested and handed over. She wanted to know how he did it. Roger explained that it was completed at Neville's safe house. Thank you very much for completing the project, she said, I have been worried since Neville's message letting us know about agents coming to take the prototype and design notes.

Roger asked, "Did they come?"

Ming answered, "Yes, and they killed each other on your office front lawn competing for what they thought was the latest prototype and design."

Roger said, "That is due to that evil bastard, Ide lying to the government causing all the agencies to go into a Shark Frenzy."

"I would like to go drinking," said Roger.

Ming asked, "Can I come too?"

"If you don't kill anybody," answered Roger.

They went off to Roger's drinking place where they met Igor and Neville, who both said they would be going when they saw Ming. Roger said to them, she promised to behave, please don't go. Igor and Neville looked at each other and agreed not to go. The first sign of trouble we will be off, they threatened. OK, said Roger.

Roger said to Ming, "I am losing my friends because of you and your killing sprees."

"What can I do if someone tries to kill me," she retorted.

Roger answers, "Nothing, then I do not lose my drinking friends."

Ming snaps back, "you're starting to hurt my feelings, and I'm getting angry."

"OK, that is enough, I'm going to get something to eat and go home."

Roger started to leave and Ming grabbed hold of his sleeve and said, "Don't be like that. Come on, we will enjoy ourselves."

Roger saw Ide and mentioned it to Igor. If this guy steps out of line throw him out, before Ming shoots him. Igor said he will be watching him for anything he does to spoil anyone's fun. After an hour or more, Ide became abusive and two guys not connected to Roger picked him up and threw him out onto the sidewalk where he continued to yell abuse and berate everyone. One of the two guys said to Ide; don't come back in if you want to keep your front teeth. While screaming and hurling abuse at everyone, Ide left.

After they finished drinking, Igor, Neville, Ming and Roger went to a steak house to dine, and a very merry time was had by all.

When Ming and Roger got back to Roger's apartment, Vivian was sitting on the steps, waiting. She said to Roger that Donald had given her key to him. Who is Donald? Ming asked, "Roger replied, Vivian's boyfriend, and he didn't give me any key belonging to her."

Vivian said good-bye and left.

The next day, Ide came to Roger's offices demanding that he give him his prototype and his designs as he was on bona fide government business. Ming opened the outside office door and shot him in his foot.

She screamed at him, "Don't come back here you lump of worm vomit unless you want me to fill your head with lead."

Ide hobbled off and got into his ugly little Ford Prefect and drove off to the nearest hospital.

Roger said, I am tired of all of these morons playing on my front lawn. Maybe we should design and build a microwave fence, so that anyone who tries to cross it will have their clothes burst into flames.

Ming said, "What about the postman?"

Roger said, "What about him?"

She continued, "He will have his uniform and letters burnt."

Roger continued; we would warn him by placing a big sign on their office lawn that reads:

"Do Not Enter Here!
Protected Area!
Microwave Radiation Hazard—KEEP OUT!
Your clothes and belongings will burst into flames if you enter here.
You Have Been Warned!"

Ming said, Oh! Yes! I like it! When do we start building it?

Roger replied; we don't start building such a thing as it would be against the law to burn people with that device. The military would love it, but after our experience with Capt. Boofhead, I'm not so sure we should design and build a prototype such as this, for them.

The dean said, coming into view, "I heard that conversation and I'm sure Karim would love it!"

Hi dean, both Roger and Ming said, we would like to go to the Maldives, just West of Sri Lanka. I'm sure there would be plenty of very rich people there who would like their property protected.

Roger said, "Why don't you come also as our Chief Procurement Officer."

The dean replied, "That sounds very tempting. Let me see what Karim says."

Roger asked why he came over to his offices. The dean answered nothing really. As I was a little bored sitting in my office, I thought I would come over and see what you both were up to. Now that I know, I will return to my office and try to start the usual processes.

Three days later, the dean came over to Roger's offices and announced that Karim was most positive about this project, and if we agree, he will do the negotiations on our behalf. The royalties would be thirty percent as before.

The Republic of Maldives is a group of 1,190 coral islets in the Indian Ocean about 417 mi (671 km) southwest of Sri Lanka. The islands were first settled in the 5th century B.C. by Buddhist seafarers from India and Sri Lanka. Maldivians are almost entirely Sunni Muslim, Islam being adopted in 1153. Originally, under the suzerainty of Sri Lanka, they came under British protection in 1887 and were a dependency of the then-colony Ceylon until 1948. An independence agreement with Britain was signed July 26, 1965. For centuries, a sultanate, the islands adopted a Republican form of government in 1952, but the sultanate was restored in 1954. In 1968, however, as the result of a referendum, a republic was again established in the recently independent country. The current President is Abdulla Yameen, who was elected in 2013 by defeating former President Mohamed Nasheed in a runoff election.

Roger asked Ming if she agreed to let Karim handle the negotiations on our behalf. Ming said she agreed, but they must include accommodation and per diem in the contract package for three people and provide their own installation contractors. The dean agreed to send this information tonight to Karim before the close of business.

Three days later, Karim replied the contract is signed and the Maldivians are awaiting the designers. Karim also added that there are many such contracts awaiting installation and would they be interested in setting up a training program to allow their own people design and install the equipment. Ming, Roger and the dean agreed.

Roger and Ming started on the design.

Roger asked his dean if he drank alcohol. He said that he did. Ming and Roger invited him to drink with them tonight and then go on to dinner. He happily agreed.

Roger, Ming and the dean went for a seafood dinner and after to a drinking place familiar to Roger. Yes, his two drinking friends Igor and Neville were there already drinking. They welcomed Roger's band with the Ming caveat, and a new round of drinks was ordered. After a couple of hours, the place was rollicking when Hopalong Tassidy Ide came in, complaining about that woman pointing to Ming. Igor gave him a stern warning that if he didn't stop making trouble, he would break one of his arms and then throw him out. He also had the support of many guys drinking there. Ide started his swearing and cursing. One of the guys who had been drinking a little too much grabbed Ide by the scruff of the neck and threw him out of the drinking place, telling him not to return if he didn't want his bad foot stomped upon. Ide issued forth a stream of invectives to the man who threw him out. The man walked over to Ide and gave him a swift kick in the pants to send him on his way.

Poor little man thought Ming; all he could do is use his tongue to fight with. Next time, she thought; I would give him a tongue lashing he will not forget in a hurry.

Roger's group continues carousing until they were asked to leave as it was closing time.

The next morning Ming and Roger planned their microwave fence. The fence had three settings: Kill, Stun and burn. It was not the same as the design of an electric fence as it did not require an Earth return to make it operate. Its operation was based on radiation as found in a microwave oven. Basically, the design is thus, if a one kilometer stretch of fence is taken, then a transmitter at one corner would burn at three hundred meters, stun at two hundred meters and kill at one hundred meters. The transmitters were all spaced at one-hundred meters, and any transmitter was activated according to the distance an intruder was found and what setting; burn, etc. was required. Overlap of microwave power was prevented by the turning off of unwanted transmitters for the required setting.

For the first and primary design, Roger's dean procured the equipment required and arranged for it to be shipped on a particular ship to the customer's port in Male, Free on Board (FOB). That means the seller delivers goods on board a vessel designated by the buyer. The seller has fulfilled his obligations to deliver, when the goods have passed over the ship's rail. Transportation of the goods to the customer's premises from Male port was to be arranged by the customer when the vessel berthed.

All of these arrangements were the responsibility of Roger's dean. Based on the shipping schedule, Roger's team would go to the Maldives.

Further contracts would be negotiated once Roger's team was in country.

Ming asked Roger's dean if he was married? The dean said that he was once, but his wife died in a car accident. They had no children, and that is why he is free to go on trips like this one.

Later in the day, the dean said their project equipment would be shipped in a couple of days to arrive in the Maldives one month henceforth. The airline flight will take 24 hours from Rochester to Male with layovers in New York and Dubai.

Roger and Ming provided detail designs of their microwave fence together with equipment requirements so that any irregular fence line could be easily designed. The microwave source and its klystron, designed by Roger for the Italian propulsion project, were housed in a thick concrete fence post away from prying eyes. This meant ten of these items per kilometer were required for one side of a square, or forty units were required to protect one square kilometer. AC power was supplied via a cable that ran under the fence line, and terminated inside each of the one hundred meters spaced concrete fence posts. The fence was supported by concrete posts spaced ten meters apart. Tomographic motion detectors were used to locate an intruder so that a particular section of the fence could be automatically or manually activated. A computer monitored the protected area and showed on a map, where an intruder was trying to get in. As expensive as the project was, the client, who in this case was the government, was getting value for their money.

Ming and Roger normalized the project costs to one-hundred meters, or the nearest one-hundred meters, based on a kill setting. This allowed them to reckon the costs for any new project and could also be used for teaching the Maldivians to design and cost their own projects.

The finalized fence design together with its procurement schedule was developed.

The time was now ready to go to the Maldives. They would catch their plane at three in the afternoon and arrive at Male at three in the afternoon on the next day to be met by Karim's contact.

By the time they booked into their hotel in Male it was late in the afternoon. There was a message waiting for them stating that they had a meeting at eight-thirty and there would be a car waiting for them at eight in the morning.

The meeting was very cordial and became more informal as the day wore on. It was with government personnel and contractors together with Roger's group.

Roger's group went through the Maldivian's requirements, making adjustments to their own design until all were satisfied and knew what needed to be done. Work would start tomorrow, and Roger's group would be supervising the work to ensure that it was installed as agreed.

That evening, the Maldivians took them to a party, set up in their honor, and they ate and drank until the early hours of the morning forming bonds of friendship and camaraderie.

The next day, the installation of the fence continued. Roger's dean informed Roger and Ming that he had been invited to provide a quotation for another project eighty kilometers south of where they are on Male Atoll. They agreed, but asked him to take some trainees with him who would start providing their own quotations. So, the dean's party left for a very good time, still on Male Atoll. The dean thought that perhaps he would never return to Rochester as the people were extremely warm towards him and the women quite forward and there was plenty of interesting and new work here. That night, he telephoned Roger to tell him that he wouldn't be back until tomorrow. Roger thought nothing about it, but after a week of not returning, he and Ming, we're starting to become concerned and thought about driving down to see him.

When Roger and Ming arrived, they saw Roger's dean surrounded by pretty women all fawning on him. Roger's dean showed them the new contract plans that would be ordered and implemented by the Maldivians.

Roger asked how are you going to construct the Microwave Cyclotron and the Klystron?

The dean said, "Can't I put in an order for them."

"Yes, but you are not familiar with this equipment," replied Roger.

The dean said, "I will use identical equipment and equivalent equipment purchase orders and your connection designs."

Roger could not argue with him because he was correct, and he was intelligent enough to understand and interpret Roger's design.

Ming asked him if he wanted to return to Rochester with them when the main project was complete. He answered that he didn't have any intention of returning now. What have I got in Rochester? I have nothing really to rush back to. Here the people are kind and friendly, and there is enough work for ten lifetimes.

Ming grimaced at Roger, who shrugged back to her in return. When they were on their way back to the hotel, Ming said, "He's gone tropo."

Roger quickly replied, "Nice way to go!" And added under his breath, "Beautiful nubile maidens come and smother me to death!"

Ming continued, "I suppose he will resign his post at your university."

"Maybe he can take furlough or long service leave or . . ." Roger said, when Ming wryly added, "Sabbatical."

Roger groaned at the thought of taking a year off from his university to be trained in love making by these lustful lovelies.

Ming asked, "What's wrong with you?"

"I was just thinking of my dean's good fortune." Roger replied.

It was late afternoon, by the time they had returned and Roger went looking for a beautiful woman. When he found the beauty, he dreamed about, he booked into a hotel for the evening. Once he had his wicked way, he didn't feel angry anymore and the beautiful woman was fast asleep on the bed, so he didn't have to feel guilty, still he left a fifty dollar note on top of her clothes.

He went for an early dinner and went back to his hotel.

After one month, as they did each three days or so, Ming, and Roger went out into the field to see how the installation teams were progressing against their planned schedule. The concrete works were nearing completion by the eight teams assigned to this work. Two teams per side of the square shape were allocated, and the cabling installation was completed.

The dean showed up with two Maldivians and wanted to see how their project was progressing as his was very similar. He inspected the form work used for casting the posts and for the trenches and coverings that would be containing the cable runs.

He expected his hardware to be shipped in within the next month and asked what they did about security against theft during the night. Night guards with dogs seemed to be the answer. The client was most excited as it meant that he would be able to store, valuable items that were easily stolen, now within the fence boundaries.

As Roger's and Ming's project progressed, more and more Maldivians looked at the project with an avid interest. Aviation people for storing their parts and planes, supermarket chains for storing their goods. There was no stopping the number of applications that could use it.

Roger suggested that cooperatives of similar materials be formed for sharing, a secure area that could be subdivided among the members, for example, airlines, helicopters, private light aircraft and warehouses.

This idea was readily accepted by businesses, especially as it would be designed, purchased and built by the Maldivians, so their money was not running away from them.

Roger and Ming achieved some notoriety with their project, which they really didn't need. TV interviews, Newspaper interviews and Radio interviews were all refused. The client of their project (the government) came to their aid by employing a media consultant to handle this aspect of the project. Roger and Ming spent some time instructing this consultant, who was very competent in his job. This took the heat off of Roger and Ming, allowing them to get on with their job.

Roger's and Ming's project was about one month off of completion, when Roger drove down eighty kilometers south of where they are on Male Atoll to see how his dean was faring with his project.

Roger met him in jail. He was caught having sex with one of the pretty nubiles when they were interrupted by the religious police who had them thrown in jail.

Roger said, "Maybe we will have you back in Rochester after all." He continued, "I was wishing I had half your luck, when I left here last time with Ming."

Roger said, "I will try to speak to the man who awarded us the contract, on your behalf. I will state that in the Maldives, all the women are so beautiful that it is a honey trap working here. Meanwhile, you can see if you can find the name of the man who had you imprisoned."

Roger returned to his hotel and explained to Ming what happened to his dean, and the ensuing conversation that he had with him.

The next day, Roger contacted the government representative and started to explain to him what happened. The GR stopped Roger by saying that he already knew what happened. Roger asked him what his dean should do. The GR said, he can change his religion to Islam and marry the woman, or he will be deported after a severe lashing and jail sentence.

Roger thanked the GR for the information. Roger explained, over an early lunch with Ming, his conversation with the GR. After lunch, he and Ming drove to Roger's dean's location, eighty kilometers south and asked his jailor if they could speak with him.

Roger explained what the GR said. The dean was overjoyed because he wasn't worried about changing his religion, and he could continue working here married to a very pretty woman.

The dean warmly said, "Thank you for your help Roger."

"I take it that I can go back and report your response to my government contact," Roger said.

The dean answered, "Please do."

A month later they were married, and Ming and Roger were there enjoying the festivities.

Roger asked his dean what he was going to do about his job at the university. The dean replied that he would ask him to take a letter back on his behalf. This letter would be for a one-year Sabbatical. One year later, I will write to the university tending my resignation.

My apartment and furnishings belong to the university. The few possessions that I have are books, to which you are most welcome. I have lived a Spartan life all of these years and have had no need for a car. The dean added a very simple closure to end a long and interesting career.

Roger and Ming were finishing their project and were on the last tests before the project handover. These were completed over the following week. The most difficult part of the testing was ensuring that the stun settings caused stun and not kill. Live test objects were not available, so Roger devised a surrogate that registered an equivalent burn, stun and kill depending on the intensity of the microwave radiation. After his tests were concluded he gave it to his dean for use in his present and future projects.

That evening the Maldivians held a going-away party for Ming and Roger with many speeches and flowing tears and Ming and Roger gave their parting farewell to Roger's dean and took his sabbatical letter and house keys.

The next evening they flew the twenty-four-hour journey back to Rochester. When they had settled into Rochester, Roger gave the Deputy Chancellor the dean's application for sabbatical leave. In return, he gave Ming and Roger their two fifteen percent royalty certificates from Karim with a note thanking them for completion of another successful project.

That night they met Igor and Neville and explained that Roger's dean had married a beautiful lady in the Maldives and was probably never coming back to Rochester. He further explained that he had a successful business there and was accepted by the locals as one of them. Roger and Ming said that they were sad to see him leave the university, as he was an important and dependable person to us because he procured material that was required for our projects and liaised professionally between the two universities on our behalf.

CHAPTER 7

PETER'S INTERROGATION

Roger being foolish discusses with Ming his Telecom project, outlining his problems. He said, he had not been capable of moving forward in his design for the last six or nine months. He hoped, all this time, that it would come to him why he was not capable of progressing. Nevertheless, the clearing of the problem did not come to him in a flash, or even very slowly. After he spoke with Ming, he regretted letting her know anything about his Telecom project. They have gained an International reputation as competent physicists and are always being observed by the Media and by people wanting to develop crazy ideas into reality. Anything Ming tells her control or her friends immediately cause a response. Ming has many friends, some of them good and reliable, but many who are evil and quite treacherous. The negative contingent of her friends has ties with Ide. Unfortunately, the positive side of Ming's personality is counterpoised with her bravado that surfaces and plays havoc with her relationship with Roger, so there exists a love-hate relationship between the two. Ming will disclose all the minute details of Roger's work to her friends, whether they are good or evil people. This leaves Roger open to attack by agents wanting to exploit his work.

Ming's friends inform Ide that Peter has been helping Roger with his design problems and has an in-depth understanding of Roger's design. This in turn is passed onto the Government's agents who arrest Peter and prepare him for interrogation.

Ide, being the instigator of Peter's arrest, claims precedence over all the other agents as being the prime interrogator when the interrogation of Peter commences. Ide informs Peter that the Government will let him go back to his University, if he can tell him what Roger's project is and does and what its present problems are.

Peter laughs in Ide's face, realizing immediately that he is a subspecies, and says he doesn't know what the Hoo-Hah is all about. Peter tells Ide that he, and Roger had been working on particle physics interactions for some years now, and he can find details of their results in the technical literature. "There is nothing to hide here. If you have specific questions, I will be most happy to answer them for you," Peter says.

Ide asks, "Why have you been hiding your results in code?" Peter replies: "Because of the competition between our country's Universities and overseas Universities. The Universities operate on worldwide grants. The higher the University's technical standing in the International Community, based on published papers and on the global recognition of their staff, the more grants they attract.

Your interference by unjustifiably incarcerating me and hounding Roger has caused much damage to the standing of the academic community in this country and to this country's international reputation. We are becoming a laughing stock among our peers, and jokes are starting to appear on the Internet that alludes to us working in a farmyard. I will be making complaints to the President's technical advisors about you and your Department and ask that you be summonsed by the government for wrongful arrest.

Not long after this interrogation finished, the door to the one-way mirror interrogation room opens, and a Government official enters. Ide stands up in respect, and the official sits down in his place opposite Peter. The official states that it was not their intention to cause damage to their reputation and on behalf of the Government, he apologizes if any damage has been done. Peter is then driven back to his University.

After a phone call, Neville informs Roger that Peter has been released and is back in his University.

"Thank God for that," replies Roger.

If they have let Peter go, I should be left alone for the moment. Roger thanks Neville and asks him if he can use his safe house. Neville states that he may return any time, but warns him always to use the proper procedures when returning. Roger returns to his office to collect his Telecom project and laptop and goes to Vivian's apartment. Thank goodness, I had a fast Internet connection put on. He makes himself comfortable with coffee and settles back into his mathematics. There is something intrinsically wrong here. What is it? He checks his prototype against his mathematics and finds everything is correct. Why don't his iterations converge? What a pity Ming cannot be trusted, perhaps she could work out why his calculations do not converge.

He composes another Stegan coded message using his new key algorithm and sends it to Peter. He states that there is something intrinsically incorrect with his mathematics, not that there is something in error with his mathematics. He also states how disappointed he is with Ming as she can't stop herself from leaking his work to the outside world.

After sending the message to Peter, he uploads his latest results to his safe place on the Internet and closes down his computer, getting ready to retire.

He notes that it is six pm, and the night is young. He hears a soft knocking on his front door and opens it to find Vivian standing there.

She asks Roger if they can have some fun and then go and eat. Roger agrees, and they go and eat Steak and French Fries and return to the apartment for the desserts. After all was complete Roger suggested that they go to Roger's drinking place and meet his friends. Vivian excused herself saying that she had a prior appointment she didn't want to break. When Roger arrived at his drinking place, he met Igor but no Neville. Igor said, "Neville was too busy to make it tonight."

After a good night of talking and laughing, Roger returned to his apartment and met Ming waiting for him.

Roger asked fairly roughly, "Why are you waiting for me?"

She answered, "Because I feel that you are angry with me."

Roger said, "Why should I be angry with you?" He continued, "You have only disclosed all the minute details of my work to your friends. Your friends have informed Ide, the guy you shot in the foot, that Peter has been helping me with my design problems and has an in-depth understanding of my design. This in turn was passed onto the Government's agents who arrested Peter and prepared him for interrogation. The interrogation has now been complete with damage to our reputations and International credibility. In addition, you passed to your control, details of my Stegan code for them to monitor my private transmissions to Peter. How do you answer this?" Ming remained silent. Roger said, "You are not welcome to my office nor to my apartment now or any time in the future. I regard you as a liability in my life."

Ming left Roger's apartment without saying a word.

Before settling down for the night, Roger sent an email to Karim explaining to him that his dean was no longer working at the university and had married a Maldivian lady and was living and working in the Maldives.

The next morning, Roger received a return email from Karim sending his congratulations, if he ever spoke to his dean again, and asked him if he was free to take on another project.

Roger replied, that he was free to do so, by himself.

Karim said his client is a very rich hobbiest who wants his hobbies to be used by the military. He desperately wants to win the intelligent mouse robot competition and will pay one hundred and fifty thousand dollars if he wins first prize, reducing by halves to ten thousand for fifth prize or less.

Karim asked him if he was interested in designing a drone mouse who could defend itself against other rodents and cats. It would be equipped with scaled-down radio controlled cameras for surveillance and with high temperature needles for self-defense. It will have a minute Alkaline Fuel Cell to provide it with power for four hours. It will use Mecanum wheels or Ilon wheels, or whatever you devise, to allow drive trains that are capable of moving it in any direction. By simply powering each wheel with a different motor and changing the directions the wheels spin, the mouse will move in different directions.

Roger said, if this means that I will be dealing with Capt. Boofhead, the answer is no.

Karim answered; I have already lodged a complaint against Capt. Kabour with his superiors. You will not be dealing with him again.

Roger asked, where do I go to do the development work and how long have I got?

Karim answered, wherever you want to go and the competition is in three months time.

Roger continued, who pays for the parts?

Karim answered; you buy the parts you need and submit a claim through me.

Roger answered, OK. I accept. Roger contacted hobbyist electronic parts suppliers like Mouser, Radio Shack, Jameco, Digikey in the USA and asked them to send to him their catalogs. If he couldn't find what he wanted among these catalogs, he would go to Texas Instruments, National Semiconductors, Fairchild, etc.

After one month his parts were in, and he started construction. His printed circuit board manufacture and hybrids were out-sourced to specialist companies that could ensure him with a quick turn around.

He had a plastic mouse body made, the same size as a real mouse, and he arranged for all of his electronics to fit into this body. Besides the electronics, the body covered the wheels making it more realistic. It could sense when it collided with objects and would change direction to run alongside of them and would stop if it was in a cul-de-sac and couldn't turn around. The control unit was used to guide the mouse in a general direction and to monitor what was in front of it. Hot needles protruded out of the front of the mouse if the control unit indicated danger or a cat was ready to attack it.

Roger had two weeks left before the competition and thought about using that time on a modification. He introduced a loud squeaking when the mouse was being attacked. He also introduced memory into its circuits so that if the mouse was successful in getting out of a maze, it could remember it for the next time it was put into the same maze, no matter where it was placed.

The day of the competition came, and Roger submitted his mouse as number eighteen. The numbers of competitors were thirty four.

When it was Roger's turn to demonstrate the capabilities of his mouse, he thought that he didn't have a hope because of the quality of the other contestants. He demonstrated how his mouse could squeak and fend off attackers and after learning a maze could escape from it from any place in the maze.

After the contestants had each shown their mouse, the competition was judged. The first prize was awarded to a club who submitted a mouse who could move and turn very quickly and, which had learnt how to escape from a maze in an amazingly short time.

The second prize was awarded to a very surprised Roger. He also appeared on television as the first runner-up in the competition for advanced mouse robotics. He returned home at the end of a long day and showered and lay on his bed and promptly fell asleep even though it was only seven in the evening.

He was awakened by his front door bell. It was Igor wishing to tell him how his drinking friends wanted him to come to his drinking place and celebrate with them. He dressed and followed Igor to their usual place. Neville and others offered their congratulations, and they all drank on to the early hours of the morning.

The next morning Karim rang him and congratulated him on another job well done and said that he was sending him a check for seventy-five thousand dollars and was awaiting his component cost receipts. Eventually, Roger submitted his receipts.

Peter sent a coded message to Roger letting him know that he would be coming to Rochester tomorrow and could he stay with him for a couple of days. Roger replied that he would be more than happy to put him up.

Roger met Peter at the airport and took him back to his apartment, just in time to meet Ide at his front door. Ide was coming to abuse Roger for letting Ming shoot him in his foot. He didn't immediately recognize Peter. Peter punched him on his face, breaking his nose and then punched him in the eye very hard making his eye swell straight. Roger stomped on his bad foot causing him excruciating pain and making him scream so loud it could be heard a block away. Peter yelled that he is never to come here again unless he wanted his arms and legs broken. Roger and Peter entered Roger's apartment, and Peter took his bags into the spare bedroom.

They went off for lunch at one of Roger's favorite Italian restaurants. After eating, they continued drinking red wine until five in the afternoon. Roger explained what happened to his dean and said, I suppose the dean's post is up for grabs. If you are interested, we can take a walk over to the Deputy Chancellor's office tomorrow, and I will introduce you to him. Peter replied that he would like to sleep on it before making any overtures to Roger's university.

Roger took Peter to his favorite drinking place and introduced him to Neville and Igor. They drank there until closing time. When they departed from their drinking place, Roger noticed that police were hiding themselves and waiting for drinkers who got into their cars intending to drive home. Roger mentioned that they would have to catch a taxi home.

Eventually, they arrived back at the apartment to meet Ming waiting. Roger said, let me introduce you to Peter, the guy you caused to be interrogated because of your blabber mouth. Ming said, pleased to meet you and I am very sorry that I caused you to be inconvenienced.

Roger said, your friend Hopalong Tassidy came around looking for a bullet in his other foot, but you were not around, so Peter gave him What For, breaking his nose and giving him a black eye, and I stomped on his bad foot.

He will be back with some of his agent friends, and you will have a chance to shoot him in his other foot and kill a few more agents. Ming said, "You're starting to hurt my feelings, so, stop now before you make me angry."

Roger asked her why she has come. She shrugged her shoulders and answered, "Because I felt like it."

They all went inside, and all drank bourbon. Peter had a very bad habit of never buying a bottle himself, but always drinking Roger's. If he did buy a bottle, he made sure that he drank most of it. He would drink everything Roger had and couldn't stop himself. The abuse that Roger hurled at him was like water off a duck's back.

They drank until Peter finished everything and as all the bars were closed, they couldn't go out and purchase more.

The next morning they went out for breakfast and drank copious amounts of coffee. Peter always drank Nescafe as it was something he developed a habit for. Ming and Roger were more discerning. They ate large helpings of crispy bacon, sausages and scrambled eggs on toast. After breakfast, Ming drove Roger and Peter to their drinking place so Roger could take his car. She went off to work at her own university.

Roger asked Peter if he wanted to go and see his Chancellor. Peter thanked Roger but said he was really not interested.

Roger said to Peter that he left his prototype with Neville for safe keeping and cannot show it to him until he retrieves it, which will probably be sometime today or tomorrow.

Roger said, you already have the calculations so, I do not need to download them again.

That evening after Roger and Peter had returned from Roger's offices, Ming returned and parked her car in Roger's driveway and was just alighting when a black SUV pulled up in front of the driveway and three agents jumped out with Ide. Ming shot the three agents dead before they had a chance to draw their weapons and Ide fell to his knees pleading for his life with Ming. Ming told him to stand up and then shot him in his good foot, warning him next time he comes looking for trouble, she will shoot him in his head like she did to his colleagues. She told him to get his cleanup squad here to clean up the mess. Crying like a baby, he thanked her and drove off in his agent's SUV.

Peter, shaking like a leaf, said to Roger out of earshot with Ming, "She must love you very much to allow you to scold her without putting a bullet in your brain or without at least shooting you."

Roger remained silent.

Ming rang her control and explained to her what happened, asking her control why they were not following the hands off Ming policy they agreed with. She explained that Roger was getting tired of his front grass being fed with blood and brains, and that it would not be long before his grass became carnivorous. Please ask Idi's control to send a cleanup squad.

Later, Ide's control apologized, explaining that Ide was not one of her agents, but had convinced her team that he was. She continued by saying that she couldn't vouch for Ide's safety as her agents were very angry that his deception caused the loss of the lives of three of their colleagues.

Peter asked Roger if anybody were collecting the bodies off of the lawn tonight.

Roger still was angry with him for gluttonizing all the drink last night, assured him that the bodies will stay there until the neighbors complain about the smell, and that may be in a couple of days.

Peter stated that he needed a bourbon or two and could they go to his drinking place. Roger replied, only if you're buying.

"Not a problem," said Peter still shaking. Roger drove to his usual drinking place, and they entered earlier than normal. They found a place to sit, and Peter bought two rounds apiece.

Peter asked Roger how can he live and work with that killer. She doesn't blink an eye when brains spurt out of a man's head, he exclaimed. He continued; I could never get a hard on, if I was with her, just thinking about what she does. Roger adding fuel to the fire, said excitedly; you want to see her when she gets angry. You have only seen her when she is happy. She is faster than Cassius Clay when it comes to pulling a trigger, and she is so accurate. I have seen her put a bullet between the eyes of three men standing with their guns drawn before any of them moved a finger. She is true Western material in real life.

Peter trembled continuously, and Roger ordered another round for Peter and himself to help him calm down. Roger knew that Ming would be coming soon. Roger explained what Igor and Neville thought of Ming and told Peter that she must behave herself around them, or they wouldn't drink with him anymore.

As expected, Ming entered looking for Roger. On seeing him, she asked if everything was alright. Are you going to buy me a drink? Roger said, we need another round. Peter, are you buying? Ugh, he uttered, and moved towards the bar. Roger said to Ming, go over to the bar and help him please. In walked Igor and Neville and Ming pointed out to Peter that he may want to include them in the round also. Neville said to Ming to go back and sit with Roger as he will take over from her and help Peter. Igor pulled up sufficient chairs to match the number in his group, then sat down. Neville asked Peter why he was trembling so much. Peter said it was because of her. Who? asked Neville. Peter blurted, pointing at Ming, her.

Neville continued with his questioning, did she grab your private parts?

Peter was beside himself with trembling and with frustration.

No, Peter croaked. She just killed three people as if she was swatting flies.

Neville, falling in with the joke, said, Oh, you'll get used to it. It was the same with us in the beginning. It's when she uses the knife that turns my stomach.

Peter said, I have to go and sit down.

He went and sat with the group making sure he wasn't next to Ming. He was really drunk as he had been downing double bourbons for the past hour or more. He made his way to the toilets and was sick.

Roger got him back to his apartment, and he was groaning and moaning all night.

Ming cooked up a huge breakfast with steaming hot coffee, but after taking a look at her, he couldn't bring himself to put anything in his mouth.

Ming left for work, and Roger went to a café with Peter to have breakfast. Peter felt better after he had eaten. Peter asked, is she as good at Physics as she is at killing agents?

Roger replied, you better believe how good she really as a physicist. Her Ion Thruster for the Italians was the best in the world and was recognized as being so by the Italians. All the projects that we have worked on together have been most successful, and she is internationally recognized as a physicist par excellence.

They went to Roger's offices, and Roger asked him why he came to Rochester. I came to get a feel for what you have been doing as you spend many months away and you both seem to always be in the news. Roger explained briefly that he and Ming, work contracts for governments and private enterprises, etc. Via a broker who arranges the contracts, royalties and payments to them and to the funding of the university for the purchasing of equipment required to perform the contract.

Roger said if something that we feel may be of interest to you comes our way, we can forward it to you for your attention and put you on to our broker so you can negotiate with him. Peter thanked Roger and said he would be interested being in the loop.

Roger said, "We keep saying no more contracts, but the offers and the project interest are still coming in high, so we don't refuse."

Roger started to arrange with Neville to get his prototype out of the safe house so that he could show Peter. Neville asked Roger if he wanted to take it back. He said no, it was only to show Peter. Neville asked Roger to bring Peter to the safe house, and he could inspect it there. When it was in Peter's hands, he carefully inspected it, for an hour or more, looking for any construction mistakes. On finding none he returned the prototype to Roger to put into storage. Roger thanked Neville, and the pair departed and returned to Roger's apartment.

Peter let Roger know that he would be returning to his own university tomorrow afternoon.

When they arrived at the Roger's apartment, they found Vivian sitting on the steps, waiting. Roger introduced Vivian to Peter, who immediately fell in love with her and got a hard on so big it threatened to tear his trousers open. Vivian noticed and her legs opened wider in front of him, so he could get a good peek at her.

Roger gave him the keys to Vivian's apartment and told him to clean the place up after he finished, which he knew he wouldn't do due to his incompetence in house cleaning. Where is the place? Vivian will show you. Peter, please lock up and return to me the keys when you come back here.

A couple of hours later, Peter returned and gave him back the keys. He said, Vivian cleaned the place and is doing the washing now. Peter continued, "Roger, can I take her back with me to my university to live with me?"

Roger replied, "You drink all of my bourbon, and now you take my woman, have you no shame?"

Peter quickly said, "No!"

They went for an Italian meal and a cheese plate for dessert before going to Roger's drinking place to continue there with Roger's usual crowd.

They caroused until closing time having very good time.

The next-day Peter asked Roger again, if it was acceptable to take Vivian back with him. Roger replied it was fine by him, but don't depend on her following you. She is a free spirit and comes and goes as she pleases. Usually she comes to my apartment every three days. We have fun, and I take her to dinner. She comes back to my apartment only to say good-bye always saying she has a prior appointment, never staying the night.

She did let her young-man boyfriend stay in my apartment once and drink my coffee and what else I do not know. I came home unexpectedly; she was not there, but told Donald that she would be back soon. I asked him to leave, and he civilly returned the keys to me. That's why she doesn't have a set of keys.

You better buy her ticket at the airport when you take her, rather than her not turning up, and then losing your money.

Peter and Roger lunched at a steakhouse and drank beer until half past two. They went to the apartment, and Peter collected his luggage, and they went to the airport and drank more beer. As expected, Vivian was no where to be seen. Peter shrugged it off as another of life's rich experiences.

Roger returned to his offices after seeing Peter off.

He had a bad feeling about his offices and checked them for anything of value. He took his extra laptop to put into his apartment. There was nothing left in his offices to say he had ever worked there. He closed and locked his offices and walked back to his apartment depositing into his lounge room his spare laptop. Nothing to do here he thought to himself. I must get myself some work. That Telecom project is really getting me down. Peter has not been able to advance it either. Maybe, I have to ask Ming to look at it.

This would mean trouble, of course, as she will tell the world.

That evening, Peter sent an encrypted message informing Roger that he is back home and thanking him for his Bourban and his woman. Roger thought that he should really go back to his offices and start a new project.

CHAPTER 8

VIVIAN'S PLOY

On his return to his office, Roger finds it completely ransacked. In his chair, waiting for him, is sitting Vivian. "What a pleasant sight for sore eyes," he remarks. "Pleased that you are happy to see me," she replies. "It appears someone has been looking for your chocolates." Roger agrees.

Roger is very much attracted to her and has succumbed to her charms more times than he should.

"I am hungry," remarks Roger, knowing that a free dinner is another thing that Vivian will not and cannot refuse. They went to one of Roger's favorite Italian restaurants close by to the University. Looking at Vivian's thighs, Roger was not so sure he wanted Italian any more. Vivian drove in her car with Roger giving her directions, not that she needed them. She knew all of Roger's haunts.

While they dined, Roger noticed two thickset Russian mafia types, sitting at a table towards the rear of the restaurant. Roger was afraid he was going to be kidnapped, so he said to Vivian that they had better leave and fast. He paid the bill, and they left with the two mafia types not too far behind.

The direction Vivian initially chose to drive in, appeared to the mafia, as if they were returning to Roger's apartment. Then Vivian stepped on the gas and sped off around numerous back alleys until they finally stopped in a motel with her car pulled in and discretely hid behind several cars and trucks. "What are we going to do here?" Roger inquired as they checked in. The front-desk check-in lady looked disapprovingly at Roger and wrote his name as, Capt. Jerkoff, crossing it out when she realized he may read it whilst paying his bill.

Vivian and Roger went to a large room with a king-size bed. When they were satiated, relaxed and sipping their second cup of coffee, Vivian brought up the subject of Roger's project, asking why different people were interested in it. By agreement with Peter when faced with this question, Roger gave her ploy the same rubbish story as Peter had given the Government agents when he was being interrogated, that is: "We have been working on particle physics interactions for some years now, and details of our results can be found in the technical literature. We have been hiding our results in code because of the competition between our Universities and overseas Universities. At present, Universities seek global grants. The higher the University's technical standing in the International Community, based on published papers and on the worldwide recognition of their staff, the more grants they attract."

Roger asked, more to himself than to Vivian, "Who are these people?"

Vivian answered, "Chocolate Smarties," and then parted company.

Roger was at a loss to know if these people were after his Telecom project details or some other project, as there has been so many projects over the past six months or more.

Maybe, he thought, next time I could let them catch me, so I can find out what they are looking for. Then an inner voice told him Don't be an idiot!

He could ask Neville or at worst, ask Ming to ask her control.

Roger went to his drinking place and met Neville, who told him they were Iranians after his Telecom project details and prototype. This project has been in mothballs for over six months. Why has the interest been renewed? Neville answered that there has been a renewed interest because of comments made by Ming to do with your recalculations and mention of Peter's inspection of the prototype.

Roger said with conviction, "Ming is banned from my apartment and my offices."

There was a chorus of guffaws mixed with voices that said almost in unison, "We don't think that will happen!" And then, everyone broke apart laughing.

And then one voice stood out from the crowd that said, "I suppose you will ask Hopalong Tassidy to explain to her that she is not allowed to come to Roger's places anymore."

The whole drinking crowd fell about laughing.

Roger returned home with a severely bruised ego. He kept thinking what he was going to do with this damned woman.

The answer was obvious; he had to work in Neville's safe house until the project was finished.

The next morning, Roger closed up his apartment and went over to Vivian's apartment to check that it was in order. Vivian had cleaned the place and all the bed sheets, and all was spick and span.

He sat in the lounge chair, sipping the coffee he had just made, pondering what he should do now. He decided that he needed to speak to his new dean, if he had one, and ask him to allocate brand-new offices to him as the old ones were continually being broken into.

He locked Vivian's place and walked over to the dean's office. He asked his secretary if he had a new dean. She answered that he had and asked him to wait until she cleared a time for him to speak to him. Half an hour later his secretary asked him what his business was with the dean. Roger said that he wanted a new office and laboratory. She returned half an hour later stating that his request had been denied.

Roger wrote out by hand a resignation, to take effect two days from today and handed it to the dean's secretary. He knew that he would have no trouble finding a new post. He then left the dean's area and walked back to his apartment.

The next morning on hearing his front door chime; he opened the door to his deputy Chancellor and invited him to come in. The deputy Chancellor wanted to know why he had resigned. Roger explained, and after finishing, the DC said that he should leave the matter to him. Roger, said if a relationship starts off unstable it will remain so and a good relationship between, he and his dean was paramount.

That afternoon, Roger's front door chimes sounded again. This time it was his new dean. Roger kept him waiting at his front door, asking him what he could do for him. His new dean apologized for his poor behavior and hoped that their relationship could be placed on a more amicable footing. Roger answered by saying OK. Thanks for coming over and he started to close the door. The new dean asked Roger what he needed to do to make amends. Roger said you could start by being more humble and stop being so arrogant, not only to me, but to everyone, you come in contact with. The dean thanked him for his constructive criticism and said he knew that he had this coming to him.

The next day a note was placed in his front door telling him where his new office and laboratory was to be located. They are presently under construction and being painted, and they would be ready in a couple of days. Roger thought that he would withdraw his resignation letter when he moved into his new office and laboratory.

Take a walk, he said to himself, and go and see your brand-new offices. He pocketed the note that appeared on his front door, indicating the location of his offices, and left his apartment. He followed the map he memorized. The new offices were fairly close, except they were in a different direction.

He was happy with his new offices. He walked to the closest coffee house and on arriving, was satisfied that it was near by. Sitting down, he could take in his surroundings.

After taking his coffee, he walked over to his dean's office and asked his secretary if he was available. She replied after checking that he was. Roger greeted the dean and asked him if he had been communicating with Karim. He replied that it was none of his business. Roger replied that he hadn't changed and was as rude and arrogant as he was a couple of days ago. My resignation still holds as I have not withdrawn it. I will ring up Karim and ask him to hold off on all payments to me and to this university until further notice.

What else do you want? The dean asked Roger.

Roger replied, that he no longer works for this university, and he will return the keys to his apartment and offices tomorrow morning. With that, Roger walked out. The dean's secretary was in tears as he departed and said, she would ring him if the dean ever left. Roger thanked her and for the services she had rendered to him over the years.

Roger went back to his apartment to take the small number of items still there, over to Vivian's apartment. He then went to his offices and cleared out all of his prototypes and stored them also in Vivian's apartment.

The next morning, as promised, Roger returned the keys to his apartment and offices.

He went back to Vivian's apartment afterwards with three bottles of Cabernet Merlot and opened the first bottle and started drinking.

After he finished the first bottle, there was a ringing of his front door chime. It was Vivian saying that she was hungry. Roger asked her what she wanted to eat. She answered; she wanted steak and crab. Roger took her to his Steak and Crab restaurant, and she ate well. Roger ate, but this time he ate steak, prawns and French Fries. After returning to Vivian's apartment, ten minutes later, she said she was going. Roger said OK.

Later, that afternoon, the dean's secretary rang Roger's phone. She asked him not to go anywhere else or to find a new job because she believed the present dean would be leaving soon as he had upset too many key people. These people have tended their resignation like yourself; she informed him. I am holding your keys, for the moment, and not returning them to the campus realtors. Please don't relay what I have told you to anyone, she said. Roger assured her that it was only between the two of them.

Roger went to his usual drinking place. He drank on all night with Neville and Igor, and they enjoyed themselves until closing. Neville said, it is not wise staying in your apartment whilst the Iranians are looking for you. Thanks, said Roger. I have rented out another apartment, for the moment; he informed Neville. This should suit my needs for now.

Roger returned to Vivian's apartment after closing time to meet her there waiting for him.

Roger asked, are you still hungry?

Vivian replied, "No; I'm scared because those Iranians are also chasing me. Can I sleep here with you tonight?"

"Yes," Roger answered. He continued, "Did they see you come here?"

Vivian answered that she was sure they didn't see her come here, because if they had, they would have seized her, whilst she was waiting.

We must be careful leaving and entering here so as not to be seen.

Vivian brought her tape recorder with her, so she could record their pillow talk. How primitive, Roger thought when he saw it under her pillow. Why doesn't she use the recorder on her mobile? It is much more discrete. Vivian was never known to show any intellect.

Why don't you stay with Donald, asked Roger?

Because his parents don't like me.

Why? Asked Roger.

Because they think, I am too stupid for him. She replied.

Roger asked, does his mother have the same intellect as his father?

I don't know, answered Vivian. Why does that matter? She asked.

It matters only if they think your future relationship with Donald, will be indicated by their relationship with each other.

For you my dear Vivian, all that matters for your success is that you remain as beautiful as you are. There are plenty of Donalds out there waiting for you to come along who do not have, problem making parents.

Roger asked, "Why don't you ask your control to send agents out to get rid of these Iranian agents, rather than you always living in fear?"

She replied; that is a good idea. "Ugh, how do you know about my control?"

Roger ignored her question as he was tired of the conversation.

The next morning, Vivian disappeared without saying anything and Roger walked over to his cafe to have breakfast. He finished his breakfast and was standing to go and pay his bill when four Iranian agents seized him, and dragged him out of the café to jostle him into their SUV.

They drove him to a house and tied him to a chair in an unfurnished room, locking the door behind them as they left.

He thought about the advantages and disadvantages of Ming and how she would have resolved this situation. What a pity she could not be trusted.

Somehow he knew that Neville would be informed where he was, but would he inform Ming? He doubted if this scenario would ever eventuate.

Not long after being tied to the chair, he heard the sounds of gunshots and a lot of yelling. The gunshots never seemed to cease. When they did stop, however, it was a non-Iranian agent who bursts into his room and freed him from his bonds. They took him back to Neville's safe house.

Roger thanked Neville for rescuing him and giving him safe haven.

Neville replied that it wasn't him, but Vivian's control who arranged his rescue.

How did I arrive here if it wasn't you who arranged for my release?

Neville replied, because I told Vivian's control to bring you here when she asked me where I should take you. You are not safe yet, as her agents are still ferreting out the rest of the Iranians. So, it is better for you to stay and work here for the time being.

Thanks said Roger.

Ignoring what Neville had suggested that he should do, Roger went back to his breakfast café and paid this morning's bill. He lunched on hash browns, fried eggs and sausages with coffee. Afterwards, he returned to Vivian's apartment and drank his two bottles of Cabernet Merlot and slept until five in the afternoon, and then went to his drinking place and drank with Neville until closing time as Igor did not come in today. Roger asked Neville what he knew about Vivian. He replied, that she is an extremely clever and patient agent and is one of our finest. Her ploy is pretending that she is a dumb broad and then slowly milking information from her victim over a period of weeks or even months.

Roger continued, is she as good at martial arts and handling a gun as is Ming?

Neville answered, yes; she is a force to be reckoned with. I don't know who is the fastest, but I suspect Vivian.

Roger felt like a small mouse, thinking about these Amazons. Well, everybody has their strengths, and I have my weaknesses, he said to himself.

One last question please Neville, what does she do with her time?

Neville answered that she spends some time teaching martial arts to the Forces, sometimes teaching new recruits the rules of engagement for international operations, etc.

Neville continued; I think you get the idea.

Yes, Roger answered Neville, and then thanked him very much.

Two weeks went by, and Roger received a call from his dean's secretary letting him know that the arrogant dean was no longer working there and had been replaced by a more congenial man. Roger walked over to the dean's office and asked his secretary if he could introduce himself. After a minute, she got back to him, and asked him to come into the dean's office and introduce himself.

Roger was met by a big, six-foot tall, jovial man who expressed his gratitude to Roger for taking the time to come and introduce himself. He said that his doors were always open to him and wished that they would have a happy and productive association.

Roger left the dean's office, and on his way out picked up from the dean's secretary the keys to his apartment and new offices.

He walked back to Vivian's apartment and lay on the bed for an afternoon nap when Vivian knocked on his front door. They went out to eat and as usual; they enjoyed themselves thoroughly. Vivian did not come back to the apartment, but picked up her car where she had parked it and drove off. Roger was not put out as she had always been her own person.

Both Ming and Vivian would be poison should they ever get the upper hand. So, it was Roger's job to adequately protect himself from both women. Neither of them was allowed in the laboratory nor in the office whilst Roger was working, and Roger would never do any research at home. If it was critical that his work was not to be seen by anyone, Roger would get Neville's permission to fabricate and test in the safe house laboratory.

Roger didn't want Ming or Vivian to think that he was working on his project with renewed zeal, because it would start another spate of abductions and break-ins.

Roger received a telephone call from Karim asking him if he was not too busy to do a quick project at home. Roger inquired what the project entailed. Karim answered by letting him know it was a Radio-Frequency

Identification (RFID) project for finding lost pets using a Global Positioning System (GPS) chip integrated with an active RFID chip. The GPS chip would relay the pet's position and details to the RFID chip that would radio it to a dedicated system receiver, somewhere on the national network, that the owner has specified and, which would display on a map the pet's location.

Roger answered that such a modified system could also be used with multiple tags and readers, by the Federal Bureau of Prisons for tracking prisoners, and by interstate shipping companies for locating missing containers.

The final Integrated Circuit (IC) chip, as a hybrid circuit, could be integrated with a GPS antenna, an RFID mobile radio antenna and a battery. This would be located in the dog's collar.

Roger said that he was interested, as he wasn't doing much at the present, and to go ahead with the usual contract details. He gave to Karim the name and telephone number of his new dean to permit them to correspond and communicate.

Roger started placing orders for equipment and components, that he required, through his university. He printed off a letter of intent for his dean and walked over to his office handing it to the dean's secretary.

He started drawing up circuits and details, thinking about how he would place the chips on the dog's collar to prevent the ingress of moisture into the hybrid circuit and to reduce the mechanical damage that may incur by the dog scratching.

He also thought about extending his basic system to incorporate finding the location of two to three hundred tagged animals, each with its own identification, scattered over a wide area each one at a distance of up to one hundred and fifty to two hundred meters away from a single reader or from many readers equally spaced at three hundred to four hundred meters. The number of readers would be according to the expected locations of the animals. As the area containing the animals becomes greater, the larger the matrix of readers becomes.

He thought about employing an electronics, hardware and software engineer to devise Active RFID Systems for the mining industry and would take it up with Neville and Karim.

It is mandatory for any miner entering a mine to tag on and where a logged-on miner leaves a mine, it is mandatory for him to tag off. The mine head would indicate on a display showing the location of any miner or tagged piece of equipment, such as a bull-dozer, at any time.

There were so many systems required around the world and so many mines unequipped with Active RFID systems. If a mine collapses, the location of the miners cannot be easily ascertained without an active RFID system.

That evening, Roger went to his drinking place and met Igor and Neville. Roger explained Active RFID systems and the need for them in the mining sector, both in-country and overseas. He asked Neville if it was worthwhile, in his opinion, incorporating a company and employing an electronics, hardware and software engineer to design an Active RFID system. It is a field that has not yet been exhausted with designers, designs or products. So, it has that in its favor, Neville said. Still, like any electronics design company, the start-up costs are high, what with the purchase of an oscilloscope, signal generator, spectrum analyzer and Computer-Aided Design (CAD) software for printed circuit board design, antenna design and also programming software for some of the hardware chips, to name a few.

Roger rang Karim and outlined his proposal to him as he had done for Neville. When he finished, Karim said to leave it with him for a couple of days.

Roger went back to his apartment after closing time. The next morning the dean's secretary rang to say that the dean was very pleased to receive the letter of intent. She also mentioned that a lady had been asking her where you are, but she never gave the lady any information. Roger thanked her very much and added that she answered correctly.

Roger went to his offices and in his laboratory, he started working on the design of the dog's tag and its reader. Using components remaining from previous projects, he finished the construction of both after a couple of weeks. The hard wired reader and tag could talk to each other. This was most suitable; the next stage was to cut the hard wiring to the reader and link the tag to the UHF or mobile section. He created a UHF section that could initially be manually dialed to a remote location and bridge the tag section so that it could send information on its GPS location as well as details of its name.

The remote location was his mobile phone situated next to him. To this, he attached his UHF receiver output circuits for giving him a screen readout or linking to a computer, allowing him to overlay a map showing his position, much like the map showing where your mobile exists, should it be stolen.

He sent off his tag design with its UHF transmitter component and dog collar to the hybrid manufacturers for fabrication. Once made, this jointly with his mobile receiver output circuits on a specially constructed, printed circuit board (PCB) for attaching to a mobile phone and computer were sent to Karim together his circuit diagrams and video recorded tests via the new dean.

That evening, Roger went to one of his favorite restaurants for dinner. Ming was sitting down by herself, and she beckoned him to join her. It had been months since he had seen her. When he was seated, she asked him if he was still angry with her. He answered that he was annoyed and extremely disappointed in her show-off behavior in front of her friends who caused him to be abducted by Iranian agents and tied to a chair until other US agents came and rescued him. You caused the problem, why didn't you come to free me? Your control would have known what was going on.

Ming apologized and said she knew nothing about my abduction.

How can I make up for it? She asked. Roger answered as fast as a flash, by keeping your mouth closed about me. Do not talk about me with anyone, especially your friends.

Roger placed his order and drank a couple of bottles of Frascatti white. After dinner, Roger returned to his apartment, followed by Ming, who was in her car.

The next morning, Ming said, I have missed you to distraction, and I promise I will not talk about you to anyone again.

Roger thought; I will not talk about you, with my friends; for two hours, I promise, a thousand times.

Ming asked, "What have you been doing?"

Roger replied, "I have just finished a dog's collar RFID project for tracking missing dogs anywhere in the country."

Wouldn't that project lead to bigger and better applications? Yes, especially in the mining industry and prisons Department to name a couple.

Why don't we start up a company and make millions?

I have thought about that, and have discussed it already with Karim. I am awaiting his answer. The start-up capital is quite high and various specialized engineers are required.

If you talk about this with your friends, we will be abducted and sent to Azerbaijan to implement it there, if the Iranians don't abduct us first. After we finish, it's anyone's guess what will happen.

It was if he could see into the future, as they noticed a black SUV prowling around the outside. Ignoring the prowling SUV, Roger said, I wouldn't mind if we went for coffee. They left the apartment and walked over to the closest café for breakfast.

Roger ordered his usual bacon, eggs, sausage and toast with a large white coffee. Ming, ordered the same.

Into the café, came three tough looking agents, definitely of middle eastern extraction. They sat and watched Ming, and Roger eat their breakfast. One of the group came over to Roger's table and asked them, with a slight Arabic accented English, if they would be so kind as to take on a project in Iran.

Roger replied, what type of project are you thinking about?

I think you would call it an RFID project.

Roger replied, would you please leave me your details, or your calling card so that I can get back to you?

The man gave him his business card and returned to his table.

The name written on the calling card was; Professor Rahman Mousavi, Amirkabir University of Technology, Department of Electrical Engineering, Tehran.

After reading his calling card, Roger gave to Ming his calling card and said; he is one of us.

Roger and Ming went over to their table and gave them each one of their business cards and talked with them until lunch time and then moved to a pizza restaurant.

The other two Iranian men were also professors at the same university in the Department of Mathematics and Computer Science and the Department of Computer Engineering and Information Technology.

They came on a fact-finding mission and also to attempt to make contacts. They had read about Ming and Roger in the newspapers and were hoping that they would be open to suggestion. They couldn't believe that they had such good luck seeing them leave for their café in the morning. Furthermore, Roger thought they wouldn't believe how lucky Professor Mousavi was, by Ming not shooting him dead when he put his hand into his breast pocket to get his calling card, not that they mentioned it to them.

They talked all afternoon.

Roger and Ming agreed to arrange their Sabbaticals so that they could arrange with Tehran's students the structure of their multi tag and reader project for their mining industry.

CHAPTER 9

IGOR, NEW OFFICES AND LINA

As Roger approaches his brand new secure offices that the University has provided, he noticed a thick set, burly man, who he immediately recognizes as Igor. They embrace each other, and Igor escorts Roger into his brand-new office. Roger can't believe his good luck. His brand-new offices are replicas of his old ones, and Igor is his trusted security man and drinking friend.

Igor gives to Roger, his mobile phone number, for him to ring day or night, the keys to his office and lab and finally, the codes to access his computer email and its University servers, because this section of the offices is separate from his previous offices.

Igor is a happy go-lucky individual who supports the Telecom project in the faith that it will benefit mankind and lead to a scientific Renaissance.

He is a burly individual heavily scarred and with a typical heavy Russian accent. It is suspected he was a member of the mafia as there are star tattoos on his shoulders, typically symbolizing his dignity and honor, and that he lives by a certain code and tradition.

Roger said, by the way, Igor, please do not let in any person, without a security pass or any women, in who may be looking for me. Igor agreed to comply with a knowing grin.

Igor lets Roger know that Lina has an office at the end of the corridor connecting all offices with the outside world. He informs Roger that he will regularly check that his door connecting to the corridor is always locked to prevent her from coming into his office and raping him, he chortles with an evil smirk.

In this world, one always finds the unfortunate runts that are cast out of the pack; Lina is one of these people. She is a frustrated, ugly, little physicist who is ignored by Roger and feels immeasurably slighted by him. She realizes that he is far above her in intellect, and although she is not privy to the project details, she objects to what he is doing on the grounds that she is not a part of it. She tries to snoop on Roger and because of this; he always closes all the doors to his offices.

If Roger held her, he thought, and kissed her and put his hand around her buttocks; he possibly would make a loyal friend for life, but afterwards, what a price to pay. He thought that it may not pan out as well as he fancies, and after that the sexual harassment charges would start flowing. How embarrassing that would be, with all of his friends and colleagues reading the newspapers and people pointing to him on the campus. He could imagine them saying, "Of all the beautiful, darling females on this campus; he has to make a play for Lina, yes that ugly little rat Lina."

Enough, Roger says under his breath. Back to work.

Roger recalls the long conversations that he, and Ming had with their Persian counterparts and plans how he is to approach his dean about applying for Sabbatical and what program he will initiate with Ming for their Iranian students. He needed to talk to Ming to come up with something they could both implement.

Ming had previously spoken to her dean when Roger broached the subject with her, and she was refused sabbatical on the grounds that there were so far, three staff members on leave and there were not the funds to keep her salary, albeit reduced, nor to employ another part-time staff member.

Roger said, I don't fancy going to Iran by myself, so I won't apply.

Roger thought to himself, whenever you want something, life will deny it to you, but it will offer you something that you are not really interested in and whether you take it or not, you are still the loser.

Roger turned on his office computer and noticed that an email containing an icon picture of Peter appeared. Making sure that his doors were closed and his hallway door was locked, Roger applied his deciphering code and then the Stegan key code to the email. The same picture reappeared with a document next to it. OK, let's see what Peter has to say!

With Peter's email downloaded to his computer, he read Peter's suggestions on where the faulty code resided. There was a total of five suggestions that he hadn't thought of. This would take at least thirty or more hours of extremely tiring work to rework. He tidied up by uploading to his secure place Peter's email and closed down this office computer.

Whether it was the thought of the work ahead of him or whether it was Lina and her rat like features causing him to have nightmarish images fill his mind, he truly didn't know. However, he really longed for a Vivian to cast out the feelings of nausea.

Roger was beside himself with excitement as his Telecom project, his main reason for existing, had finally, after months of being stalled was going to come back to life.

He had to control himself and work on the prototype only from his laboratory and not take anything back to his apartment that could compromise the project. Once he had isolated the fault, he had to work on the prototype in Neville's safe house.

Furthermore, he had to try to control his work habits in order not to arouse suspicion in the mind of Ming and Vivian.

Maybe he should take a long holiday and visit his ex-dean in the Maldives, or go out to Safi to check on his postgraduate students. He would think about it or take on a new project.

Roger had memorized the first of Peter's suggestions and after downloading his code from his safe place on the Internet, he started to implement the changes. So keen on getting his project restarted, he worked seven hours straight until he exhausted this initial suggestion. He heard a banging on the outer corridor door and heard Ming's voice calling him. He quickly closed down his computer and locked his office door, before opening the outside door to Ming. She wanted to know what he was doing. He said that he had fallen asleep whilst thinking about Karim. She said she was hungry and wanted to go to a steak and fries restaurant to eat. Roger locked the outer door and left with Ming. They ate well and discussed working in Iran. They downed three bottles of Cabernet Savignon and left for Roger's apartment.

Roger was exhausted, and Ming asked him if he had another high-powered screwing machine.

He said yes, but it is not that which has caused him to be so tired, because he hasn't been around for some time.

What do you mean by HE?

Nothing, I am only joking.

What is it then Drakey boy?

I have been thinking about Karim, Iran, Amirkabir University of Technology and Professor Mousavi and company. My conclusion after your sabbatical refusal is that, this project is a dead duck.

Ming said, she also believed that this was the case.

Roger said, I contacted Karim about working in Iran, he told me after a couple of days that they could only offer an Assistant Professorship. He didn't mention any other contracts, but that doesn't mean too much because I didn't ask him to look further afield than RFID.

A contract through your university would be permitted because it brings money into the university, whereas sabbatical takes money out of the university.

The next morning they ate breakfast at Roger's café. Ming went to work at her university, and Roger went to his offices, locking the doors behind him. He downloaded Peter's email, read and memorized the second suggestion contained within it and closed the email. He then downloaded his code and started looking at how Peter's suggestion would affect it. Eight hours later he completed his calculations, and again to no avail. It was night time, and he was very hungry.

On many occasions, he heard banging on the door leading to the outside world and guessed it was Ming. He closed down everything and locked his offices and walked to his car to drive to a restaurant. Ming was waiting for him and accused him of having sex over the Internet. A bit difficult I would think he replied laughing. You must teach me how you do it. Ming was in no mood for his comments as she also was hungry. When he said he was going someplace to eat, her mood lightened, and she became as soft as a pussy cat.

Ming asked with a little-girl voice, "Can I come?"

Roger answered, only if you promise to behave and don't kill anybody.

She answered tersely, why are you being bad to me again and making me angry?

They went off to a Spanish restaurant called Tapas 177 and ate Seared Sea Scallop served with Parmesan rice pilaf, sherry braised mushrooms, sweet red pepper gorgonzola sauce, balsamic reductions & sauteed spinach and drank three bottles of Rioja red.

Roger fell asleep straight away on getting into bed. This did not impress Ming, who was looking forward to her dessert. Ming castigated Roger, something terrible, but he was too fast asleep to worry.

The next morning she made breakfast, and they chatted over coffee. Ming went to work, and Roger went to Vivian's apartment to see if

Vivian had been waiting for him. She had not, so he went to his offices and wanted to start on the next cycle of checking Peter's third suggestion. Something warned him not to do anything today as people were getting interested in what he was doing. He sat in his office chair thinking about what he should do. He thought that he would memorize Peter's third suggestion and go to Vivian's apartment and start working on it there, when he heard a tapping on his office door. It was Lina. What does she want? Roger asked himself.

Roger answered the door and asked her how he could help her. She replied; she wanted him to help her solve a particular set of equations. Roger looked at the equations and explained to her the fastest way to solve them if she was going to do it by hand. If she wanted to use a computer, she may use the software package MathCad. She was bending over him, whilst she was talking to him and showing to him her excuse for breasts as she was not wearing a bra. Roger didn't know whether to laugh or cry at her sexual antics and her pin prick mammary glands or to pick her up and throw her out of his office.

After she accepted his methods to solve the equations, she left.

Roger left his offices and went to Vivian's apartment where he downloaded Peter's email and memorized his third suggestion. He downloaded his code also and started working on the changes required. He heard a car pull up outside and on looking out of the window, noticed that it was Vivian. He memorized where he was in his code and closed down his computer. Nothing was on his computer that indicated what he was doing.

Vivian asked him what he was doing home. He said he felt like having a sleep.

Roger continued, "I came here this morning to see if you had left a note in the door."

Roger asked, "What are you doing home at lunchtime?"

She replied, "I haven't seen you for such a long time; I was checking to see if you were home."

Roger said, "Next time, leave a note on the door indicating the date and time you came and when you think you will come back. I will do the same."

They both went to get some lunch. Vivian went off, saying that she would be back this evening.

Roger continued from where he left off and by six that evening, he had finished the third suggestion. He was starting to feel very tired and due to his lack of success, the strain was taking its toll. He sent an email to Peter on his lack of success before closing down.

Vivian returned, Roger said that he wanted to sleep. She asked him if he was ill and wanted any medication. He said, he was not sick and had been thinking deeply now for three days, and that had caused him to be very tired. She said ok and left. Roger went back to his own apartment and found Ming waiting for him. She wanted to know what was making him so tired. He said the same thing to her. Maybe, I should go and visit my old dean, he said. No you don't, I will not tolerate you getting laid by those nubile lovelies, said Ming. Roger grinned at the thought. They had an early night, and Ming didn't complain.

The next morning Ming went to work and Roger went to his offices. Lina came to his office before he had a chance to sit in his chair. She asked him to solve the same set of equations. Roger knew that there was no escape from this woman, so he acquiesced to her request. He opened Mathcad and showed her how to change her system of equations into a matrix and enter the coefficients into the spaces provided and then go ahead and find the inverse matrix and so on. She started bending over him again showing her bare mouse breasts. He didn't want to look, but she was being very persistent and coming over quite strongly. He wrote her answer on a piece of paper and passed it to her. She thanked him and then left. He thought the next time he came here; to his offices, he will bring Ming to sit with him.

He left his offices and went to his café for breakfast.

As he left his café around ten in the morning, three men grabbed him and bundled him into a Chevrolet Suburban. Inside the vehicle, he was bound and blindfolded. The vehicle drove for two hours, and then he was transferred into an Embraer Phenom 100 personal jet that traveled for five hours. At the end of this journey he was taken to a hotel, Hotel Copacabana Cuba, La Habana located in the residential zone of Miramar, twenty kilometers from the International Airport. He didn't know this due to his blindfold. He was taken to a room and pushed into it with the doors being locked after him. All the windows were blacked out and locked. However, after a while he moved his blindfold sufficiently to see that the cracks in the window frames showed it was still daylight. He estimated that it was around six in the evening.

He was grateful that he had a toilet and drinking water. His bonds were loose enough to open a fawcet so that he could drink water.

Hours went by, and then he was roughly pushed out of the room and onto a stone staircase. He descended for about three-quarters of an hour and walked straight for at least another two kilometers. He was shoved into a room and dragged onto the floor. Nothing was said to him for another hour, and then his bonds were loosened and his blindfold removed. He saw before him one of the roughest, ugliest men he had ever seen in his life. The ethnic mix of the Cuban is African, Spanish, Indigenous and European. Looking at this man, Roger was still not able to determine his origin or to where he had been taken. However, he estimated that it was around nine at night, and he was feeling hungry. He noticed that the toilet was a hole in the floor in the corner of the room and there was no water to be seen. He fell asleep, to be awoken around midnight by his rough jailor who only spoke Haitian Creole. This man kicked him to get him standing and motioned him to start walking again until they arrived at another staircase. They walked down this stone stepped spiral staircase for another fifteen minutes and entered a small windowless jail cell containing a pail for his toilet, a jug of water and a bug infested mattress. His jailor exited the cell locking it behind him and turned off the electric light from outside.

Roger went back to sleep on the floor, estimating the time to be twelve thirty.

He estimated that he slept for six hours, making it six-thirty in the morning. Around eight in the morning his cell door was opened, and a white man entered. He spoke English with something like a Spanish accent. Dr. Redman you are to design Cuba a Hadron Collider like America has. We will give you three days to complete your mission. I give you fair warning, if you do not complete the design in three days, we will put you between the walls of knives.

Roger thought, this guy is a joker, and he is joshing me on an empty stomach.

What have you got to say? Asked the man.

Roger answered, "Bring me a deep pan anchovy pizza; I am hungry, and then I can answer you properly."

The man laughed and then Vivian appeared behind him with a large grin on her face.

Vivian introduced the man as Colonel Emidio Guardo of the US army who is a Cuban by birth. He is my boss and teacher, she said. We wanted to give you a lasting impression of Havana, Cuba and what could be better than introducing you to the catacombs deep underneath the city. These catacombs were built by the Cubans when the Spanish were in power. There are lifts down to them from the Hotel Copacabana Cuba, located in the residential zone of Miramar, Havana. You were in this hotel last night, before you descended into the tunnels. There are fully equipped air conditioned laboratories containing electronic instruments in these tunnels with easy access to this hotel.

They went into the hotel restaurant, and Roger ordered a bacon, egg and sausage on toast breakfast, and a take away deep pan anchovy pizza with a cheese crust filling and a couple of diet cokes.

Whilst they were eating, the colonel explained that one of their main exports is cigars. The Cuban tobacco industry was nationalized by Fidel Castro's communist government in 1962, in which all cigar brands of Cuba became the property of the government. As a result, the government created Cubatabaco to handle all productions and distribution of Cuban tobacco products both locally and internationally until 1994, when the firm of Habanos S.A. was formed to export cigars and cigarettes worldwide.

Habanos S.A. is the government arm of Cubatabaco that simply monitors the promotion, distribution and exports of cigars & tobacco products around the world. To control distribution and protect against counterfeiting, Habanos S.A. set up a network of stores called La Casa de Habana in different countries except the United States, which has had a trade embargo enforced against Cuba since 1962.

This is leading me to our problem at the moment. An extremely large amount of our cigars is being smuggled out of the country, and it is very difficult to stem the flow of these smuggled goods, for various reasons.

What I am asking you to do, is to design an RFID chip that can be placed on or in each carton of cigars manufactured. Once these cigars are sent out of the factory or placed in storage, this chip will contain the following information: identity of the contents, where it is destined, and the mode of transport to be used or is being used to convey it to its destination.

Why don't you buy this technology as it is already developed? Said Roger.

The colonel answered that it is manufactured mainly in the US, and I have already said; the US has had a trade embargo against Cuba since 1962. Outside of US we have not yet been able to source it.

We feel that it is better to ask you, as you are by Vivian's recommendation, a trusted entity.

If you agree to develop this chip, please let me have your business plan and your proposed costs. Our air-conditioned electronic laboratories are at your disposal.

Roger agreed to look into it this afternoon.

After lunch, Vivian booked him into the hotel and took him to his room.

Later that afternoon, Roger outlined his plan to the colonel. He would need to recruit a hardware engineer for the interfaces, a software engineer because all the radios are programmed for operational frequencies in transmit and receive mode and for specific data to be sent, digital data rate, etc. He required a radio frequency (RF) engineer to design the antennas, and the duplexer over the frequency bands required. He required a technician to build the prototype circuits for testing and for ordering and purchasing the parts. He also required a printed circuit board layout engineer familiar with Computer-Aided Design (CAD) Software, such as Altium. A total of five people, besides himself would be required for at least two years.

Roger outlined the salary, including his own, and the electronic parts and outsourcing costs. He required an inventory to be made of all of their test equipment, to ensure everything required existed in the laboratories. Test benches equipped with magnifying glass lamps, vices, files, saws, soldering iron stations, and fine tools such as side cutters, long nosed pliers, tweezers, etc. were required. A Laptop computer, with a high-speed connection to the Internet is necessary for each engineer and installed with any specialized software that he requires to do his job.

The matter of accommodation of the non-local staff and their per diem requirements as well as their home leave entitlements are to be addressed separately. Please let me know if these five people are local people or are expatriates from the US, if you want me to include this estimation with the main business plan.

Is that all? Asked the colonel. Roger replied, yes, for the moment.

I will get back to you when I have more information for you. Meanwhile, get yourself a mobile so that we can communicate easily. Vivian can give you my mobile number when you are ready. With that, he left and Roger and Vivian went out to do some sightseeing. Not that there was much in Miramar. They returned to their hotel where they were entertained, quite well, with a choice in the little bar or in the lobby.

When they got back to Roger's room, Roger continued eating his pizza. Vivian was not interested in eating cold anchovy pizza. Vivian said, there is a twenty-four-hour pizza place here in the hotel if I want one.

The next morning they ate a reasonable omelette breakfast at the hotel and decided to take a red bus tour from the bus stop right next to the hotel. The hotel is along the ocean and is on the route of the forty minute open top Double Decker daily, get on-get off, bus tour of old Havana downtown.

They toured and ate out and thoroughly enjoyed themselves, coming back only to sleep or swim in the pool. They found at night Vedado, has the lion's share of clubs and musical venues, from the swanky to the seedy, while Miramar and Playa are the locale for titillating cabaret and raunchy discos.

La Habana Vieja is brimming with bars, tango houses and cultural centers. The main strip of Calle Obispo is the place to begin an old town bar hop, where a seductive musical soundtrack and spontaneous street side grooving to provide some of the city's best free entertainment. As the bars close at twelve midnight, the clubs get into full swing, continuing until the early hours.

After a week, the colonel returned with an update on the RFID project. He informed Roger that they are sourcing their own engineers, and he should start placing orders through him for components, etc. He said they should have a list of their instruments ready by this afternoon. Most of the components he requires, they can purchase and have delivered within one week.

The contracts are with him and will be signed in one or two days. The colonel said he realized that in order for him to leave his university for some time, they had to release him for one month every four months and fly him back and forth to Rochester and also give his university a letter of intent and a grant. Roger thanked him very much for his understanding and cooperation and thought to himself that this would stop his dean squeaking.

As promised, the colonel gave Roger a list of test instruments that they had in their laboratories. Roger scanned the list with his eyes and noticed that the Network analyzer was missing. All else seemed to be in order. Roger gave a sheet of paper detailing the electronic network analyzer he required. It was an Agilent Technologies E5071C (9kHz-8.5 GHz) ENA series network analyzer.

The colonel was pleased and said he would attend to it immediately.

Roger prepared a list of components he required straight away as well as the Electrically Erasable Programmable Read-Only Memory (EEPROM) Chip's programming software and hardware.

He would wait for the hardware and software engineer to come, before placing more orders on programming the radio chips.

The next day, the colonel came back to tell Roger the private jet would take him to Rochester tomorrow, and to give him his letter of intent, and his contract signed by a four-star general.

That night Vivian and he, had a very good time going to Vedado, visiting and drinking at clubs and musical venues. They returned early in the morning and bought a large anchovy pizza to soak up the drink.

The next day, Roger returned to Rochester. He went back to his apartment and found Ming living in it. She crudely asked him, in English full of expletives, where he had been for the past month or more. He told her. She said she wanted to work there also. Roger said, it was electronic design and testing work, but he would ask the colonel if he could take a clever physicist on board. She was placated for the moment.

They went out for dinner, and Roger ate steak and fries and two bottles of house red. Ming drank one bottle of house white and started to get maudlin.

The next-day Roger went over to see his dean and gave him the letter of intent and explained that he thought the project would run for two years. The dean was beside himself and thanked Roger very much. This is the way; it should be, the dean thought to himself, patting himself on the back for doing nothing.

Roger was looking forward to working on his Telecom project. He went to his offices and after locking the doors, he downloaded Peter's fourth suggestion and memorized it before turning off his computer to lose the downloaded email. He then downloaded his code from his secret hiding place on the Internet. He was just starting to work on his code, when there was a knocking on his office door. He turned off his computer and answered the door. It was Lina. Roger quite tersely asked her what she wanted. She was unfazed by his rude tone and continued to tell him that the inverse matrix he solved for her was incorrect. Roger said, Lina, I am not here to solve your problems. She answered, but I have nobody else to turn to. Please help me, she asked, as she wiggled very vigorously, her little mouse breasts at him. Roger thought; she will send her nipples flying off like bullets at the rate, she is shaking them.

Why don't you go over to the High school and ask the maths teacher to solve it?

They can solve that? She asked incredulously.

Roger near to shouting, said yes.

She left frustrated by Roger's annoyance with her and his lack of interest in her.

Chapter 10

DESIGN CORRECTED

Roger gave up trying to get any work done at his office. He decided to go home and seriously start working on his design code from there. He was going to keep following his more successful procedures by not leaving the deciphered Stegan code on his work laptop, nor download his master design to his laptop whilst the doors of his office and laboratory were unlocked or there was anybody in his apartment.

On arriving home, he noticed Ming's car in his driveway. Not too much work on my design is going to be done tonight, if I stay here. He thought to himself as he drove on past his apartment towards Neville's safe house. Always use the proper procedures when returning, Neville's words echoed in his ears.

Once in Neville's safe house, Roger downloaded his master design and started going through the mathematics of combining it with the fourth of Peter's suggestions, by independently deriving and comparing line by line, section by section. After eight hours, he had not made any headway and had revised completely four of the five suggestions. He sent off an email to Peter, letting him know of his results. Roger started work on the fifth suggestion when an email prompt from Peter signaled a new message. Peter asked Roger, Did you change your reference coordinate system from spherical to an oblate spheroid? Roger had not and now it became clear why there was a problem. Roger worked frantically for the next six hours and was ready for another internal test. This time it was successful. Everything converged. He let Peter know his results, and it looked like they were now in a position, at long last, to start modifying the prototype. Roger uploaded his corrected design to his secure place on the Internet ready for tomorrows effort.

He went for breakfast of bacon, eggs, toast and sausage with a large mug of coffee. When he finished, he returned to Vivian's apartment and went to bed. He woke up in the afternoon to Vivian's smell. She smothered him with her body and tried to stop him breathing. That is a wonderful way to wake up, he said sleepily biting her. He asked her, how long have you been here? She answered by saying, long enough to make coffee. After coffee, Roger showered, and they went to a crab and steak meal at the Black & Blue Steak and Crab restaurant, in Monroe Ave and drank two bottles of house red.

Vivian asked, when are you returning to Havana?

Roger replied, in just over three weeks time.

Oh Good! She exclaimed; that is the same time that I return, so we can enjoy ourselves again.

They returned to the apartment, and they had fun until she left at midnight.

The next morning, Roger went back to his apartment and found Ming waiting for him. Roger asked her if she was coming to breakfast with him. They went to his usual place to eat. Ming wanted to know what he has been working on. He told her he had been working on an RFID problem. Why is your project clouded in secrecy? She asked. Roger explained how Lina was always bothering him and wanting him to play with her breasts.

"I don't want to go back to my offices and work there, because she will use some excuse to tap on my door and bother me." He said.

"Poor Drakey," she said mockingly. "All the girls are trying to kiss him."

Roger angrily retorted, "So, I go to a brothel, and work there in peace as the lady is not too interested, after I have paid my money."

Ming grinned, and Roger asked her if she was going to work. She said she was returning to work after she finished her coffee.

Roger went back to Neville's safe house and took his prototype out of its box and looked at how he could modify it to reflect his latest code.

He could not modify it easily, due to the change in the coordinate system making the configuration greatly different. He thought; it was better that I put it into my offices for some future thief to steal and start on a new prototype in Neville's safe house.

He started building the new prototype and continued day and well into the night for two weeks or more, stopping only to eat and sleep. At each stage of its construction, his tests proved that the prototype was working correctly.

He sent an email to Peter in the afternoon, explaining that his new prototype performed properly at each stage of its construction.

After he was finished, he physically compared the two prototypes and noted that the recent unit looked completely different. He placed a fine sliver of silver paper in the hinge area of the old prototype box that would easily fall out if anyone opened the box and stored the new unit on a shelf out of the way, waiting for its own box.

He thanked Neville for the use of his safe house, letting him know how difficult it was for him to do anything in private.

He took the old prototype in its box to his offices and stored it on an easily accessible shelf at the back of his laboratory.

He returned to Vivian's apartment to meet her there drinking freshly brewed coffee. Want some? She asked.

She poured him a large mug full and then sat opposite him.

What have you been up to? She asked.

Roger answered that he had been working on a private project of his, that didn't receive any money. He told her he did it because he found it interesting.

She asked, "Was Ming with you?"

Roger looked at her eyes for a long time for an indication of what she was thinking and not seeing anything, he answered, "No. I haven't seen her for over a week now."

Vivian asked, "Do you want her to come to Havana?"

Roger replied, "It's your patch, and you can't have two queen bees in the same hive. Based on that, my answer is no. However, if you were shifted elsewhere, my answer would be yes, because she is very productive, and she has expressed a desire to work there."

Roger anticipating the next question added, "No, I do not love her."

They went out for dinner and ate steak with fries washed down with a couple of bottles of red.

Once back at Vivian's apartment, she got into her car and drove off.

Roger drove over to his apartment and met Ming, who proceeded to tell him how hungry she was. She said she fancied an Italian meal. She ate a Carbonara with plenty of Parmesan cheese, and Roger ate an antipasto with a feta cheese salad.

Ming was no longer complaining after this and Roger topped it off with a cheese plate. They drank a couple of bottles of house red, and Ming had to drive them home because Roger was positively dangerous.

Ming wanted to play, but Roger was in no state to oblige and told her to stop carrying on before he was sick all over her. She stopped pushing him.

The next morning, when Roger got out of bed, Ming had left for work. He went to Neville's safe place because he wanted to modify his prototype to accept an activation code to make it turn on.

Again, he takes a week to modify his prototype so that the activation code MOUSETTES needs to be entered before the prototype responds to any commands. Once finished, he tidies up after him by uploading his new code and design notes.

During this time, he slept and showered at Neville's safe house and used his staff to have his clothes washed and pressed. He ate out occasionally and brought pizzas back many times.

He realizes that he has only two or more weeks left before he has to return to Havana, and both Ming and Vivian are highly suspicious that his work is more than what he says it is, because he has not slept at either home for over a week.

Roger goes back to his apartment and meets Ming still living there. He puts up with impertinent questions demanded by her, such as: "Have you got another jiggy?" "Where have you been?" "Have you been playing with Mousettes?"

He answers, "Yes, but I haven't seen any of them for over a week now." Roger continued, "Why don't you live in your own place rather than spying on me all the time?"

Full up with righteous indignation, she starts her ranting and raving act, which continues until Roger leaves and drives off to Vivian's apartment.

Vivian's apartment was empty, and he could relax and work out what he was to do next.

Roger returns to his offices at the University and following his locked door procedure; he downloads his corrected design to his office laptop. In addition to the MOUSETTES activation code, he changes the design to build into it a fail-secure mechanism; that is, if the prototype is attempted to be initiated without its second level of proper codes, namely, DRAKEY, it remains inactivated. In addition, he builds into it a third level of security in the form of a voice recognition circuit that recognizes his voice only and allows the unit to be activated when he speaks I say, open sezme. Roger afterwards re-uploads the modified design back to its safe place. He then, starts to build a new prototype, knowing that it will take him a week or more to finish, but he anticipates that it should be completed before he returns to Havana. His new prototype is constructed faster than before, because he is now very familiar with the postioning of the components. He doesn't worry that it is stored in his laboratory as nobody will be able to activate it, and if they try with the wrong codes or voice, nothing will happen.

The prototype in Neville's lab is a working unit without the second or third-level security circuits. This unit can be used by him later if he runs into problems, which may happen as on the new unit, there is no code reset mechanism. Occasionally, he goes out to eat, keeping away from places that Ming or Vivian would frequent.

Roger returns to his apartment that afternoon to meet Ming waiting for him. Ming complains, "I give up with you."

Roger replies, "Ming you are not my wife or my mother or any other woman in my life who thinks that she has the right to control what I do, or where I go. Please keep your comments to yourself." He continues, "Coming home to you is always a stress full occasion."

Ming bursts out crying, "Don't you realize that I love you so much, and you are never off my mind."

Roger pulled her close to him and held her tight. Her crying turned to sobbing, and it took a long time for it to subside. He carried her into the bedroom and lay her on the bed, taking her shoes off. She wanted to laugh at how ridiculous he was, taking only her shoes off, but her sobbing was ruining her laughter.

"What's wrong with taking my panties off, you Drake!" She said, in a mixture of sobbing, laughing and indignation.

Over dinner, Roger told Ming that tomorrow he would be flying back to Havana and would see her in three months time unless the colonel wants to bring her out to work with him before that time. She was a little crestfallen, but picked up after half an hour with Roger's encouragement.

Vivian already knew Roger would return tomorrow because she had discussed this with him, and she was returning also.

Roger had locked his offices and informed Igor that his latest working prototype, and his non-working prototype was in his laboratory and to make sure his girlfriend with the mouse titties didn't steal them. Igor guffawed and said he would take care of it.

Roger returned to Havana and met Vivian waiting for him at Havana Jose Marti International Airport.

Roger asked, "Are we still booked into the same room or is it different now?".

Vivian answered, "It was the same room, as the room was a permanent booking."

They got into the car that was sent to pick them up and was driven back to the hotel. After going to their room, they went to the dining room and ate dinner and drank three bottles of house red. Vivian wanted to sleep, and Roger was most relieved.

The next morning, the colonel welcomed their return over breakfast and introduced them to Roger's five new Engineering staff. Namely: a hardware engineer, a software engineer, a radio frequency (RF) engineer, a printed circuit board layout engineer and a technician.

Roger thanked the colonel for the introduction, and then he outlined what the overall project was to achieve and how it was to be done. From the broad concepts, he started narrowing down, giving specifics of each part of the project and adding breadth to the project. Once this was completed, he defined the time line and the major milestones that the team had to reach. After three hours, he was finished and so was his five Engineers. The scope and depth of the work made them very tired. Roger stated to his Engineers that brain storming sessions would start with each Engineer tomorrow to ensure that each facet of the project would move in the right direction from the start. Chip manufacture choices would be among the first to be agreed upon. Although these sessions were for each specific Engineer, any Engineers or all Engineers were invited to attend and contribute to the final decision, with the Engineer responsible with this area of the project having the concluding decision on what components, etc. were to be used.

Roger asked them to use their laptops and Internet connection this afternoon, so that they could prepare for tomorrow's sessions.

They all got up and went to lunch.

Vivian showed Roger a fine eating place in Miramar called La Fontana. They had the crab créme soup of the day, and a main course choice of rabbit cooked in a classical Spanish way, washed down with a dry white Chardonnay wine from Chili.

When they returned to working, Roger spoke individually to each member of his staff to determine if he had any problems with what was discussed in the morning and explained what he wanted him to do if he did have a problem.

Roger was careful not to be friendly, and spoke seriously without being unfriendly. He would do this with each member of his staff for the duration of the project.

The next day, they had to choose what chips, software, etc., they required by discussing the pros and cons of each manufacturer and submit to Roger their final choice. They had to be ready to defend their choice if asked to do so. This same modus operandi existed throughout the project, from design to testing and final testing.

Roger knew that once they got into the habit of working this way, the number of mistakes that they would make would be significantly reduced.

Roger had to be confident that they knew how to correctly operate the test equipment and taught those, who didn't know.

So, day after day they followed a routine of designing, checking, bread boarding, testing and bouncing their ideas off of each other. It eventually became a part of their nature. After four months and what would be the same at the end of every four months, Roger submitted a progress report to the colonel showing the milestones and their position on the timeline from project completion. He was pleased with the progress of his team and was ready to go back to Rochester. He was also pleased with the cohesiveness of the team. Each member of the team bonded properly with each other member giving a synergy to their thinking. Furthermore, each person responded well to individual suggestions or suggestions from the group.

Every day and every night Vivian was with him. What was it she wanted to know? Was it that she was the colonel's eyes on the RFID project? Or was it something to do with the Telecom project? What were Vivian's qualifications? There was so much Roger didn't know about her. It may be no use asking her as she may not wish to disclose anything about her work. Neville really would be the best source, and he would ask him on his next leave to Rochester. Vivian was an excellent guide, knowing many good restaurants and cabarets throughout Havana. In many ways, he preferred her to Ming. She didn't go around openly killing people. She wasn't prone to volcanic tantrums, and she wasn't rude to him. He couldn't trust either of them, and they both liked being fed.

He told Vivian that he would be returning to Rochester on his three monthly leave in two days time. She exclaimed, what a coincidence; that's also when I return.

Roger thought, this is not a coincidence; she has been tasked to find out what my Telecom project is all about.

Vivian said, we must have fun the whole night for two nights because when you return you will be with Ming for at least two nights.

Roger asked her why she always wanted to be with him. It wasn't like this six months or less back.

She looked directly into his eyes and said, "Don't you know?"

Roger answered, "No. I don't know."

She said, "It's because it's my new job."

Roger asked, "What is your new job?"

Vivian answered, "To report everything you say or do, here or in Rochester."

Roger queried her some more, "What am I working on in Rochester?"

She answered, "You are working on a revolutionary new form of telecommunications that does not use electromagnetic radiation to propagate."

Roger was stunned. "How did you find that out?"

She answered, that it was due to a Stegan Coded message to your colleague Peter some six months or less ago, that was easily deciphered because Ming obtained the Stegan key.

"Does the whole world know this?" Roger asked her.

She answered, "Just about."

This means that when I return to Rochester, I have to be very watchful. Roger said.

She agreed, "However, one of my duties is to protect you."

Roger answered, knowing that he would immediately throw her off balance, "Yes, I have heard how fast you are."

Vivian's eyes flashed in anger that she was known by these credentials.

Roger asked, "Vivian, what qualifications do you hold?"

She answered, that she held a PhD in Mathematical Physics from MIT and could understand his code in all its fine detail.

Roger continued, "What group do you belong to and what group does Ming belong to?"

Vivian answered, "I belong to International Operations where we protect the country against external threats. Ming belongs to Internal Operations that protect the country against inside threats."

I have two of the most beautiful women in existence as companions, and both have a PhD and are adept at killing bad guys. What more should I wish for?

Roger sank back into his insignificance, flanked by his Amazonian protector.

Roger talked to every individual on his team explaining what goal he was expected to meet in his absence and asking each person how he thought he was going to attain it. He inspected the work log of every member to see how they chose their components, how they were using the software to program their chip and how they were doing their testing. He did not believe in choosing a replacement for him from his team because he thought it would produce unnecessary competition between them, that would not be technical but political. He told each team member to ask the group first if he had a technological problem that he could not handle and if the group couldn't answer it, the colonel would contact Roger, and he would look into it. If the team member had a non technical problem, then he should take it directly to the colonel.

Roger returned to Rochester and went back to his apartment. Ming had been expecting him, so she was waiting for him. After unpacking his bags, they went out for dinner. Ming wanted to know if she was going to be offered a job there. Roger told her not for the next four months at least, as they already have someone reporting everything, I say or do. Why? She asked. Because you gave your Internal Operations agency my Stegan code key when I was detailing my problems, some six months or so back, to Peter. Since that time, the whole world knows what I have been working on.

Who are you to cheat on me? Roger said sternly to her. I have told you before that you are a liability in my life.

Your agency must have been patting you on the back and saying; our Ming is the best, look at what she has done. She has got details of the greatest invention since the discovery of electromagnetic waves, and her stupid lover is no more the wiser. She is definitely the best spy there ever was. She is the model for all who follow in her footsteps.

Roger added, there is no way I could ever love you, because you are not one with me and always fail me.

What worries me most are that some foreign agency group will abduct me when you or my other Amazonian Protector is not around.

Ming answered; I admit I failed you six months ago, but not now. When I look back at what I have done to you, I am filled with remorse and regret. Please forgive me Roger, please forgive me.

Roger thought to himself, if I believed that, then I would believe that pigs fly.

They finished dinner and returned to Roger's apartment.

Ming didn't make any comments when Roger showered, went to bed and was gently snoring five minutes later.

The next morning Roger went to his offices and checked on his prototypes, and Ming went to work. The sliver of silver paper was missing from his non-working prototype, but the unit was otherwise undisturbed. The working prototype was not touched.

Roger sent a coded message to Peter telling him what had happened to the two prototypes in his office, and the modifications that he had made to his latest prototype, saying that he wanted to test the new prototype.

Peter replied that he was not available for the rest of this month as he had to go to an International conference on Mathematical Modeling in Amsterdam.

Roger found Igor and explained that someone had tampered with the prototype, detailing how he knew. Roger said that he should change the locks to his offices as he was sure that his girlfriend has a spare key. Igor, greatly bemused, said that he would get onto it straight away.

When Ming returned in the afternoon, Roger let her know that he was going drinking at his usual place, hoping to meet Igor and Neville. He invited her to come so that she could easily protect him.

They went and dined on Chicago Stuffed Pizza at Chester Cab Pizza and from there to Roger's usual drinking place.

They met their usual crowd there, and they caroused until closing time.

The next-day Ming went to work, and Roger went to speak with his dean.

His dean welcomed him back and said everything was in order. He asked him about Havana and the night life there. Roger played it up a little as he could see from his sparkling eyes that he was delighting from the stories about the cabarets and drinking places. Roger was loth to suggest he come out there with him as he had already one dean defect and losing another one would look like he was doing it on purpose.

Roger returned to his offices where he met Igor, who gave him the new keys to his offices. He thanked him for changing the locks. Entering his offices, he noticed Lina skulking around. "Why have you had the locks changed?" She asked.

Roger said, "Because someone has been in my laboratory, opening my prototype box. I have passed the box to the police for them to check the fingerprints they find."

Roger thought; we would not be seeing too much of her in the near future.

That evening, Roger returned to Vivian's apartment to meet a smiling cat.

Roger asked, "What are you so happy about?"

She replied, "I am happy to see you and want to have fun, then eat and afterwards have fun again."

What a plan, Roger said.

The next morning, Roger went to his offices and set up more traps. He restored the sliver of silver paper on the hinge of his non-operational prototype and for the new prototype, he placed a square of silver paper underneath, in alignment with one side.

He carefully locked the doors to both offices and went looking for Igor. When he found him, he explained what he had done and took him back to his offices to show him, because he believed Lina had used a master key to enter the offices.

The next morning, Igor checked the traps and found that they had been sprung. He called Lina and told her that if she didn't give him the master key immediately, he would call the police to arrest her straight away for trespassing. She gave him the key with Igor's assurances that the matter would go no further unless there are more break-ins. When Roger came to the offices, Igor gave him the master key. Roger thanked him and said to him that he should hold the key as it is a security matter.

Roger reset all the traps just to make sure that the matter was closed.

Roger inspected his latest prototype, from all angles as if it was a Henry Moore statue. It is truly beautiful; he thought.

Roger returned to his apartment at lunchtime to meet Ming there. He asked, why aren't you at work? She answered that she was still feeling dreadful from his scolding. Roger thought how long will she feel awful. He bet with himself that it would be finished in two days hence, and she would be back selling him out again. I suppose Vivian is the same.

What is there to hide? They know everything except the theory and how to operate it.

CHAPTER 11

LINA'S DECEPTION

Sometime during Roger's and Igor's absence, before Igor confiscated the master key from Lina, she let herself into Roger's offices and photographed his prototypes. She didn't have access to his design because Roger always closed down his computer, whenever he went out, locking it in one of the office drawers or taking it with him.

Lina was now on the lookout for someone who would be willing to pay her for the photographs of the prototype. As she walked towards Roger's apartment, she came across Ming, whom she remembered as one of those people Igor, was told by Roger, never to let into his offices. She recognized her from a signed photograph of her on Roger's desk, saying, "To Roger, with all my Love Ming."

"Hello Ming," calls Lina. Ming turns and sees Lina, whom she doesn't recognize. "Do I know you?" Ming replies.

"I work in the same building as Roger, the new one in which he now works, given to him after his old offices were ransacked."

"Please take me there," she asks Lina.

Lina says, "It will not do you any good as the security people will not allow you or anyone else to enter without a security pass. However, I've something that you may be interested in." Continuing, "It is a photograph of the prototype Roger has been building. Moreover, you will have to pay me for it."

Ming takes Lina's mobile number and replies that she will get back to her.

"You have to be dreaming, you ugly little piece of vomit!" Ming says under her breath.

Ming informs Roger what Lina has been doing. Roger calls Igor and Igor has Lina arrested for illegal entry into Roger's offices and trying to sell photographs of his private property. She is placed on remand in custody awaiting trial.

Igor, being the university's security man has to write up the case and includes the breaking into Roger's offices using a stolen master key and trying to sell the photographs of his private property.

The day of the hearing arrived, and everyone had to present their evidence. The first to explain his report and the stolen master key and how it was discovered was Igor. Followed by the offer of the photos to Ming and then by Roger explaining his prototype traps and new changed-out keys.

Lina pleaded guilty and asked for the lenience if the court. She was sentenced and was told she would be free after a short time on good behavior. She was dismissed from her job at the university.

It was a relief to Roger that there would be no more snooping, and that he could stop looking over his shoulder every time he was in his office or went into his laboratory.

Nobody went to visit her in jail.

Outside the courtroom, Ming asked Roger to take her to his apartment as she wanted to tell him how much she loved him in private. When they returned to the apartment, she was sobbing again and said she thought that she was going through menopause.

Roger said, "It could not be possible as you are only eighteen years old and women have to be at least twenty-five before they experience menopause."

"I am thirty-three years old, she blurted out whilst she sobbed, nearly choking herself as she laughed."

She yelled at him, "What gives you the idea that I am so young?"

Roger replied, "It's because your elder sister is so young?"

"I don't have an elder sister, nor any sister, where did you get that information from?"

Roger remained silent, because he knew that it wouldn't be long before he would be in big trouble.

After he wiped her tears dry and kissed her eyes and made her very excited, they showered and went for lunch. Again, she wanted crab, so they went to Joe's Crab Shack and ate crab.

After lunch, she went back to work, and Roger returned to his offices. The prototype sat undisturbed on his desk like a work of art, and Roger loved its form. He sat thinking about a way to test it without Peter. To involve Ming or Vivian was too dangerous. He just had to wait.

Roger returned to Vivian's apartment and found her waiting there. "How long do we have left in Rochester?" he asked.

She answered, "About two weeks."

"What do you know about my latest prototype?" He asked.

She replied that it was a fail-safe mechanism that had several layers of security to prevent unauthorized activation. Without proper activation, it couldn't be used for anything.

Roger asked, "From where do you get this information?"

"When I build this prototype I do not discuss it with anybody, I just build it. So, how do you know?"

Vivian answered, "We have Neural Networks where all of your decisions are mapped into them and, which give us probabilities of what decision you will make next."

Roger asked, "Can you tell me what is my first-level code?"

Vivian answered, "MOUSETTES and the second-level code is, DRAKEY. We cannot get the third level because we haven't yet built a voice synthesizer of your voice, and we cannot determine what words you entered."

Roger asked, "Has Ming also got all of this information?"

"Yes, the same information." Vivian replies.

Roger asks, "Do you have any of my designs or design notes?"

"No." She answers.

Roger says, "It shows you where we are heading, it will not be long before the emanations of your brain waves from a distance will be deciphered into your thoughts." Continuing on this line of thought, he added, "And then there will be the thought control police in a truly dystopian society. We can see how our society and other societies in the world have moved more away from a utopian to a dystopian society as time has passed."

Roger continued, "I am truly afraid, because every agency in the world will be wanting to obtain the theory behind the new telecommunications to create military applications for their own hegemony."

The working prototype is only proof of the validity of the theory.

Vivian asked, "Why haven't you tested the prototype?"

Roger answered, "Because it is the opening of Pandora's Box. If only my eyes were on it, it would be a very simple matter, but with the eyes of the world on it, the proving of the concept makes the project dangerous and very difficult to contain."

Roger continued, "If the prototype was shown to work, do you think you could protect me against inside US agencies and outside US agencies? I do not think you, and Ming together would be able to offer the same measure of protection that you presently offer. We have already seen how an internal US agency the Foreign Agent Control Group thought Ming was a spy and on several, occasions tried to kill her. She almost had to wipe out the whole group before they stopped. Agents do not seem to be chosen for their intelligence, Ming and yourself being the exceptions."

Vivian said, "You're probably correct."

As it is mid-afternoon, I am going for something light to eat and coffee if you want to join me. She said ok. They walked to the group of shops near the university and sat down in a sandwich bar to eat salmon and tomato sandwiches.

Near them were three large men dressed in dark suits each packing a gun in a shoulder holster. One of the men leaned over and called Vivian a slut. Why did they call you that Roger asked? She said that they were trying to provoke me for winking at them. She turned her legs towards them and opened them. The men couldn't believe what they were looking at; a free peek at a very beautiful woman. Vivian asked them why they were rude to her? One of them said loudly that he noticed her in a downtown brothel. They laughed and started making more rude comments. Vivian said that he was looking at his mother not her. They all fell silent. Vivian added that all of downtown Rochester knows your sisters are poxy harlots.

The man who started the trouble got up, and Vivian got up and ran out of the door, followed by the four well-dressed men. Roger got up and followed just in time to see the fourth man fall with his throat cut and blood spurting all over the roadway. Vivian rang her control and let her know where she was and what had happened. Her control told her that they were Russian agents who came to steal the Telecommunications prototype. She added that she would send the cleanup people.

Vivian told Roger what her control had told her. She asked Roger if he wanted them to go back inside and finish their sandwiches and coffee. He agreed, and they continued as if nothing had happened. Roger thanked her, because if she hadn't protected him, he would be on his way to Russia now in a diplomatic bag. When they left the sandwich bar, there were no dead men or was there any blood on the road. Roger said, if foreign agents are coming into the country to steal the prototype, we must expect more trouble like this to come our way in the days to come.

The problem stems from both you and Ming, when either of you find something new, through the filing of your report to your group control, the world gets to know about it and then in comes the bad guys to grab the goodies for themselves.

Vivian agreed, but reminded him that they are out of Rochester in two weeks henceforth, and Havana will be more subdued.

Roger said, let's go for an early dinner and see who tries to abduct me tonight. If it does happen, maybe we should return to Havana earlier than planned.

Vivian was silent, then she said, "I was hoping that you would test your prototype before you left Rochester."

Roger could see that she was on a one way track and couldn't switch her focus to anything else but the testing of the prototype. It was no use arguing with her as nothing would come of it but anger. He was sorry to find out that she was so single minded as he now realized that she really was on a par with Ming.

They went for a Spaulding Steak & Ale meal at the Governor's Inn Hotel and restaurant. Afterwards, Vivian did her disappearing trick and Roger went back to his apartment to find Ming watching television.

Roger relayed to her what happened tonight. She said that she already knew as Vivian's control had told her control.

Roger said to her that he was thinking about returning to Havana early.

Ming replied, "Why don't you take me on a holiday instead, if you could bear to be away from your darling Vivian for a couple of weeks."

Roger said, "Where do you want me to take you, Russia?"

Ming retorted, "Why can't you speak to me sweetly instead of always making wise cracks?"

Roger replied, "It would be better if I go somewhere by myself."

Ming demanded that he take her to dinner. He replied he had already eaten, and that she should speak courteously to him.

Ming yelled, "You take your slut to dinner, but not me."

Roger left and went to Vivian's apartment and slept soundly there. In the morning, he awoke to the smell of bacon, eggs and coffee. She said that breakfast was ready, and then she tried to smother him to death with her body. He nipped her on a sensitive part, and she cursed him. He laughed and got up to eat a hearty breakfast.

Vivian asked, "Why didn't you sleep with Ming last night?"

Roger replied, "She got angry when I said to her that I would take her climbing on Mount Everest for two weeks."

"What did you say?" She asked.

Roger said, "I would go off by myself somewhere."

Vivian asked, "Where are you going to go?"

Roger answered, "Mount Everest."

Vivian asked, "Please take me to Italy or France for two weeks."

Roger didn't answer because he didn't want to hurt Ming's feelings by taking Vivian with him anywhere for two weeks.

Vivian pushed him for an answer.

He asked her, "Are you in love with me?"

She laughed and said, "You conceited shit! Do you think every woman is in love with you?"

Roger said, "No, I didn't ask about every other woman; I asked about you."

Vivian said, looking into his eyes, "Yes; as a matter of fact, I am very much in love with you as I know you are with me."

Vivian, "It would be very hurtful to Ming if I ran off with you on my month off, when I am with you in Havana for three happy months out of four."

"Yes, you are right," she said.

Roger went back to his apartment and then took Ming to lunch. Ming asked, have you decided where you want to go for the next two weeks? Roger said that he was not going anywhere as he hadn't given it much thought.

Ming asked, "What about testing your prototype before you go back?"

Roger answered, "I have to await Peter's return. He would be quite annoyed if he wasn't included."

They went drinking with Neville and Igor and caroused all night. There was no incident when they left their drinking place.

Ming and Roger ate at Roger's usual café the next morning and they both noticed four nefarious looking individuals dressed in dark suits, each dressed with a breast holster sitting at the back of the café. Excuse me, Ming said, give me time to get the first guy's gun, then, please come outside bringing the rest of them with you, as she got up from the table and walked outside. The lead guy went outside to put her down, but ended getting a hole in his head. The other three, like stupid sheep, went looking for their boss, but instead, each got a hole in his head. Ming rang her control who sent a cleanup squad and told her that these were Bulgarians looking for the prototype.

They went back to Roger's apartment and discussed what they wanted to do today. Roger said, things were heating up here, and it was getting too dangerous to stay. Since I returned there were four Russians dead and today four Bulgarians. What will there be tomorrow? I am scared for you, even though I know how competent you are. Probability is not working in your favor as you are not infallible. It only takes a stray bullet from a boofhead to kill you. Roger continued; I really would like to get out of Rochester for a couple of weeks without the hassle of going international.

They decided to go to California and would fly out and hire a car on arrival at Los Angeles. When they arrived, they did just that.

They stayed in a different hotel every two nights and each night went to a new pub, club or bar and thoroughly enjoyed themselves. After two weeks they returned to, Rochester refreshed.

Roger was due to fly back to Havana tomorrow, which he did. He caught the same plane as Vivian, and because she arranged it, he found himself sitting next to her.

She asked him, how was their trip to Los Angeles? He said, fine, but nothing exceptional. Did Ming enjoy it? She asked. I think so, Roger answered. Roger asked if there had been any trouble during his absence. Vivian replied, nothing. You must have taken it all to California. Roger said, nothing happened there, not even a bar brawl.

I thought about you all the time and missed you something terrible, he said to her. She warmed to him, and her chillness melted away. Thank you, she replied.

She was sitting in the window seat, and he was next to her in the middle seat and there was nobody next to him. Roger told how difficult it was to get to the toilet from that seat.

"Look at what you have done," She exclaimed quietly, "You have made me wet my slacks."

A few minutes later she returned from the toilet after changing her slacks.

Roger laughed as he commented on the fact that it was obvious that she had wet her slacks whilst wearing them.

He continued by telling her how everybody between them, and the toilet were smiling. When she was sufficiently embarrassed, he put her mind at ease by telling her that he was only joking.

When they were back in Miramar, they both showered and dressed and ate dinner in their Copacobana hotel.

Roger wanted to take an extra cheese, anchovy pizza back to his room. That evening they went downtown to the Tropicana.

The Tropicana is the oldest Cabaret show in town, and it's located in Havana. Both Vivian and Roger were very disappointed with the dinner and outdoor theatre with many dancers in elaborate costumes. However, it has been reported by other customers that it's a third rate stage show, with a style from the fifties, with poorly performed dancing.

The whole thing appeared to be a state-run money spinner milked daily for hard currency. On top of the eighty-five dollar tickets, a drink before the show is five dollars, and if you have a camera, you will be charged another five dollars or fifteen if you take a movie.

It may be more advisable if you are going to spend one-hundred dollars, to eat at the best restaurants and dance the night away in old Havana for a whole weekend rather than go here.

The next morning, they all met for breakfast and the colonel welcomed them back. He explained to Roger how pleased with the progress his team was making with the RFID project. After breakfast, Roger spoke to each of his team members to determine how they had progressed and if there were any problems. They had all progressed well and were extremely cohesive with no apparent problems. Roger looked at his milestone chart and timeline and noted that they were a little ahead of where he expected them to be. He wondered what it was that made them so motivated. It had to be something internal to the group that generated a desire to progress, because they progressed synergetically and this fired them to keep outperforming themselves for the next cycle, like an increasing non stable oscillation. Roger wondered what would become of it all. Would they burn themselves out or would they become a super mind with the ability to design anything asked of them? Roger could now see himself at the brink of two major changes in mankind. These changes were the birth of a super race that could create a single potent mind from many that comprised its parts and secondly, the new physics based on Hadron technology.

Roger realized that he had to monitor constantly his team's progress and creativity. His team didn't need him to tell them what to do; they knew and not only that, but they knew better than he, how to achieve it. All that his team required was a starting point and a finishing point with some milestones for suggestions. What a marvelous thing was happening before his eyes. Something a million computers linked with each other as a neural network would not be able to achieve. Here we had countless trillions of neurons working together that could not be achieved by computers.

It was a demonstration of anarchy at its best.

Roger wondered what would happen if he created a group ten times larger and trained them to work together as he had done with his own team. Would he be able to take the Hadron technology and advance it well into the future?

He went to lunch with Vivian and ordered Ropa Vieja, which is; shredded beef brisket, bell peppers, onions, tomato wine sauce and moros (black beans and rice cooked together).

She said that he was a little quiet and asked him what was wrong. He answered nothing, absolutely nothing.

She continued with her questioning, Is your team doing well? Roger said, "Yes, they are progressing."

She persevered, is there anything you want to tell me?

Roger answered, only that I think you are the most beautiful woman alive, and I love you dearly.

Vivian was quite put out, "You have done it again!"

What asked Roger, "You have gone and made me all wet again. You shit! You did it on purpose!"

Roger guffawed. I am so lucky having a woman like you my darling Vivian.

She replied; you have never called me darling before. Oh, I love you so much, she happily cried.

After lunch, Roger went to his team asking them questions about how they felt about the project and whether there was anything, they thought could be improved. There was nothing that they thought could be improved as they had everything under control.

He looked at their prototypes and observed that they had been professionally laid out using the shortest of printed circuit board tracks and very high density component count. He checked their test procedures and the software they used. Again, he couldn't fault them.

Roger felt quite inadequate as he had created a team that far surpassed what he could do in one month, and this is one of his main areas of expertise. He could understand his feelings of inadequacy when it came to Ming or Vivian because their fighting skills were alien to him, even though they never showed him any sign of their strength, he knew that they had it, and that they controlled it.

He sat and watched his team work and most of the time they were absorbed in their work, but occasionally they came together and had a quick discussion and then went back to what they were doing. Roger felt a shiver down his spine, because these men were changing from men into some sort of high intelligence androids working in unison.

Again, he had the feeling that he was in the process of changing the course of mankind, and he didn't like what he saw.

He thought, if he tried to stop this project, his team would probably kill him, because it was no longer his project anymore, and he had no part in it any longer. This led him to think about expanding the team numbers to ten times the current size. He thought that when he had made them to be at the equivalent level as his present team, they probably would build into their project some sort of protection mechanism to prevent any outside interference and to make themselves fairly invulnerable to most forms of intrusion. He was sure that they would expel him from their group, as he was no longer at the same intellectual level anymore and not as dextrous. He could see the group slowly changing their members, one at a time, into their own retrained creations to perform specialized jobs, requiring a higher intelligence, until the final group became unrecognizable from its original composition.

Roger didn't want to let anyone know what he had achieved because, like the Telecom project, it would become uncontrollable, with major corporations and governments throughout the world breeding these superb designers, who in their turn would be phasing out humans as we know them today. He felt that it would become a self-perpetuating entity that initially would run alongside mankind, eventually replacing him by its super intelligence counterpart.

Roger's head was spinning as he imagined the ramifications of his RFID project.

He wondered what would happen if he never came back to Havana. The most likely thing would be that the prototypes and designs would be given to the Colonel for him to progress, and the group would be disbanded.

Roger asked Vivian if she wanted to go out for coffee. During coffee, she asked him what was troubling him. It is not the Telecom project; he answered; it is another project of mine that also has wide implications. Please tell me, she said. Roger said no, as anything from your mouth would also change the direction that the world was heading. Vivian said, take it that we are one, and I am not at liberty to tell the government anything that you prohibit me from letting them know.

Let me think about what you have said, then after an hour Roger responded; what makes you more loyal to me than to your own government? I find it difficult to reconcile that there is anything in this world that would shift your beliefs. Furthermore, and more important, I don't want to burden you with this knowledge as I know enough about you now to know that, as time passes, it will deeply disturb you.

Roger knew that Vivian would disappear in a few minutes to go and lodge her latest report.

True to form, after coffee, she excused herself and wasn't seen until eight at night. The colonel appeared around seven in the evening and asked if there was anything he could do.

Roger thanked him and replied that there was nothing he required.

Roger ordered a spicy pizza and took it to his room to eat with a bottle of white wine that he purchased earlier.

Roger noticed an icy reception when he went into the laboratories to inspect the project. It was like; you have no right to come in here. Roger ignored it at first, but it became more apparent as the months passed. When he was due to go back to Rochester, Roger informed the colonel that he should be very careful when entering the laboratories as the team may take a dim view to him entering and inspecting their work. He should enter with two armed guards. The colonel laughed at Roger and wished him a good leave and looked forward to seeing him on his return.

Vivian asked Roger why he had given the colonel such a stiff warning.

Roger answered, because it is what I feel. If he does not heed it, there is nothing more that I can do.

Vivian said, is there anything that I can do?

Roger said yes, leave instructions to arrest and incarcerate all team members immediately if the colonel dies for any reason, no matter how innocent his death appears.

Vivian said to Roger, now I understand your reticence in explaining anything to me. This is like a horror movie.

Vivian gave the instructions to the next in command of the Havana base, and he said he would fully comply with her wishes and inform her immediately if anything went awry.

We will go back to Rochester tomorrow Roger said. I don't know, which is worse, here or Rochester. We may have to come back earlier than we expect for you to play out your horror movie, which believe me will be worse than you expect. How can you defend yourself against five foes who are ten times more intelligent than you are? Go and report that to your colonel, before we leave.

The next day they were on their plane back to Rochester.

CHAPTER 12

THE PROTOTYPE IS STOLEN

Government agents storm Roger's offices looking for his prototype and design plans. Initially, Igor is immobilized and tied up with tie wraps and gagged before he can do anything. The agents start looking for the prototype and its design notes. Once they find the prototype, they carefully bag it and then look for the design and design notes which do not exist in paper form.

The agents leave with the new prototype only.

Lina who has spent the last three months in jail has been released on good behavior and uses one of her relatives working in the university administration to have her reinstated back in her old job. She is very happy as she sees the possible end to Roger's project, but is peeved over not receiving any money. She stays in her office not wanting to be seen by anybody and not become involved.

Roger enters his offices and notices Igor bound and gagged. He quickly releases him and listens to him relate what happened.

Roger sets up his work laptop and sends a coded email off to Peter, who has recently come back from Amsterdam, explaining to him the latest events.

Roger notices Lina skulking around and asks her what is she doing in this building. She explains why she is back, and that she will never make trouble again and would he please excuse her. Roger said, not a problem as you keep a far distance from my offices.

Roger hurries to Vivian's apartment and tells her what has happened. She rings her control who informs her that the colonel is dead and that the five engineers have been arrested and put behind bars and will stay in jail until her and Roger return. Roger requests Vivian to ask her control to keep each of the five engineers in spaced apart cells so that they cannot communicate with each other. This is a matter of urgency as they will break out of their jail if they can communicate and formulate something together. Should any one of them escape, then all others must be executed by a firing squad. This will stop them from wreaking havoc on Havana. The colonel didn't listen to me and paid for it with his life. If the Havana control doesn't listen to me and do what I ask, the whole of Havana will pay dearly for it.

Vivian asked, what will they do?

Roger answered, what can five men each with an IQ that is ten times your IQ, who is hell-bent on getting payback for breaking up their team, think of doing? I am sure we could not imagine. However, whatever it is, it will not be handing candy out to passer by's.

She also asks her control to inform her of who stole Roger's Telecom project prototype.

An hour later, Vivian informs Roger that her control in Havana will carry out his instructions without delay, and it was Ming's group who stole the prototype.

Roger went back to his apartment. Ming was not there. From there he went to Vivian's apartment to see if she wanted to eat. She was happy to go to, so they went to eat crab again and French fries with two bottles of house white and returned to Vivian's apartment to sleep after a very busy day.

The next morning Vivian was up to her body smothering tricks again and had made a bacon, egg, sausage, tomato and toast breakfast with hot coffee. Roger complimented her on being so thoughtful and wanted to know when she bought all of these breakfast items.

We will have to return to Havana soon Vivian said. Roger agreed and added that he needed to get the RFID plans and test results, if his team had left any. Maybe we should threaten them with execution if we cannot find any, or if they do not produce the circuits, plans and working prototypes.

The local time in Rochester is the same as the local time in Havana, so whatever news we get from there will be on our time said Vivian.

As she was talking, her phone rang, it was her Havana control who lets her know that trouble has started in Havana. One of Roger's team members escaped and so the US agents started executing the other team members, but they were most unsuccessful, instead they were executed until all team members were free. The Cuban authorities in order to contain them to Havana has grounded all airlines in and out of Havana, closed their borders and put up road blocks throughout the country.

They issued an edict saying that anyone harboring these criminals would be shot together with their families.

Roger asked Vivian, what are the nationalities of these team members? Vivian replied that they were Cuban.

Roger suggested that they arrest their families until they surrender. If they do not surrender within three hours, their immediate families will be summarily executed.

Vivian informed her control who answered, that this has already put into place, and the clock is running down from two hours, not three. She added, her control informed her that each team member would be shot dead-on sight, and there no longer would be any arrests due to the gravity of the team member's behavior.

By late afternoon, all team members had been shot dead and order had been restored.

Roger wept as he felt that it was he who was responsible for what had happened.

Vivian said to him, there is so much that you are not telling me. Roger answered, yes, you know nothing, and it is better for you and the rest of the world to remain in ignorance, because you saw what happened. The world is not yet ready for this technology.

Roger and Vivian returned to the laboratories below the hotel Copacabana to look for circuits, plans and prototypes. They found nothing because his team had collectively remembered everything and had no need to record anything or make any prototypes.

What do we do with the RFID project? Do we start again? Roger asked Vivian. She answered; I was having the time of my life with you. Why should we stop? Well, you better arrange everything once again with your control; to employ Engineers, to place component orders, pay the university, and everything else we did. We will start again tomorrow and after the initial arrangements, we go back to Rochester to continue my one month's leave whilst things are getting underway here.

Vivian informed her control what she discussed with Roger, and her control told her that she would appoint another intermediary to act in the same capacity as the previous Colonel.

Roger prepared order lists for the new engineers to inspect and approve. He made lists of approved Printed Circuit Board (PCB) manufacturers and lists of Hybrid Circuit Manufacturers. He checked that each engineer had his software on his computer. When he was all done, he said to Vivian, we can go back to Rochester when we wish.

They left for Rochester one day later as everyone was happy with the initial preparations.

Whilst they were in the plane with Vivian in the window seat and Roger next to an empty aisle seat, Roger said to Vivian that he wanted her to go to the toilet . . . . She squeaked at him; you dog, you have done it again!

Done what? Asked Roger. He looked down at her slacks and noticed a large wet patch spreading out from between her legs. Have you urinated in your slacks again? He asked her guffawing. She was quite put out. He told her to take her spare pair of slacks out of her bag and go to the toilet and change herself like she did last time. Don't stand up to get your extra slacks as everyone will see why you are squeaking? Roger, please get my spare slacks out of my bag. He did as he was asked, and she could change her slacks without getting out of her seat. Now that you are settled, would you like to sit . . . he didn't get further than that because she hit him in the stomache, making him groan. The airline hostess noticed that there was some extra movement going on in his seat and came over to see what was going on.

"Is everything ok here?" she asked.

Roger said that this strange lady had tried to make a pass at him. The airline hostess smiled and said, "I don't think so sir, more than likely she was trying to confirm your gender."

Roger lay back and tried to get some sleep as they still had a few hours to go before landing.

He thought what he had to do in the three or more weeks left to him in Rochester. He would use his prototype in Neville's safe house to test the project with Peter. The only difference between the units was the access codes required by the stolen unit. Even though the agents who stole the latest prototype, had two of these codes, they didn't have the third, making the unit quite unusable. He was proud of himself for having the foresight to build that third level of security into the prototype. Even though they held the prototype, it was nothing but metal and wires, etc. without any functional use.

He needed to monitor what was happening in Havana to ensure all was ready for his return.

He also needed to have a conversation with Neville to determine what Ming was doing, as he didn't meet with her when he was last in Rochester. Perhaps, it was because she was instrumental in the theft of his Telecom project prototype and didn't want to face him.

When they arrived back to Vivian's apartment, they showered and went to bed to get over the strain of flying home. They slept until evening and decided not to go anywhere tonight. Roger rang for a large anchovy and tomato with extra cheese, and cheese filled crust to be delivered to Vivian's apartment. They ate and drank white wine that they had previously purchased and went to sleep.

The next day they went their own ways, and Roger went to his offices. Everything was the same as what it was before leaving for Havana, except Roger's Henry Moore sculpture was missing.

He noticed Lina hovering around her end of the corridor and said loudly to her, don't come down here!

Roger confirmed with his dean that payments were still being made to the university. His dean asked him if everything was in order in Havana. Roger, replied that everything was as it should be. There had been a change in management. Yes, I noticed that, Roger's dean said. Roger went back to his apartment and made a coffee for himself and then returned to Vivian's apartment. He asked her if she felt like going drinking with his friends. She said that she had things to do.

Roger went to his favorite drinking place and met both Igor and Neville. They enjoyed each other's company all night. Roger was not able to get Neville by himself, so he could not discuss what Ming had been doing.

Roger went back to his apartment and slept there. The next morning he went to Vivian's apartment and met her waiting for him. Why are you waiting for me? He asked, is everything ok?

Vivian answered him by relaying to him what her control told her. The Telecom prototype is becoming a very hot property with agents killing each other indiscriminately in an effort to possess it. Obviously, there is nothing they can do with it, but because of the mentality of the agents, that is not significant. What is important is possession. It is a bit like the very rich owning a famous painting; they cannot look at it all the time. I'm not sure that it would appreciate faster than its cash value placed into a high interest rate deposit account. It appears it has something to do with mindless possession of the work of art that makes the owner feel more special than all those who know he owns it. Give the same man an ice cream wrapper and tell him it is the most valuable object in the world that he could possess and once convinced he would kill to prevent it from passing into another's hands.

Roger said that he agreed. My prototype, I believe, he said, could pass as a Henry Moore sculpture as its form is most pleasing from all angles. I'm sure the possessors of the Prototype do not see it that way and probably would never see it that way. As Plato said; . . . eye of the beholder.

With this saying, even Lena has a chance of finding someone who thinks she is a humdinger.

However, when I think about it some more, perhaps not.

They went off to lunch and ate Pasta, and Antipasta topped off with a couple of bottles of house white and returned to Vivian's apartment to sleep it off.

Roger asked, how long have we got before we must return to Havana? She answered that we still have two weeks.

Later, that afternoon, Roger went to Neville's safe house to inspect his prototypes and noticed that the working prototype had been damaged beyond repair. It looked like some sort of heavy object had fallen on it. Neville apologized, saying it was a bumbling fool he had employed who lifted more than he could handle, and he toppled over allowing his load to fall onto the prototype. Roger said to Neville, not a problem.

He then left Neville's safe house and returned to Vivian's apartment. Vivian had returned, and Roger explained what had happened to his other working prototype.

Vivian wanted to go out to dinner, so Roger said they would go wherever she wanted to go.

After a nice evening meal, they returned to Vivian's apartment.

Roger was feeling more and more dismal as his numbers of failures were mounting. He thought about how he would handle his new team in Miramar. There was no need to change his initial policies as they were quite sound. He pondered over where the changeover occurred. It seemed to occur when he went on leave for the first time. Exactly, what did I do at that time? Recalling the events back at that time, he thought the main difference between the usual management style, and his management style was: *He told each team member to ask the group first if he had a technological problem that he could not handle . . . .*

In other words, he threw the design of the project onto the group, rather than letting the individual sort it out for himself. This accelerated the group's ability to come to grips with the whole project rather knowing next to nothing.

The second mistake Roger realized, was not to relinquish the growing knowledge given to the group, when he returned from leave. From this day forwards, these questions would be directed to him or the Internet for the three months he was in Havana and answered by the team member researching the Internet for the one month when he was on leave.

Knowledge obtained from the many questions asked by the team members and answered by the collective group was highly undesirable, because the questions posed by the team members to the group, month after month, made the group become more knowledgeable and powerful each time it answered them. This was shown previously, to continue until the group became another entity that would control each member of the team and rebel against the colonel and Roger.

Roger now had the solution to his immediate pressing problem as he knew that he had to prevent any team member from asking his colleagues what was the answer to his question. Although the team member asking the question didn't know, within the group, it was more likely than not to have one member who did know. It was the answering of this question to the knowledge of the group that was the root of the problem. He would instruct his fresh team with the new procedures that they must follow on his return to Havana.

Vivian said to Roger that he had been quite pensive during the past hour. Was everything all right?

Roger answered cheerfully, yes; I have been thinking about how I must instruct my new team in Havana when I first meet them.

Roger asked Vivian, what has Ming been doing?

You don't know? Vivian said.

No, I don't know. If I knew, I wouldn't be asking you. Roger tersely replied.

There was no answer from Vivian. Roger went back to his apartment, but didn't find Ming there. He had a good idea that she was keeping away because she knew that he would, give her what for, when he did finally come across her.

He returned to Vivian's apartment; dog tired, and fell asleep immediately his head touched the pillow.

The next morning he awoke to Vivian's smothering trick and gave her a severe nip that earned him a sharp smack across the back of his head. He arose and ate with Vivian a hearty breakfast with coffee.

I only hope that I give you as much happiness as you give me; he said with a mouth crammed with toast, egg and sausage.

You filthy pig! Didn't your parents teach you never to speak with your mouth full.

He repeated what he said, but this time his mouth was crammed with toast, bacon and runny egg yolk.

Vivian got up from the breakfast table and went to sit someplace different to finish her meal, cursing him some more as she moved.

After breakfast, Vivian did her disappearing trick again, and he knew that he wouldn't see her again until later this afternoon.

He went back to his offices to start work on a new prototype, but when he started he found that he didn't have the mind anymore. So, he locked up and went back to his apartment to sleep even though it wasn't even midday.

He slept until four in the afternoon and then drove to a delicatessen to buy some different cheeses, Jarlesberg, Aged Goat Cheese (Garrotxa), Pepperino pepato, Camembert and Boursin together with cheese biscuits and Baguette Bread and four bottles of Argentinian Merlot. He took everything back to Vivian's apartment. Without waiting for Vivian, he then started eating and drinking, enjoying himself immensely. Who needs company he thought? No such luck he thought as he heard the front door open . . . and along came Jones.

"What are you eating without me?" She squealed.

"Um . . ."

Roger asked Vivian, "What was at the end of the tunnel leading to the laboratories under the Cococabana Hotel?"

"I don't know." She said.

"We must go exploring when we go back. I think the tunnel must lead to the outside world or dungeons full of silver Spanish pieces of eight. Take your pick." Roger said.

The tunnels extend either side of the laboratories. Does anyone know in the hotel where they go to? We should do an Internet search to see if there is anything there. We should search under tunnels under Cococabana Hotel. Vivian came up with nothing, as did Roger. The guy who may know is the guy who forced me down the staircase into the tunnels when I first came here. He may be associated with the hotel or with US intelligence.

Vivian asked Roger what was he going to do about his Telecom project?

Roger answered, nothing at the moment. It was Ming, who started the latest furore and as a consequence, I can do nothing with a stolen prototype. I need to build another one, but I haven't got the mind, nor energy for it at present.

Just leave me to my cheese please.

Vivian asked Roger, "Why didn't you buy salami also?" Vivian said she was going back to the delicatessen to buy; Cacciatore hot salami, spicy Hungarian salami and Spanish salami and more sliced Jarlesberg cheese and black grapes.

Roger asked her nicely, "Are you going to share it?"

Vivian answered, "Of course, between me and myself."

She left Roger to keep feasting on his cheeses.

Half an hour later she returned finding Roger still stuffing himself. She opened up the salami packet and spread the selection on the table next to the other fare. The two of them enjoyed a magnificent spread and washed it down with the Merlot. When they finished gorging themselves, they lay back on the bed and fell asleep on each other.

They awoke around midnight to the tap-tapping on the front door. From behind the door, Roger asked who it was. A man's voice answered that it was Donald. Roger let Vivian know it was Donald and asked her if she wanted him to let him in. She said no, as she was leaving. Roger did nothing while she dressed and then went back to bed after she had gone. He slept soundly for the rest of the night and awoke at eight in the morning, showered and dressed, put the cheeses and salami into the refrigerator and left to go to his café for the usual breakfast with a large pot of coffee.

He returned to his apartment and noticed that nothing was different from when he came last. Ming was certainly keeping away from him.

He sent a Stegan coded email to Peter explaining all that he knew over the past three or more days and informed him that he had to build another prototype for testing with him, but it would not be straight away due to his other commitments. He told him that he would be back in Havana in two weeks time.

He went back to Vivian's apartment and found her eating cheese. "You rat! Eating cheese without me," he exclaimed.

Roger continued more subdued, "Has your control in Havana informed you about employing the new engineers."

She replied that she hadn't. Vivian then went on to explain that her Rochester control called her last night because she wanted to know what to do about the stolen prototype, whether to join the chasing race or not. Vivian said that she advised her to keep out of it as it would serve no purpose.

Roger complimented her on her correct response to her control.

Roger thought, so Donald is a runner for her control, and that puts an end to that.

Roger then went about devouring the remaining cheese, salami and cheese biscuits with Vivian. They finished off the last bottle of Argentinian Merlot, like there was no tomorrow.

She said, I was hoping that you were not coming this morning, so I could eat your portion and drink your bottle of wine.

Roger said, just like you can have fun by yourself.

She looked at him and said to him, "Why don't you shut up?"

"Look what you have done!"

Roger looked at her panties, they were sodden. She had spilled wine over herself.

Roger said to Vivian, we still have another week and one-half before we return to Havana and there is no point going back early if I do not have the staff to work the project, unless we explore the tunnels in the meantime.

Having said that, Vivian receives a phone call from her control telling her to take Roger back to Havana straight away as there are many agents from the Eastern European block countries who have entered the US over the past forty-eight hours and the word is about that they wish to abduct Roger and force him to surrender the prototype codes to them. Please leave your apartment immediately and declare yourselves to the airport staff asking them to direct you to the private jet going to Havana that is waiting for you. Park your unlocked car at the airport near the terminus and put the keys in the closed sun shield on the driver's side for Donald to drive back to your apartment.

Vivian and Roger left that afternoon and were picked up in Havana about four and a half hours later. After the immigration and custom's formalities, they were driven to the Cococabana Hotel. They showered and slept to late in the evening. There was a note at the reception to let them know that they had a meeting at eight in the morning.

The next morning, Vivian smothered Roger nearly to death and got a good bite on her buttocks for her efforts. They went down to breakfast and introduced themselves to a Colonel Schiffer, who was the previous colonel's replacement. He hadn't quite lost his German accent and sounded and looked a little like a Gestapo hangover.

Roger asked, "Have the five new engineers arrived?"

The colonel replied that they had not yet arrived, as they are having difficulty recruiting anybody suitable. The death of the previous five engineers tarnished the recruitment, and they may have to go to the British Virgin Islands, Jamaica, Haiti, or Puerto Rico if they cannot find anyone in Cuba. The advertisements have been distributed to the above-mentioned countries, and we are hoping to hold interviews in a couple of days.

Roger imagined he heard the colonel clicking his heels where the full stops ended the sentences. He thought to himself that he was being extremely unfair, taking the Mickey out of him like this as he was probably a truly nice, kind and gentle person. However, Roger had learnt never to give anyone the benefit of the doubt. So, he was afraid that if he was dining with the colonel, he would be clicking his heels where the full stops punctuated his sentences. Consequently, he reminded himself always to wear running shoes when around the colonel to prevent any embarrassment.

Roger outlined how the RFID project would be set up and monitored and how there would be no replacement for him when he went on leave. The colonel said that would not be the way it would be done. It would be done his way or not at all. Roger thanked the colonel for being so direct with him and said that it would not be done. He asked the colonel to arrange as soon as possible a flight back to Rochester for Vivian and himself. The colonel backed down very quickly and said that we should not be too hasty about throwing in the towel. Roger persisted about returning to Rochester. He said, I learnt a long time ago that if I don't get on with my colleague immediately I will never get on with him. The colonel was now starting to panic, he said, I didn't mean what I said, as it came out different to what I intended.

Roger said, I quote you;

". . . *that would not be the way it would be done. It would be done my way or not at all.*"

This seems pretty clear to me.

Roger asked, "What did you mean then?"

The colonel answered, "I don't know what I meant, but it was not that."

Roger said, if Vivian and I are to stay here, please give me immediately a signed declaration that you will in no way interfere with any policy or instructions that I give my team regarding the design, testing or implementation of this project, and you will do your utmost to cooperate with me and progress this project to my satisfaction.

The colonel agreed and presented him with the signed declaration an hour later.

Vivian and Roger caught the blue bus to old Havana, where they purchased two very strong torch lights and two boxes of AA Batteries, together with six spare torch globes and a compass for determining the direction that they would be walking. This would be a backup to their mobile phone compass.

They lunched in old Havana and bought three bottles of Cab Merlot and returned by blue bus to the hotel.

Chapter 13

NEVILLE'S REVELATION

Roger said to Vivian that there were a few people watching us with interest, whilst we were buying the torch lights. Vivian said, yes, I noticed. Vivian said, maybe we should wait a couple of days to see if we are going to be questioned over these items before we set out on our expeditions. If we are questioned by the authorities, our answer is, so that we can see around the laboratories if the power fails.

After a couple of days, they set off with a packed lunch and walked for a couple of hours down the left hand tunnel from the laboratories. They didn't come across too much of interest, not even an air vent. After another two hours of walking they ran out of the tunnel as it now descended. They went down like they were walking to the center of the Earth. Down and down they went, one hour or more until they reached an open space, chiseled into the rock was directions that were no longer readable. They photographed these inscriptions. Where should they go? Go left or go right? Roger looked at his compass and informed Vivian that if they went left, they would continue in the same direction as they had been walking before they descended. Vivian kept a detailed map, including bearings of where they had come from and where they were going. She agreed with that, but said they had been walking nearly South-West which fifteen kilometers from Miramar should bring them underneath Playa Baracoa near the sea. After a picnic lunch with a drink of water, they continued South-West on for another fifteen kilometers until they ran out of the tunnel, as it now ascended, up and up it went, kilometer after kilometer until they reached an opening to the sky. This should be Mariel Bay, Bahia del Mariel. They carefully climbed out onto a narrow path that winds to the top of the cliff. Vivian took many photographs, in case they had to come back this way. From the top of the cliff, they could see the town of Mariel. They walked there taking many photos again and couldn't find a hotel or restaurant. They caught a taxi back to Miramar and showered and went to bed. They had their exercise for the week.

When they arose some hours later it was already dark. They dressed and went to the hotel restaurant and had dinner and two bottles of house red and listened to the hotel band.

They discussed what they were going to do tomorrow. They were going to follow the tunnel to the right of the laboratories and eat a packed lunch when they got hungry. Roger asked Vivian if she had her gun with her. She replied that she had a Sig Sauer 220 with her. Roger asked her to strap on her holster with the gun and bring it with her when they go out tomorrow.

Why? She asked.

Roger answered, that he just had a funny feeling tomorrow will be different than today.

They awoke and went for breakfast. After finishing their coffee, they returned to Roger's room and arranged their items together with the packed lunch that they ordered and collected at breakfast and put them into a backpack that Roger had purchased for the occasion.

After catching the lift to the laboratories, they started walking down the passage that continued right, past the laboratories. They walked North East for about two and a half kilometers and then East for about two more kilometers. Vivian said, look for a vent or upwards passage way because I estimate that we have just walked half a kilometer North under the water comprising the entrance to Havana Bay. This should bring us directly under Morro castle where there should be dungeons. "There they are, ahead of us!" Roger exclaimed.

They came across eight dungeons, four each side of the passage way, and they were so dismal. How could anyone throw anyone into any of these dungeons? They were soaked from seepage of the entrance to the bay and small and dark. Sleeping in these dungeons meant sleeping on a cold wet floor. There must be steps leading upwards, and there were. They discovered these just past the dungeons, and they would have risen to somewhere in the bowels of the castle. The dungeons didn't seem to be used for anything as the locks were old and rusted and all the cell doors were open. Vivian took many photographs. The passageway turned sharply South-East, and they walked for another half a kilometer. Vivian said she estimated that they were now under the Castillo de San Carlos de la Cabana or the old Fort. They noticed more dungeons, like the ones they had just passed. There was an upward winding stone staircase. Roger said, let's go up and see where it goes. They climbed for about an hour until they reached an area full of small rooms that they supposed were torture chambers from looking at the various mechanical contraptions contained by these rooms. Roger said to Vivian that she should make a special note of where they came in, otherwise they could be wandering around for ages trying to find their way out. Some of the rooms still had grisly human remains locked into mechanical machinery. They found the staircase going upwards again and continued going up. They walked up for another half an hour and came to an iron grill that had a carpet or rug over it. Roger pushed, and the rug lifted, showing an expensively furnished office. Fortunately, there was nobody in the room, so Roger and Vivian came out of the staircase and closed the grill and rearranged the rug. They both walked to a large door in the room and opened it and entered a hallway leading to a secretary's reception area. Fortunately, because it was lunch time she wasn't there either. They walked out of the reception area and caught a lift back to ground level. When they exited the lift, they saw the place inundated with tourists. They walked across the bridge to Habana 61 Restaurant and ate there. Whilst eating there, they noticed four typical Eastern Block agents staring at them and obviously talking about them. "How did they find us here?" Roger asked.

Vivian replied; I suspect it was Colonel Schiffer, still smarting over your tongue lashing.

Can you kill him without being suspected? Roger asked her. She replied, I sure can. I can put my stiletto into his neck, severing his spinal cord without much blood being spilt. Roger shivered at the thought, but then as Ming had taught him, it's either him or me.

Vivian said, let me get rid of these idiots first. They paid, and left the restaurant and walked to the Parque Martires Del 71 They stood next to the Statue of Máximo Gómez and waited for the four agents. Vivian shot the four agents through their forehead before the first fell. We will let the old man who lives in the statue clean up the mess. It was on National News that night, that four Russians were assassinated outside of their famous Statue of Máximo Gómez.

Roger and Vivian returned to their hotel and both noticed that Colonel Schiffer was surprised to see them. He was relaxing on a sofa, and Roger went and sat in a chair opposite him. Vivian walked behind him, and whilst he was talking to Roger, she severed his spine by inserting her stiletto into the side of his neck, missing any major arteries. He sat like he was still talking to Roger when Vivian said to Roger, let's go back to our room and have a nap.

They left the Colonel sitting there as if he was thinking. Vivian rang her control and let her know what happened. Her control said she was lucky that it happened now rather than later, when the place was full of people. She informed her that Ming was continuing to chase after the prototype she stole from Roger. She continued by saying, there seems to be a lot of Eastern Block agents still pouring into the country, but Ming is doing her best to keep the numbers down. She said that she would look for another local control for her. Vivian asked if any interviews had been set up for selecting the five engineers. She didn't know, but would find out and get back to her.

"Now, wasn't that a fun day." Roger said to Vivian, who was nude before he finished the sentence. They had a lot of fun that afternoon and then showered and dressed for dinner.

"Would you like to go to Habana 61, for dinner?" Roger asked.

"Yes, it sounds good." Vivian responded. They hailed a taxi and went to the restaurant that had Lobster as well as grilled fish, mashed and fried yucca, cuban rice and beans and a very varied menu of an international cuisine fused with cuban tradition and they enjoyed themselves listening to mellow jazz rock. Afterwards, they walked along the Malecón Malecon that runs alongside Havana Port and they caught a taxi back to their hotel. The police were there investigating the death of Colonel Schiffer. They didn't require them, so they returned to their hotel room and dozed off after good food, good exercise, good drink and their own good company.

Roger said, tomorrow, I would like to go back to the tunnel that we took left of the laboratories and explore the branch that turned right and so doubled back on itself.

The next morning with a packed picnic lunch, from the laboratories, they walked for about three hours down the left hand tunnel from the laboratories. They ran out of the tunnel as it now descended in a winding staircase. Down and down they went, one hour or more until they again reached an open space, and found again the chiseled inscriptions in the rock that were undecipherable. This time they walked down the right hand tunnel. Roger looked at his compass and noted that they were heading North-East. Three kilometers from their turn off the tunnel kept on the same bearing. Vivian estimated that they were below the Latin American School of Medicine. They discovered eight small rooms, four on either side of the tunnel. Roger entered one of the rooms after forcing the rusted door, expecting it to be another dungeon but instead he found it full of sacks of black silver coins that he judged to be pieces of eight.

Vivian, he said, "We have found the mother lode." They took four coins each and left the rest untouched. Looking into each of the other seven rooms without breaking the door of each, they saw the same story of a room filled with pieces of eight.

They kept walking down the tunnel looking for a vertical staircase and noticed it twenty meters further down.

They started to ascend the winding staircase, knowing it would take them an hour or more before they may or may not be able to exit.

An hour later Roger came across a grill baring his exit. He gently pushed on it, and the grill opened enough for him to notice that he was in a mortuary. He was not able to open the grill sufficiently for them to escape without making a great deal of noise. Roger told Vivian what he had seen, and she recorded it. They climbed down and made their way back to the hotel; dog tired. Once back in their hotel room, they showered and slept until evening. They ate at the hotel and relaxed to the hotel band and then went to bed around eight.

They agreed that tomorrow morning after breakfast, they would investigate the same tunnel until they found its exit.

They started off after breakfast at the hotel. Roger said to Vivian that they shouldn't leave their coins in their hotel room because if the cleaner came across them, there would be very big trouble. They agreed to store them in a small plastic bag in the toilet cistern.

They walked down the left hand tunnel from the laboratories, and once they were below the Latin American School of Medicine; they saw the eight small rooms, four on either side of the tunnel filled with silver coins. From there they continued walking North-East for another three and one-half kilometers without coming across anything of interest. Vivian remarked that she thought that they were below the town of Santa Fe and heading towards the Hemingway Marina. After walking for another one or more kilometers, they noticed ahead of them more rooms. When they reached these rooms, they noticed that there was one room either side of the tunnel, again with the door lock rusted. Roger kicked open the door to one of the rooms. Inside they found old books and maps that were still in good condition. They carefully stored these documents in the back pack and then went over to the other room. Roger kicked this door in and found nothing of interest except an old lead crucifix of the type people hung on their walls. Vivian stored this carefully in Roger's back pack. Vivian said, if we keep walking for another three kilometers, we should be walking alongside the Hemingway Marina and possibly find an exit pipe before we reach the Rio Jaimanitas. They kept walking and as Vivian expected, they found the vertical staircase. Vivian went first, and she walked up the spiral stone staircase for about one kilometer until she reached the staircase grill. She gently nudged it and could see the sky; she kept pushing until the grill gave way, and they could climb out onto a wide ledge overlooking the North-East end of the Marina. They carefully put the grill back into somewhere near its original place. As luck would have it, they were right next to the Carretera Panamericana. They were about eight kilometers from their hotel and thought it better to get a taxi than walk. When they arrived at their hotel, they showered and changed their clothes and carefully hid Roger's backpack among their other clothes, they went to lunch. Roger wanted a cheese crust anchovy and tomato pizza with a couple of bottles of house red. They ate their pizza and drank their wine in a fairly open place to ensure their privacy, as they both knew that they were possibly being monitored by non-friendly parties. They would never discuss the Telecom prototype or the Colonel or anything private, in their hotel room as they were sure the room was bugged. Vivian's control rang her during lunch and said that she, and Roger would be flying back to Rochester tomorrow morning as they are experiencing delays in finding Engineers and a new Colonel. They will return to Havana when these people have been found.

What perfect timing Vivian said, Roger agreed. That evening they enjoyed themselves going to jazz clubs and drinking bars. In one bar, a young American kept making dirty passes at Vivian and Roger told him to stop it or he would regret it for the rest of his life. He got worse and was spoiling for a fight. Vivian stuck her forefinger in a pressure point in his neck and he fell paralyzed to the floor. No blood, no screaming, no cursing. Roger bent over and said, "I told you so." And they went to another place to drink.

The next day they collected their coins and documents, left the hotel in the special hire car that took them to the airport and then caught the private jet to Rochester. Once home and recuperated, Roger started looking at the documents they returned with. There were maps of where the Spanish ships had stored their gold, and other booty in the same tunnels as they had found the pieces of eight. The Spanish had secret doors fitted in rooms along these tunnels never to be found by searching for them. These doors would lead to rooms filled with ingots of gold and jewels. The maps showed where the doors were and gave instructions on how to open them. Roger memorized these maps in all their detail, not wanting to make copies for security reasons. There was also an old book called Don Quixote by Cervantes, published in 1605. This was the first part of the two-part book. The second part was published in 1615 and was also among the papers Roger found. These rare books, probably first edition, would fetch a fortune on the open market.

Roger put these books, the maps and four pieces of eight, together with the crucifix, into a plastic bag and put these into a plastic container that clipped down either end.

He asked Vivian if she wanted to store her maps with the books and maps from the tunnel. She said she would prefer to keep her things in her own safe place.

Roger said, "Trust and confidence in each other is what it's all about."

Vivian said, "What is that supposed to mean?"

Roger tersely answered, "You work it out!"

Against his better judgement, Roger gave two of the loose four pieces of eight to Vivian.

Roger arranged to keep their joint things with a commercial storage company, so they had twenty-four hours a day access. He took the items down to the storage company and personally put them in a special cubicle that had a padlock with two keys. After padlocking their things away, and signing the required forms to him allow access if he lost the key, Roger returned to Vivian's apartment. After her wanting to keep her hand-drawn maps to herself, which Roger felt were just as much his, he decided not to give her a key to the storage place, nor let her know its name.

Neville contacts Roger and arranges to meet him for lunch at the "Il cucchiaio d'argento" a favorite Italian restaurant that they both frequent and enjoy.

When they both have arrived, seated and have placed their orders, Neville explains how the agents from the different countries are each vying for the prototype with Ming leading their own merry band.

Neville said, "Everybody now knows, that your project develops a new form of telecommunications that does not depend on electromagnetic waves and, which travels over very large distances instantly without the need of bandwidth et cetera, et cetera."

Roger replied, "Yes; it was Ming, who let the world know, even though she promised to keep her mouth closed.

"You will knock around with clever women, who eat people like you for breakfast," remarked Neville.

Roger said, "Changing the subject, could you have two of these coins discretely valued, giving him one of the pieces of eight and this book, which he wrote down on a piece of paper; It is an original edition of Don Quixote by Cervantes, published in 1605. This was the first part of the two-part book. The second part was published in 1615. I will give you both books when you find a suitable buyer.

Neville replied, "You are a man of many surprises, yes, and I can take my ten percent commission?"

Roger answered, "No, take five percent." Neville agreed.

Vivian has the other two pieces of eight, which I know she will try to sell herself. It may be worth waiting as, undoubtedly, she will sell for a very small amount, not realizing their true worth, and this will cause a high demand for the coins.

Neville said thanks for that information. You are quite right; it will cause a high demand from buyers all over the world. OK leave it with me.

After lunch, Roger goes to his own apartment and finds that it has not been disturbed so he returns to Vivian's apartment and also finds it empty. He lies down on the bed and falls asleep after a hefty lunch with Neville.

Later, that afternoon Vivian returns and smothers Roger to death and gets a nasty nip for her efforts.

She said she was talking out of place by preferring to keep her things in her own safe place and apologized for being so stupid. Roger said, OK, give me your two pieces of eight as I can find a good-paying buyer. Vivian said that already she had sold her two coins for ten dollars each.

"They are worth eight hundred dollars each," Roger shouted at her from the top of his voice.

"Check the Internet." Roger said, still in a very agitated voice. Vivian looked and felt very stupid and by Roger remaining silent after his last outburst, didn't make it any better.

Vivian's control rang her to let her know she had caused considerable excitement by walking into a Rochester coin dealer, selling him two pieces of eight for ten dollars apiece rather than eight hundred dollars a piece. Her control said;

"What do you think you are up to?"

"You know every agent in the world will be trying to abduct you now, to find where the treasure is hidden!"

"Sort it out." She yelled at Vivian.

Vivian gave all of her maps to Roger for him to hide. He went directly to the storage place and deposited them in his cubicle, and returned to Vivian's apartment. He said to Vivian, you better take what clothes you may need, because we are moving into your allocated apartment, wherever that may be. It is not safe now in my apartment, nor the one that I rented. They moved all of her belongings, and Roger was surprised to find how pleasant her apartment was and how close it was to Vivian's old apartment and also that they could watch for prowling vehicles. Vivian gave a set of keys to Roger.

After Vivian unpacked her belongings into her own apartment, Roger said, "Now wasn't that fun."

Roger delighted to see how much she enjoyed herself.

That evening they dined on steak and French fries with two bottles of house red, then went back to Vivian's true apartment and slept it off until morning. Roger awoke to the smell of eggs and bacon and fresh brewed coffee.

Where are you going this morning? He asked her.

Nowhere, in particular, why have you got anything in mind? She replied.

Maybe we could do our own recruiting for the Havana RFID project if you could tee it up with your control.

That is a good idea. Vivian rang her control and asked if it was possible. After a couple of hours, she rang Vivian back and asked her to go ahead with her recruiting, but to limit it to the Caribbean. Roger wrote out the job specifications and experience level required, and Vivian put it onto job sites for immediate action. Vivian negotiated with her control regarding what the salaries were to be and where the accommodation would be located and other administrative matters.

Both Roger and Vivian caught the US government, private jet to Havana and settled back into their usual hotel room.

Roger and Vivian conducted interviews with the candidates, and selected those who would become the successful four engineers and one technician. Furthermore, they employed an administrative assistant as there was no colonel, for the moment, as one could not be found. Roger had to play that role for the present, taking advice from Vivian's control with help from Vivian.

The next morning after breakfast, Roger called his new team together, including the Administrative Assistant (AA) and outlined what the overall project was to achieve and how it was to be done. From the broad concepts, he started narrowing down, giving specifics of each part of the project and adding breadth to the project. Once this was completed, he defined the time line and the major milestones that the team had to reach. After three hours, he was finished and so was his five Engineers. The scope and depth of the work made them very tired.

That afternoon he called his team together again to explain the problem that Cuba is facing at the moment:

An extremely large amount of cigars is being stolen from the factories and smuggled out of the country. It is very difficult to prevent this from happening and reduce the outflow of these smuggled goods, for various reasons.

What I am asking you to do, is to design an RFID chip that can be placed on or in each carton of cigars manufactured. Once these cigars are sent out of the factory or placed in storage, this chip will have programmed into it, the following information: identity of the contents, where it is destined, and the mode of transport to be used or is being used to convey it to its destination.

To design and implement this, I have recruited:
1. A hardware engineer for the interfaces,
2. A software engineer because all the radios are programmed for operational frequencies in transmit and receive mode and for specific data to be sent, digital data rate, etc.,
3. A radio frequency (RF) engineer to design the antennas, and the duplexer over the frequency bands required,
4. A printed circuit board layout engineer familiar with Computer-Aided Design (CAD) Software, such as Altium,
5. A technician who will build the prototype circuits for testing and who will order and purchasing the parts,
6. An Administration Assistant (AA) to help whenever required.

Roger's closing remarks were:
- He would talk to every individual on his team explaining what goal he was expected to meet and asking each person how he thought he was going to attain it.

- He would inspect the work log of every member to see how they chose their components, how they were using the software to program their chip and how they were doing their testing.
- He told each team member never to ask the group if he had a technological problem that he could not handle, but keep trying to find a solution himself on the Internet.

The administrative assistant was there to let Roger know if any team member was having an insoluble problem that required Roger to intervene.

For non technical problems, then he should take it directly to the administrative assistant (AA).

In summary, Roger said that was a lot to take in for the first day. Tomorrow, you will start your designs and start sourcing your components.

The next day, they had to choose what chips, software, etc., they required by discussing the pros and cons of each manufacturer and submit to Roger their final choice. They had to be ready to defend their choice if asked to do so. This same modus operandi existed throughout the project, from design to testing and final testing.

Roger knew that once they got into the habit of working this way, the number of mistakes that they would make would be significantly reduced.

Roger had to be confident that they knew how to operate the test equipment correctly and taught those, who didn't know.

So, day after day they followed a routine of designing, checking, bread boarding, testing and bouncing their ideas off of Roger, never off of each other. It eventually became a part of their nature.

After three months, Roger wanted to take his leave. He told his team to keep working like they had been doing, whilst he was with them. He told them that it was important that they solved their own problems using the Internet. He would inspect their log books on his return to assess their progress. He pointed out the milestones that they should reach during his absence and wanted to view their prototypes and have them demonstrate them to him when he got back.

Roger and Vivian returned to Rochester.

CHAPTER 14

IGOR'S NEWS

The next morning, Roger went to his offices with the view to begin constructing his new Telecom prototype. On seeing Igor, Roger smiled and warmly greeted him. Roger asked Igor, "What have you got for me, my friend?"

"Nothing yet," Igor replied, "but I should have something for you soon."

"Oh yes, like what?" Said Roger, with a questioning look.

"Well, I found out from an old colleague of mine, that the prototype has been booby trapped by a hostile faction and will explode if tampered with," said Igor.

"Oh NO!" Exclaimed Roger. "That means that Ming will die, because she believes she only has to contend with the unlocking code that will not trigger any explosive device. Igor, let me see if I can stop Ming's faction from playing with the prototype."

Roger rang Neville on his secure personal mobile phone and when he answered, he explained what had happened. He asked Neville if he could do anything to stop any of the agents from playing with the prototype, especially Ming, who would be leading the Government's contingent.

Neville said that he would ring him back.

A few minutes later, Neville rang back to let Roger know that the prototype had exploded half an hour ago, and all agents were dead. "They are still trying to collect all the body parts of those present," he said.

Roger let Igor know what happened and thanked him for trying to save the day.

"What a waste, beauty and brains," said Roger, to Igor, as Igor was walking out of the offices. Igor turned and returned a rueful smile.

There was nothing here to do, so he closed up shop and returned to Vivian's true apartment.

He met Vivian and explained that her co-worker Ming and Ming's cohorts were dead due to an exploding booby trap that was fitted onto his Telecom prototype by a foreign agent. She rang her control who confirmed the story. I'm so sorry Vivian said.

It was still morning, so they went for coffee at the local coffee shop. The two of them noticed foreign agents having coffee at the back of the shop. Vivian and Roger sat behind the four agents and listened to their conversation that was in French. They picked up enough words to know that they wanted to abduct them to find out where the pieces of eight were being hidden. After their coffee, Roger went to pay the bill and returned to where Vivian was sitting. The four agents were staring at each other when Roger and Vivian left the café. After they had walked to where Roger parked his car, there were cries coming from the café as the waitresses discovered four of their customers were sitting on their chairs' stone dead. The waitresses couldn't remember who was sitting next to them, or near them, so they couldn't help the police in their enquiries.

Roger said to Vivian that this was getting to be too much, and they should think about emigrating to a different state.

Neville rang Roger and arranged a meeting with him for lunch at a steak and crab restaurant. Once they were seated and their orders placed, Neville said, "I have had the coins appraised and each was valued at eight hundred dollars."

Roger said, "Yes, I agree, that is around the value I had expected."

Neville continued, "I have a buyer who will pay three hundred and thirty thousand dollars for both the Cervantes books."

"I agree also," said Roger.

Neville asked when could he give him the remaining items? Roger replied, after lunch. Neville said that would be most satisfactory. After lunch, Roger went to his storage place where he left untouched the four remaining coins and took the stored two books. He met Neville in a coffee shop and handed them over to him together with the second coin that was still in his pocket. Neville said that he would be in touch within the next two days to pay him the sum of: three hundred and fifteen thousand, and twenty dollars after his five percent had been deducted.

They parted, and Roger went back to Vivian's true apartment to find her there.

Vivian asked, "What have you been up to this morning?"

Roger replied, "Having lunch with Neville and wheeling and dealing."

"Did you get what you wanted?" She asked.

"Yes, eight hundred each coin."

Vivian added, "We should have taken a hundred, each and that would have made us eighty thousand each."

Roger answered; it doesn't work like that, the larger the number of coins, the smaller their total value. If you tried to sell two hundred coins in one go, the value may fall to ten dollars a coin.

Vivian remained silent, then she asked, "How many coins did we take?"

Roger replied, "Eight coins, four each. We have both sold two coins each that leaves us with four in the store."

"When can I have my other two coins?" She asked.

Roger answered, when you want. It would be better to hang off for a week, to let the market recover so that you are able to get your eight hundred for each coin.

OK, she replied.

Roger asked, do you want me to sell them for you?

She replied, no; I am capable of doing it myself.

That afternoon Roger went back to his other apartments to check that they were all in order. His apartment had not been touched, nor had Vivian's apartment. He thought that he would sleep at his own apartment tonight. He went to his offices to check that they were in order. He saw the rat skulking around at the end of the corridor, but when he looked in her direction, she scuttled back into her room and closed her door. Thank goodness Roger thought.

In his laboratory, he looked at his components and made a note of what else he required. He walked over to the administration office and wrote a list of components; he immediately needed, and another list that he would eventually require to rebuild his sleeping project. He was filled with a desire to finish this project once and for all, but he knew the politics of the Havana RFID, and the Pieces of Eight project would prevent him from doing so, and the turmoil that his Telecom project would bring to the world was something he really didn't want to see. He already could see in his mind's eye what would happen if he could flood the gold and silver markets with his pieces of eight, or if he trained his engineers to form a cohesive synergistic entity.

He drove to his cheese delicatessen and purchased the same range of cheeses and salamis together with different breads and biscuits and four bottles of Cab Merlot and the two kilos of black table grapes.

He spread them on his dining room table, uncorked a bottle of wine and was just about to start eating when his front door chime sounded. He went to see who it was, and saw that it was Vivian. He opened the front door and in, she rushed, smelling the fare. She got herself a sharp knife, a cheese knife and a fork and a large plate and sat down to start gorging herself.

Roger said to her, he didn't buy this spread for her to share. She answered that she couldn't care less, and he didn't have a hope in hell of stopping her. She challenged him, "Come on, try it and die!"

Roger remained silent.

She said, "What's wrong?"

Roger said, "Saying that, is in bad taste."

She quickly answered by saying, "not as bad as the smell and taste of this cheese," referring to the Taleggio.

Roger picked up his car keys and left the apartment. She came running after him, but she was too late; he had gone. He went to the local supermarket and bought sliced Emmental cheese, sliced Jarlesberg cheese, bacon, ham and a sliced whole-meal loaf. He went back to Vivian's place and cooked himself the best Cheese and Ham/Bacon fried sandwich a hungry man would ever want. He sat down at the dining room table with four of these tasty hot melt sandwiches piled on a large plate when . . . Along came Jones.

Roger yelled, what are you doing here? She took a plate and sat down at the table and started to eat his Cheese and Ham/Bacon fried sandwiches. Roger got up, very angry and left. This time she wouldn't know where he went. It was already evening, and he drove back to his apartment and starting eating the cheese and salamis and drinking the wine. After an hour and a half, he was satiated and finished another bottle of red before taking his shoes, shirt and trousers off and falling asleep on his bed. He blissfully slept all night and awoke to his door chimes ringing repeatedly. He got up and noticed Vivian at the door. It was eight-thirty.

She said to him, "I've told you before, you are not to eat cheese and salami without me."

Roger started eating the cheese and salami with the French Baguettes and enjoyed it as much as he did the previous night. The Boursin was one of his favorites, so he finished this off before Vivian the Vulture could get at it. By the time the two gannets had finished eating, there wasn't too much left.

"Why are you so angry?" She asked him gently.

I am capable of doing it myself, you say. Well, you have shown by selling the two Spanish silver dollars for ten dollars each, that you are not really capable of doing it properly. Why don't you leave it to people who are more capable than you, or is that too much for your over-inflated ego to handle?

She snapped back at him, "What makes you think that you are more capable than me?"

There you go with your ego tripping you up again, said Roger. I am not going to sell them, but I know who can sell them for me for a small profit. He said.

She was completely deflated.

That afternoon, Neville rang to say that he had his money. Roger thanked him and arranged to meet at their usual coffee house. Neville gave him a cash check for three hundred and fifteen thousand, and twenty dollars for the two books and two coins, each worth eight hundred dollars.

Roger found Vivian and told her that they needed to put money into their accounts. Fortunately, the three of them banked at the same bank and so transferring money between accounts was not going to be a problem. How much she asked; Roger replied, if you give me one of your coins, it would be one hundred and fifty-seven thousand, five hundred and ten dollars.

What for? She asked. It was for the two Cervantes, Don Quixote books and two of my coins. How much did you get for the two books? Three hundred and thirty thousand, and add one thousand six hundred for the sale of my two coins less five percent on this for brokerage, divide it by two, and you can see how much each of us made on the deal.

They went down to the bank and arranged the transfers between the accounts.

Afterwards, Roger said to Vivian, "Dinner is on you tonight."

Gladly, she said. They dined very well on Filet Mignon and fresh fruit with a house cheese plate. Vivian feigned forgetting her purse, but didn't let it get out of hand.

How long do we have left here Roger asked? Vivian rang her control, who said three more weeks. Please ask her if everything is going well with my design team in Miramar.

Her control rang her back after half an hour to let her know that all was well in Paradise.

Roger arranged with Igor to store his ordered components in his laboratory when they arrived. He said to him that there would be two consignments arriving at different times. Igor said that he would take care of it for him.

I have to do an Internet search on the crucifix before leaving Rochester, he thought to himself. Better to let someone have it who appreciates it rather than it be hidden away in a box.

That evening, he started researching Spanish crucifixes used by soldiers and explorers in Cuba around the 1500s and found nothing out of the ordinary.

Roger thought the best action was to give it to Neville to determine if any of his contacts knew if there was any history associated with it.

The following morning, Roger went to his storage place and took out the crucifix. He arranged with Neville to give it to him later that day. Once Neville had received it, he asked for a couple of days.

A couple of days later, as promised, Neville met with Roger at their coffee shop. Neville said that none of his contacts could place the crucifix as anything out of the ordinary. Neville gave the crucifix back to Roger, who weighed it in his hand and said to Neville; I can see that it is lead, but it seems to be too heavy for lead. Roger took out his penknife and dug it into the crucifix feeling something hard under the lead. He then pared the crucifix to discover a gold stem and on further shaving revealed a diamond stud. There you are, my friend, he said to Neville if you can have all the lead removed, I'm sure your contacts will be able to identify and value it.

I wouldn't be surprised if it was owned by Panfilo de Narvaez, who helped conquer Cuba in 1511.

Neville was most taken aback and agreed to do as Roger asked. Give me a couple more days he muttered, as he got up to leave.

Roger went back to Vivian's true apartment, and they went to lunch.

"What have you been doing?" She asked.

Roger answered that he had been wheeling and dealing over the diamond-studded gold crucifix.

"What diamond-studded gold crucifix are you talking about?" She asked.

"The one I found in the empty dungeon," He replied.

Roger explained about the metallic lead coating disguise and the hidden diamond studs.

"How much is it worth?" She asked.

"Don't know, but I expect it to bring a quarter of a million."
Roger said.

A couple of days later, Neville rang to say he had a couple of buyers. The highest buyer was two hundred thousand. Roger said to Neville that he could hang out until the offers reached three hundred thousand. You will get your five-percent brokerage fee of course. Neville said he was satisfied.

A week later, Neville rang Roger to say the highest bidder was two hundred and eighty thousand. Roger said that he agreed and asked him to close the deal.

Vivian agreed to buy the dinner again tonight as payment for her one hundred and thirty three thousand dollar portion of the sale.

A couple of days later, Neville said he had Roger's check and where should they meet. Roger said, at our bank, so I can give you your share immediately. They met at the bank, and Roger arranged for the transfer of fourteen thousand into Neville's account and one hundred and thirty three thousand into Vivian's account.

Vivian said they had one and a half weeks remaining of their leave.

Roger and Vivian left the bank and went to their delicatessen and bought a fare fit for a king and a queen. Salamis and cheeses and different breads and whatever took their fancy.

After buying black grapes, and four bottles of Cabernet Savignon, they went back to Vivian's true apartment and gorged themselves on this delightful food until they couldn't keep their eyes open.

Roger awoke to being smothered again. He nipped her quite hard, and she jumped off giving him a smack over the back of the head.

"Don't do that!" She yelled.

"Well stop trying to murder me in my sleep!" He yelled back at her.

They had their fun and then went back to their cheese and wine and ate and drank again until they fell asleep once more.

When they awoke it was already evening and Roger remarked that she hadn't killed anybody today because they hadn't left the apartment.

"Do you want us to go out and look for trouble?" Roger said, provoking her, or "are you happy smothering me to death?"

"Come on pussy cat, come and lie on your comfortable cushion."

She came over to smother him again, and he gave her a very painful nip. "She yelped." Backing away whilst Roger was in peals of laughter and trying to avoid the smacks across his head.

"I have told you not to do that!" She yelled.

"Come on angry cat, let me give you a nice kiss." She came over to him determined to give him a hefty whack on the back of the head, but he grabbed and swung her around and gave her another painful nip. This time she was a true angry cat and Roger laughing uncontrollably ran as fast as he could to the bathroom, to lock himself in, until she calmed down.

Fifteen minutes later she asked him to open the bathroom door as she wanted to go to the toilet. He opened the door and exited the bathroom.

Roger said that if he had more time he would rebuild his Telecom Prototype. Next leave, I will start he said.

Roger thought of what he was going to do when he returned to Havana as there was nothing to do here in Rochester except to keep Vivian and himself out of trouble's way.

The sale of the Cervantes books, the crucifix and the coins started a renewal of attempted abductions by foreign agents as shown by the break-ins made to Roger's and Vivian's apartment and Roger's offices in an attempt to find Vivian and Roger.

Roger was always worried by probabilities and thought it only a matter of time that a bullet would find them by the sheer number of firearms that could and would be fired at them.

Vivian rang her control and explained that although they had about six days leave remaining it may be safer to go back to Havana straight away. Vivian's control agreed and said that she would arrange for a return flight for tomorrow.

An hour later, she said Donald would take them to the airport tomorrow, and the Havana control would arrange for them to be met and taken back to Miramar.

The next day, five days early, they were settled back into their Cococabana Hotel.

They dined at the hotel restaurant and had a bottle of wine each.

The next morning, Roger started on a three-day inspection of his team's log books to assess their progress. He wanted to confirm the milestones that they should have reached were actually reached during his absence, and he wanted to view their prototypes for layout and constructional quality and have each team member demonstrate the operability of his prototype.

After a week, he could make a proper assessment. To his relief, his team had progressed as he had expected. Some advanced and some retarded in the progress of their work. Roger now knew who he had to tutor and whom he could leave to his own devices.

Over the next week, he counseled his weaker team members and formulated a plan that was suitable for them and, which would help develop their abilities. He asked them to criticize their own work until he was satisfied with their evaluation, and then he asked them to rectify their work until it was up to a satisfactory standard. He never directly criticized their work, that was up to them.

He carefully watched each team member over the next three months to make sure that each team member was satisfied with his own work, and that he had good reason to be satisfied.

He noticed that over time, the morale of the team improved.

Roger was aware he had to be constantly on his guard for any misdirections he could make, that would lead his team into self-sufficiency and move the knowledge base over to the group.

Roger also asked that, at the end of each day; each engineer uploaded to his name on Roger's server their latest circuits and test results. Each engineer had his own code to enter Roger's server and could download his most-recent circuit or drawing for modification, which he should do every morning.

Roger was very busy with his team and didn't have time to go exploring with Vivian. He asked her if she was becoming bored. She answered that she was happy things were progressing well with his team, and she would bide her time until he was ready.

Night time was her time, but usually Roger was so tired that he couldn't summon the energy to eat out. He said to her that he would take his six days leave owed to him whilst in country, now that all had settled down, and they would go exploring again.

That afternoon, Roger informed his team that he would not always be around for the next day or so as he would be taking some of the leave owed to him. If they needed him for anything, they should let the Administrative Assistant know, and she would inform him.

They had breakfast the next morning and headed off with a packed picnic lunch. From the laboratories, they walked down the left hand tunnel until they found themselves having to descend the winding staircase until they again reached an open space. They walked down the North-East right hand tunnel until they arrived at the eight small rooms, four on either side of the tunnel. Roger walked up to the last door on the left-hand side and paced ten meters past it along the corridor. He was looking for a finger hole at eye level and one at waist level. Once he found them; he put his forefinger from each hand into the holes and pushed. He heard a mechanism inside the door release, and the door swung open. They went inside the room one person at a time, and the second person was tasked with holding the door ajar. If the door closed when they were both inside, there was no way out, and they would die in there just like they could see from the remains of two unfortunates whose skeletons told the story. Vivian looked around and told Roger that the room was full of jewels and sacks of gold pieces of eight. Roger told her to take ten gold coins and under no circumstances touch the diamonds as they have been booby trapped. Vivian did as she was told and came out of the room. Roger let go of the door which immediately swung tightly closed, showing no indication of where it was. They had their picnic lunch, with water and Roger reminded Vivian never to speak about what happened whilst in their hotel room, because he was sure that it was bugged. They then made their way back to their hotel room and were extremely tired by the time they arrived back. Roger put the ten gold coins into a small plastic bag and hid it in the toilet cistern. They both went to dinner in the pizza area and had a couple of bottles of house red with their dinner.

Roger wrote on his napkin: Gold is sixty-six times the value of silver, so eight hundred dollars for a silver piece of eight would bring about fifty-three thousand dollars for a single gold piece of eight.

He constantly wiped his napkin on his wet red-wine covered mouth until there was no writing left to read.

When they were out of hearing, Vivian asked.

"How did you know where the room that stored the gold was located and how did you know about the booby trap?"

"The map showed where the first hidden room storing the gold was located with reference to the fourth seen room on the left-hand side. The second hidden room was ten meters on from the first hidden room and so on for the third and fourth hidden room. The fifth, sixth and seventh and eighth rooms are on the other side of the tunnel, numbered until the eighth is opposite to the first. It was very explicit in the instructions. Skull and Cross Bones over the diamond."

She asked, "How about the door?"

He answered, "The same, a very graphic closed door with a Skull and Cross Bones over it."

She asked why they didn't go into the other hidden rooms?

Roger answered because each of the other seven rooms contained some form of death, in a form typical of Spanish cruelty.

The second hidden room contains poisonous spiders, such as black widow spiders and harmless tarantulas, etc.

The third hidden room contains the blue scorpion *Rhopalurus junceus* which is an endemic species from Cuba, and its venom is used in cancer treatment.

The fourth hidden room contains smallpox as shown by the map diagram of a man covered with sores all over his body.

The fifth hidden room contains syphilis or gonorrhea, shown by a man discharging from his penis.

The sixth hidden room contains something that drives a man insane as shown by a man holding his head and screaming.

The seventh room does not show what it contains. Maybe it contains something beyond description for its day. The same for the eighth room.

Roger said, "There is nothing left for us to do here anymore. I will finish this contract, and then we will move away. We can come back here in five years time perhaps, to top up. If we try to take more then, the markets will collapse, and we will be identified."

She agreed, and Roger thought she was clever enough to take advice this time, and so he did not feel the need to elaborate.

Once out of the tunnels and back into the open, they dumped the torches and the small number of batteries that were left, leaving no trace of their exploits.

They returned to their hotel room and showered and went to bed.

The next-day Roger returned to work and continued inspecting their daily uploads to see if there were any problems. All seemed to be on track.

They worked like this for the next three months, and the project progressed as well as expected. Nobody had any major problems, and each team member was on a par with every other member when it came to standard of work and reaching his milestones.

Roger inspected all of their log books and interviewed each team member about his contribution to the project asking him about his relationships with the other team members and asking if he thought there was anything that could be done better.

He told his team that his three months were complete, and he needed to take leave. He said to them that he really didn't need to remind them that they solved their own problems using the Internet, and he would inspect their log books on his return to assess their progress. Again, he pointed out the milestones that they should reach during his absence and wanted to view their prototypes and have them demonstrate them to him when he got back.

That evening, Roger and Vivian went to the La Maison, which is a beautiful mansion with garden and swimming pool and has been a favorite place to many tourists for many years. They had dinner here and drinks while the late show was on.

They moved to the Irakere Jazz Club in Miramar, a well-known club, once called Johnny's dream that offers a program of group performances, international and jazz latino all performed by national Cubans.

Vivian informed her control that they were due to return to Rochester. Her control agreed and arranged for Donald to pick them up at Rochester airport. The next morning after taking their gold coins from the toilet cistern, Roger and Vivian returned to Rochester.

Chapter 15

THE PROTOTYPE IS CONSTRUCTED.

Roger entered his office and opened up the lab door and looked at the array of components he had been using previously. He returned to his office and sat in his chair, contemplating what he was to do next. He heard a soft tapping on his office door. Turning around, he saw that it was Lina. Roger asked, "Yes, Lina, what can I do for you?"

Lina looked at him for a long time and then asked him what his project was all about. Roger answered "Telecommunications."

Lina asked, "Why are so many people and Governments interested?" Before Roger could answer, Igor appeared and said, "Ma-am, I'm sorry to inform you, but you are in a restricted area, I am asking you to leave. Please leave now!" Lina did as she was told and Roger said nothing, as he knew that Igor was protecting him. After she had left, Igor said to Roger that he would have signs made up stating, "Restricted Area, Please Do Not Enter." Roger said, "You better clear this with Admin beforehand, otherwise you will be giving your girlfriend an excuse to make trouble for you. If you want to pass your girlfriend on and make a lifelong friend, introduce Lina to Ide. They are made for each other."

"You have a lady visitor named Vivian, waiting for you outside," said Igor. "Thanks," replied Roger.

"You know I was going to do some work tonight," he said to her with a resigned tone in his voice.

"That's no way to greet a hungry lady," she bantered.

They walked back to the apartment and by the time Roger had unlocked the front door, Vivian had already entered the apartment and was rummaging through the refrigerator for the leftover cheese and salami spread.

The next morning they went to breakfast at Roger's usual café.

They didn't notice anybody out of the ordinary sitting in the café. After fifteen minutes, four mafia looking hoodlums walked in and sat down at a table next to Vivian. One put his hand on the inside of her thigh and asked her if she wanted to pla. He was dead with a stiletto severing his spinal cord before he could finish his sentence. Vivian was up and finishing the other three off before the first one fell. Vivian told the café owner that these people were terrorists, and she was a government agent. She told him that she had already arranged for people to come and clean up, and the squad would be here within five minutes. They came, and Vivian paid the bill and she and Roger left. Her control lets her know that they were Afghanistan this time after codes for the Telecom Project.

They went to a supermarket to buy coffee, etc. In the supermarket Roger noted more agents with their guns bulging. Vivian and Roger quickly left the supermarket before Vivian had to put them down. Roger said, we should just give up and go home. As they quickly walked back to their car in the supermarket parking lot, they saw the agents trying to cut them off. Vivian signaled to Roger to crouch down beside him. She indicated to him that he should stay put whilst she moved up between the rows of cars to where the agents were. Like sheep, she thought all huddled together. She crept up to the one closest with his back to her and stuck him in the side of his neck, severing his spinal cord. She swiftly dispatched the other three before the first hit the ground. After that she rang her control letting her know where she should send the clean-up squad. This time they were Iranians, her control informed her, wanting Roger to tell them the prototype codes. When the clean-up squad arrived, Roger and Vivian went back to Vivian's true apartment.

Roger rang Neville to arrange with him the sale of two gold pieces of eight. Neville was most excited and asked if he could meet with him straight away. Roger and Vivian met with him at Roger's usual café, and Roger said he had ten pieces, but he thought it wise only to sell two pieces now. Still, Neville could let his customers know he had more pieces if they asked and were extremely interested. Neville asked if he had any idea of the value of each. Roger said gold was sixty-six times the value of silver now, so possibly each coin's value is more than fifty-three thousand dollars. Neville took two pieces and said he would get back to him in a couple of days.

Roger received a telephone call from Neville after a couple of days informing him that he couldn't find a buyer.

Roger asked, "You couldn't find any buyer?"

None, said Neville.

OK, keep trying and let me know if you do find anyone, said Roger.

What do you think is the problem? Roger asked.

Neville replied, probably the estimated cost that you have put on it. Maybe its better to let it find its own level.

Roger agreed, and so Neville would try this out and get back to him once the fish started biting.

Vivian asked what happened? Roger told her that Neville could not find any buyer. OK dinner is on you tonight; she triumphantly crowed. They went to Jines Greek restaurant and ate Mousaka and drank two bottles of Red Rock Merlot.

The next morning Vivian made breakfast for them both, and they ate and sipped coffee. She asked him what he was doing about his prototype. He said that he was still thinking about constructing a new one, but he always seemed to run out of time. If he constructed a new one, then it would be stolen, so he wondered if there is any point to building, having it stolen, building it again, ad infinitum.

Roger asked Vivian, "As Colonel Emidio Guardo of the US army was the main source of inspiration for the RFID project, who has now replaced him?"

Vivian answered, "It is some group; the control in Havana knows in the US Army administration, that is still funding it."

Roger asked, "Who do I report to, in Havana?"

Vivian replied, "Me, silly boy!"

Roger told Vivian that he wouldn't be around for a week or more, as he needed to construct the prototype once more, in a quiet and safe place.

Roger arrived at his offices in the morning to start building the prototype afresh once again. He met Igor, who had arrived early to ensure Lina didn't come prowling around Roger's office and laboratory. Roger locked the front door of his office that had access to the passage that ran down the length of the building, past the other offices and to the outside door.

"Where do I start," Roger said to Igor and mainly to himself. "Why don't you employ a technician," Igor said.

Roger replied "Security. How do I find someone I can trust in a hurry?"

"If you trust me," Igor said in a low voice, "then I can work as your Technician."

Roger shook his head, "I trust you, but it takes many years experience to work as a competent technician." Igor, not wanting to push himself out, said nothing.

After a couple of minutes, Roger asked Igor if he had ever worked in an electronics development environment before.

Igor answered "Yes."

Roger asked, "For how long were you working and what were you doing?"

"My latest work was on heat-seeking missiles. That was for two years, but I had worked on other defense systems for around twenty-eight years."

Roger asked, "Did you use storage CROs?"

Igor answered, "Yes, also Spectrum Analyzers and Electronic Network Analyzers for the RF work, PCB fabrication and so on." I am impressed said Roger. "Why are you working as a security guard with your experience?"

Igor didn't answer, but asked, "What are we doing first?"

Roger downloaded his design and explained to Igor how the circuits worked and interlinked. Each night, the work computer was updated, and the design replaced to its Internet safe place and downloaded the next morning for the new day's work.

Both men worked days and nights for nearly a week to get the prototype finished to Roger's satisfaction. Roger activated the prototype and then gave it three levels of security code. The first security code was an alpha code: PRIMARY, The second again as a numeric code: 1123581321 and the third as a voice code activated on Roger saying opensezme. All coded to maintain a fail-secure mechanism if the prototype was attempted to be initiated without its proper codes.

As the prototype was completed it needed to be put in a safe place. First, Igor took it to a carpenter who made a specially constructed box to hold it safely. Then, Roger arranged for it to be kept in his secret commercial storage place as Neville's place had been shown not to be as secure as he had wished.

Roger gazed at the prototype and said to Igor that it was another beautiful Henry Moore sculpture. Igor smiled.

Roger sent a Stegan coded message to Peter letting him know that the new prototype was now completed and ready for testing, and that he would inform him when the testing was to occur, which would be in three months time.

Roger met Vivian in her true apartment and explained to her that his new prototype had now been constructed and was awaiting testing.

"When are you going to test it?" She asked.

Roger said, "I will test it when I return from Havana on the next leave cycle." He continued, "You know that, by reporting this to your Control before we leave, puts us in grave danger when we come back."

I am thinking of asking Igor to come with us, as he helped me build the prototype; which leaves him open to attack if it gets known, and he can help with the completion of the RFID project and eventually work as the colonel.

Vivian had no objections to his proposal.

Roger walked back to his offices and met Igor. He asked him if he would like to come to Havana with Vivian and himself when we return.

He asked, "What would I do there and how long would it be for?"

Roger told him about the RFID and the need for another colonel and that if the US military was happy with him, he would continue to work for them after the RFID project was finished.

If he agreed, then Roger's remaining time in Rochester would be spent arranging with the university for his release, and Vivian's time would be spent arranging with her control as well as the Havana control for Igor's change of duties.

Igor agreed, and the wheels for Igor's transfer were put into motion.

Roger, thought to himself that he wouldn't be surprised if Igor never comes back, like his ex-dean, as his work would be interesting, he would hold a responsible position, and this project would need to be implemented in many places where the US had set up manufacturing plants.

After all, had been arranged, Donald took them to Rochester airport, and they were flown to Havana, where they were picked up and driven to the Cococabana Hotel. With Vivian's help, Igor registered and was given his room a few doors away from Roger's room. She also arranged per diem for him and a hotel account for drinks, etc.

Once they had freshened up, they had a late lunch in the hotel restaurant. After lunch, Igor went exploring and Roger and Vivian went back to their room for a nap. They arranged to meet with Igor at six that night after telling him he could go and return free of charge on a red bus to Old Havana. They asked him to purchase an SIM card to use in his mobile, so they would always be able to communicate with each other. They each gave him their mobile number. Later, that afternoon, Roger received a phone call from Igor, that allowed him to record his telephone number. Roger gave the number to Vivian.

That evening they took Igor to some of the bars and cabarets in Vedado. The cabarets he liked very much were Cabaret Turquino and Cabaret Parisian. The music in the Santiago de Cuba square goes on all night and is a very high quality.

Knowing Igor, that was a good introduction for him and would enable him to enjoy himself every night.

The next morning they met for breakfast in the hotel, and Roger said that after breakfast, he wanted to introduce Igor to his team. Vivian pointed out, the all-night pizza place, should he feel hungry at any time. They told him that also they played music in the foyer.

Roger took Igor down to the laboratories and introduced him to each team member and also to the Administrative Assistant, who will be your main helper. After the introductions, they spent the next couple of days going through each member's log book and interviewing each about his contribution to the project and checking that he had no interpersonal problems with any of the other team members, and then he checked their progress in meeting their milestones. He explained to Igor that each team member was to upload each day his work for the day on Roger's server under his own name for Roger to inspect for problems.

After these exercises were complete, he was there to answer any problems that they may have.

These procedures were to be followed for the next three months during which time Igor would become familiar with all aspects of the project and the strengths and weaknesses of each team member as well as the administrative side of the job.

Igor, expressed his gratitude to Roger for giving him this opportunity, as he found the work most interesting and stimulating, and he now could see how a team of motivated people could become very creative.

Roger said to Igor that the team had now been working on this project for nine months and when this present three months is completed, they should be ready for production, which will be exciting for everyone.

Roger said to Igor that he needed him to help in the testing of the Telecom prototype, so he should pencil into his diary that his Rochester return occurs when Vivian, and I return. He can return to Havana whenever he wanted within the one-month leave, but not after. Vivian would give him the contacts' name and telephone number with whom he was required to liaise to leave and return to Havana and Rochester. In time, he would be the man whom everyone had to clear with if they wanted to purchase parts, take leave, book cars or the private jet, etc., and he would know the fine details of the Rochester, and Havana control personnel. He eventually would become the Havana control.

As this latest tour neared its conclusion, Vivian checked to see how her Havana control and how the US military felt about Igor. All results were positive and if he continued like he had been doing, he had a job for life and would start moving through the ranks.

Roger transferred, all the circuits and notes that each member of his team had uploaded onto Roger's server, onto his laptop so that he had a complete record of the project.

Roger said to Igor that he would not be returning to Havana after this tour had finished as it would be he who would be taking over everything. He would be liaising with the US military over the RFID project production for attaching an RFID to each of their cartons of cigars and the control centre for monitoring each carton on a national map.

As they were getting ready for dinner, there was a knocking on their door. They answered to a corridor filled with police who arrested them on charges of stealing national treasures. Of course, they objected to the charges. The police put them into jail and then they carefully they went through all of their belongings. After finishing with their belongings, the police checked every part of their room, including the toilet cistern. Roger said that he would lodge a complaint against them for false arrest. He asked the police, where did they obtain these federal treasures? Bring here the people who say they have sold us national treasures and show us the national treasures that they say they sold to us, Roger said angrily, but politely.

Vivian rang her control and asked her to send a US government representative to witness what the Cuban government is doing to them. The US representative came, and Vivian and Roger explained what was going on. The representative asked why this matter hadn't been taken to court by the police. The police knew they didn't have a case, so they remained silent. Eventually, the police let them go without any apologies.

When they were out of earshot from anybody, Roger said he thought, that one member or more of his team must have reported that they noticed us exploring the tunnels, especially when I took leave when we first came back during the last tour here. It is lucky that we were not greedy and took more booty, otherwise we would be sitting in a cold, damp cell on a bug ridden mattress for the next, who knows, number of years.

Roger went to dinner with Vivian in the hotel. Igor, as usual went to one of his drinking pubs, as there he had made his own set of friends.

Vivian told Roger that she would be transferred to another project after his prototype had been tested as there was no longer any need to protect him or get any more information from him.

Roger said nothing as she had said it all.

The time was drawing near for Roger and Vivian to leave. Roger said to his team in the presence of Igor, they should be getting ready for mass production. They all nodded their heads and spent the next four days demonstrating every aspect of the project to Roger and Igor. After their testing was successfully completed, Roger expressed his satisfaction with their efforts and hoped everyone had personally grown with his part of the project. He also told his team that he was handing everything over to Mr. Igor Ippolotov, as he would be returning to the USA in the next couple of days. Roger said, however, Mr. Ippolotov would come with him for a couple of days to help tidy up some outstanding issues in the USA that he has. When he returned to Havana, he would be working with them on the production plans and on the central monitoring unit for the next month or so.

That evening, Roger and Vivian each gorged themselves on a large flat pan pizza and drank three bottles of house red.

They went to bed a little tipsy.

The next morning during breakfast, Vivian arranged for the three of them to return to Rochester.

Once they arrived in Rochester Igor disappeared, and Vivian was busy with her controller arranging with her, the details of her new project. Roger rang Neville, who said he found a buyer who was prepared to pay twenty-five thousand dollars for each coin, which is a far less than the fifty-three thousand dollars expected. Roger agreed, and Neville gave him forty-seven thousand, five-hundred for both coins after he deducted his five-percent brokerage.

Roger went to his storage place and took out four gold pieces of eight, leaving him with four pieces still in storage.

That afternoon, on meeting with Vivian, Roger gave her four gold pieces of eight and twenty-three thousand five hundred dollars for her pieces of eight coins. He explained that he only got twenty-five thousand dollars for each coin, which was less than half of the fifty-three thousand dollars that he expected. Still, if you release them slowly onto the market, you will make a cool ninety-five thousand, and that will permit you to buy a few daiquiris.

Roger said that she was buying tonight. She agreed.

Roger opted for Lobster and crab meat with two bottles of house white. Not to be outdone, Vivian ordered the same.

Over dinner, Vivian asked Roger if he would allow her to witness the Telecom prototype test that he would be conducting with Peter. Roger said yes, on the condition that you tell me what your next project is, after me. She went silent. After a while, she says, I am sworn to secrecy never to reveal that information to anyone. How incongruous, I am going to show you something that has never been seen by mankind before, and you will not show me something that is of no value to mankind.

Roger didn't say anything more to her on this subject, but thought how childish she was.

Vivian thought how she really didn't like arguing with him because he was so dogmatic. Thank goodness she would be finished with him in a couple of days and wouldn't have to put up with his arrogance any longer.

The next morning, Vivian was up and gone before Roger woke up.

Roger sent a coded message to Peter to let him know that he has scheduled the tests to commence tomorrow at ten in the morning, if that was suitable for him. Peter replied that the time and day were fine with him.

Roger would inform Igor that afternoon when he comes to his offices.

He wasn't too worried about Vivian because he anticipated that he would be seeing her tonight.

Roger walked over to his offices and met Igor. He let him know about tomorrow's schedule.

That evening, as Vivian didn't come home, Roger went to his drinking place and met Neville and asked him what was Vivian's new project?

Neville answered that she was chosen, from over twenty other seasoned contenders, for the task of escorting the president's wife wherever she went.

Roger said, yes, she can do the job competently, as I believe she is faster with her hands than Cassius Clay was in his hay day.

Thanks said Roger, now knowing that possibly he would never see her again.

Sorry, my friend, I have stolen your drinking partner.

Neville said, yes, I know, and we all appreciate what you have done for this highly intelligent person. He has been dying inside as a lowly unappreciated security guard who has not had the opportunity, until now, to realize his full potential.

I am glad he will be present during the testing of your Telecom project because he is a great believer in the effect that this technology will have on the future of mankind if used properly. He has always been a supporter of your project and defends it against naysayers, not that there are many in our drinking group. After closing time, Roger returned to Vivian's true apartment because in the morning, he needed to clear the small quantity of his belongings from her apartment.

The next morning he looked out of his front window and noticed an SUV slowly driving up the road. Roger thought that he was in for some trouble now as his Amazon woman has left. He grabbed his belongings and waited until the SUV was out of sight and then ran out of the front door towards his car. He got into his car and drove to Vivian's apartment. There was no SUV in sight, so he parked his car in his drive and ran into the apartment. He arranged his clothes into their drawers and wardrobe in his bedroom and the foodstuffs into the kitchen and refrigerator. After that he checked out of the front window for a prowling SUV. Not seeing one, he drove to his offices and checked again. He then parked his car outside and went into his offices. Igor was already there. Roger informs him that he is now going to get the prototype and informs him about this morning's prowling SUV outside of Vivian's apartment. Igor said he would be vigilant.

CHAPTER 16

THE PROTOTYPE IS TESTED.

Roger takes out the boxed prototype from his secret commercial storage place, as today is the prototype testing day. He takes it back to his laboratory to a nervously waiting Igor and sets it up ready for testing. As expected, Vivian didn't come, as she would have been adjusting to her new job.

Igor asks, "How does the prototype operate if it doesn't use standard electromagnetic propagation principles?" Roger replied, "It uses the principles of Quantum Mechanics."

Igor asks Roger to explain briefly.

Roger answers: "We first have to consider the double slit experiment and entanglement to see why we cannot rely on our classical understanding of the world when dealing with quantum mechanics and to see what is the meaning of the dual particle-wave nature of matter.

Take a solid plate with two equal upright slits, cut out and now fire at it ball bearings, each having a diameter less than the width of a slit. After a sufficient number has been fired, two unrelated vertical patterns would be seen on the wall behind the slits. If the solid plate was immersed in water and a splash was made in front of the screen, two different water waves would come out from behind the screen. These waves would cross over and interfere with each other, forming many vertical lines of maximum and minimum wave intensities, with one maximum intensity vertical pattern centered between both slits and a vertical wave pattern of minimum intensity either side of it. The same pattern is repeated either side of the main pattern, and so on.

Just described is the classical result, where we see what happens when we use a real-life size ball-bearing. If, everything remains equal, except that the ball-bearings are reduced to the size of electrons (Diameter of an electron $d \approx 5.63 \times 10^{-15}$ m) and fired at the two slit screen, we do not get the same two vertical patterns as before, but a multi-banded interference pattern like those produced by waves. Even if, one electron at a time is fired at the screen over a longer period of time, the same pattern is built up. That is, the single electron goes through both slits at the same time and then as it is in a superposition with itself; it interferes with itself on the other side of the screen as a wave would do.

Here is the interesting part; when a monitoring device tries to observe, which slit a single-electron passes through, the electron reverts to a particle, as if it was aware that it was being watched. That is, the wave function of the electron collapses into a particle when being observed, showing the dual particle-wave nature of the electron."

Igor asks, "How are we going to test both transmitter and receiver both ways, when we have only one prototype? We need two transmitters and two receivers."

Roger replies, "A good question for someone with only electromagnetic knowledge."

Roger continues, "We have come a long way from the basics, namely: if we extend our minds to action at a distance, which is the interaction of objects that are separated by arbitrarily large distances, we get into the realm of Entanglement. One particle of an entangled pair knows what measurement has been performed on the other, and with what outcome, even though there are no known means for such information to be communicated between the particles. At the time of measurement, also, the particle may be separated by arbitrarily large distances. Much like an electron that knows it is being observed when it goes through a slit, even if it was being observed a million miles away.

If we generate entangled pairs locally, say a pair for each bit of a PCM codeword, then one-half of the entangled pair for each bit, instantly extends all over and to the ends of the Universe and is received by anyone with a properly coded PCM receiver/transmitter chip to decode the entangled particle coming in. The receiver contains a photocell to supply power to the PCM chip to operate, even at the far reaches of the Universe. The other half of the entangled pair is read out on the local prototype, as it is the local half of the pair.

The far end person or persons, once receiving the local transmission, uses the received half of the entangled pair to read the message into its receive buffers and in addition, stimulate another entangled pair to combine with a message from its transmit buffers to transmit back a new message to the sender and to the rest of the Universe."

Roger could see Igor's eyes were glazing over, so stopped his lecturing. OK Igor, we are beginning our tests to Peter now.

Roger rings Peter and says, "Now we start."

Roger entered into the prototype the activation codes and watched the front screen LEDs to see if the codes had been accepted, and the prototype activated. They both heaved a sigh of relief when the unit LEDs gave an OK readout and gave a confirmatory single BEEP indicating that the prototype had been properly turned on and was ready for transmission.

"Here we go with our first transmission," says Roger. He transmits to Peter from his computer, a picture of himself comprising millions of bits and awaits Peter's response.

A minute or so later, a copy of a photograph of Peter's face with the annotation, "All received well here, congratulations and have a drink for me!" Appears on Roger's computer screen.

Both men smiled at each other and started packing up, to send the prototype to its commercial safe place. When the prototype was returned, Roger goes back to his offices and picks up Igor. They adjourned to a restaurant where they both celebrated by dining and by Igor drinking, copious quantities of Vodka and Roger red wine.

The next day, Roger awoke lying on his bed, fully clothed late in the morning. He was in his apartment, and he remembered his celebration with Igor the previous night, but couldn't remember how he got home.

Igor returned to Havana the next day.

Roger felt extremely depressed as: yesterday's successful Telecom project testing was the result of two year's work and had left a large hole in his thinking; the RFID had reached its proper conclusion, and he was no longer involved with it, and finally; Vivian had moved on to bigger and better things, and he missed her like he missed Ming.

Like Vivian, he now had to move on.

He decided to improve, in the short term, his Telecom project by making it more flexible. His major problem was the governments vying for its theory and test results. It was a reality now that it had been tested, and the theory verified that it was a modern-day Pandora's box. He realized that it opened newer fields than he could ever imagine. As only Igor and Peter knew of the prototype's success, and nobody knew where the prototype and the theory was stored, it may be better to leave them untouched.

His problem was that he was a marked man and agents from all over the world wanted him for their own designs. He thought that he should go away somewhere until things settled down.

He rang Karim and said he was available should there be any suitable project for him.

Karim replied, "Well done on the successful completion of the RFID project in Havana. I will put my feelers out and get back to you. Give me a couple of days."

After a couple of days, Karim rang him back to let him know that there was no open position available at this time.

Roger decided to modify his prototype by adding video circuits and putting a far end video transmitter/receiver pair in the next room that was watching television. In addition, he placed a second video transmitter/receiver pair as part of the prototype next to him. By turning on the distant end transmitter and the near end receiver of the video circuits, he could watch the television by controlling the arrangement using his near end transmitter and far end receiver.

To modify the existing prototype to accept the new video circuits was not a simple job, so Roger started building a new prototype from scratch. He built into it video control units that allowed the far end to be controlled from wherever his viewpoint was, that is, local or distant. This meant building two new prototypes, which allowed him independent communications from wherever he was.

He sent a coded email to Peter letting him know of his plans, and that he would be sending by courier a completed unit when it was ready.

Three weeks later, Roger completed the two units with a self destruct mechanism built into each and sent one to Peter, to commence testing when he received it. Roger sent the activation codes for each unit. His voice coded unit being replaced by a picture of P.A.M. Dirac a pioneer of Quantum Mechanics.

The self destruct mechanism could be self activated or activated by either unit. When in self activated, mode it was used to prevent tampering, that is after three unsuccessful attempts to activate, it would blow up with bangs, sparks and fire, leaving an unrecognizable molten mass of plastic and metal. When activated by the distant unit it was a theft disabling mechanism.

When Peter was ready, he sent a coded email to Roger stating that he was ready. They both activated their units, and they could both see each other's image and listen to each other as if they were face to face.

Peter said, "I've got to give it to you; your creation is something truly amazing."

Roger said, "Thanks, but I am not sure I should release it at this time because I think it would cause instability in all facets of life throughout the world."

Peter replied, "Yes, but that is not your responsibility. You are not God, so don't act like you are."

Roger replied; you may be correct, and I will think about what you have said some more.

Roger checked that all of his new circuits and notes had been uploaded, and nothing remained on his computer.

His new unit was the size of a miniature video unit, with fewer controls. Due to the lack of bandwidth constraints, the video picture was perfect and instantaneous. The transmitter could have been over the other side of the universe, and the picture would still be as pristine due to the entanglement principle that he used. In addition, it would be in real time as there would be no delay in transmission like there is in electromagnetic transmission. So, a thousand light years happen immediately. This means that a transmitter sitting on the edge of the event horizon would inform the receiver what is happening at the moment of the big bang.

Roger was not sure how he should hand over his invention to his hegemonistic government. This would take more thinking and more soul searching. Whoever he handed it to, would exploit it as if they had been its inventor. This type of intellectual theft, he despised. He could see in his mind's eye, the various panels that would be set up on the television networks each with their neat trimmed white-bearded residential head monkey. This ape would be gesticulating and would be pontificating about the prototype's pros and cons as if he was the one who knew every aspect of its design, operation and capabilities, and who was going to make the decision on how it was to be used.

Media, Government and Military are all ministries of fear and misinformation. They can never give the same story because each has its own conflicting agenda.

Roger kept coming back to the same decision not to release it to anyone or any group at the present time. However, as Peter had the other working unit, and he would like to demonstrate it to Igor when he returns off of leave, he decided to build another unit. This unit would permit conference calls to be allowed or not allowed.

Two weeks later Roger had his updated unit fully equipped with conference calling; self destructs mechanism and recording of close and distant events. He tested it out by himself, and recorded events in the near and far units to his satisfaction.

The size was still the same. He had another box constructed to store his new unit.

He uploaded all of his new circuits to his Internet safe place and after checking that there was nothing left on his computer, he switched it off.

He took both of his boxed units to his commercial safe storage place and put them under lock and key.

He locked his lab and office and walked over to his car. Vivian was running towards him.

"You want to take me to lunch?" She said.

Roger answered, "No! You take me to lunch to celebrate your appointment as the First Lady's bodyguard."

She was completely flattened. "How do you know that?" She asked.

Roger asked, "Are you taking me to lunch or not?"

She agreed, and they went to a steak place and drank two bottles of house red. She persisted, asking him how he knew. Roger answered by saying if you do people favors, then they will do you favors and that is how I found out. Don't worry, it wasn't whilst I was in my drinking place and some inebriate says, "I noticed your girlfriend on TV last night walking just behind the First Lady."

However, I'm sure many have seen you and recognized who you are.

Vivian asked, "How did your prototype tests turn out?"

Roger didn't want to let her know just yet, so he said that he hadn't tested it yet as Peter fell ill and hasn't fully recovered.

"What is wrong with him?" She asked. Roger answered; he caught Chicken Pox, and then Chinese Flu virus followed by Mongolian Maiden's Malt virus.

Vivian said that she hoped that he would recover quickly.

Yes, I also hope he gets over it soon so that I can test out my prototype. Roger answered.

Vivian asked Roger if he had any belongings in her true apartment as she had been told to vacate it today. Handing back to her the keys, Roger answered that he had nothing there.

She left, and Roger waved her off.

Roger was feeling a bit down after she left, and wished she hadn't come. To compensate, he went to his delicatessen and purchased a large selection of cheese, salami, French breads and cheese biscuits and four bottles of Cab Merlot. When he returned to his apartment, he spread everything out on his dining room table in readiness for an eating session.

He ate and drank like there will be no tomorrow, enjoying his solitude without having to worry about that other gannet, named Vivian. After two bottles of Red, he slept until the evening. He then went to his drinking place and met Neville there. They caroused, enjoying themselves, until closing time. Neville told Roger that Igor would come back on leave the day-after tomorrow.

Roger said, "Good."

Roger returned to his apartment and continued eating his fare for the next two hours and again fell asleep.

He awoke to a knocking on his front door and the sound of the chimes; it was Vivian, who said, "I have told you before, never to eat cheese and salami without telling me first."

She moved straight to the dining table and started stuffing herself and whilst doing this, she opened a bottle of Red and quaffed it between mouthfuls of cheese, salami and bread.

Looking at her, you would have thought that she had never eaten a spread like this in her life before this time.

Roger asked her, "What are you doing here? You will end up getting the sack if you keep running off like this."

Vivian answered that it was all above board because she was not in her working time. Furthermore, she was being shifted to Capitol Hill, so she couldn't come here again when she felt like it.

Roger asked, "When do you have to return to your job?"

She answered tomorrow morning, first thing.

Roger asked, "Are you going to drive your car to Capitol Hill?"

She answered, "Yes, probably tomorrow."

Roger continued, "Have they given you an apartment?"

"Yes, like the one I have here."

"Are we going to have fun?" She asked.

The next morning she left as she said she would do.

After Vivian had left, Roger went down to his commercial storage place and took out his two prototypes and brought them back to his offices. Later, that morning, Igor arrived at Roger's offices and after scaring off Lina, who was scurrying around at the end of the corridor, he greeted Roger, who escorted him into his laboratory. After locking the doors, Roger showed him the two new prototypes and activated them. He gave one to Igor and kept the latest one for himself. Roger demonstrated all of its most-recent capabilities to Igor and said he should now be able to make conference calls to Peter. Roger called Peter, letting him know Igor was with him, and since the last time they had spoken together that he had made two new prototypes, each more advanced than the previous one. He said to Peter that he wanted to test the conference call feature between the three of them. Roger switched the feature on and immediately the three of them could see and speak to each other as if they were all in the same room. Each person could move their finger across the screen to select with whom to talk or the pair to whom they wanted to talk. Roger discussed the extra features he added, such as the various combinations of video recording.

He was satisfied that the tests were successful like everyone else who was involved. He packed up the prototypes in their boxes and took them back to his commercial safe storage and placed them under lock and key. He paid for five more years of storage and instructed the storage owners, that if the lot was not claimed by the end of this time, it was to be destroyed.

Igor went his own way, and Peter returned to work.

Roger went back to his apartment to take a nap until it was drinking time. He awoke around seven and finished off the food that Vivian had left for him, which was still a substantial meal. He finished her unfinished bottle of wine and then went to his drinking place and caroused with Igor and Neville until closing time. Igor mentioned that he would be returning to Havana the day-after tomorrow, and would call by Roger's offices tomorrow morning.

Roger opened his offices at quarter past-eight in the morning knowing that Igor would be there at eight-thirty.

At eight-thirty as anticipated, Igor arrived, and they warmly greeted each other.

Roger suggested that they went to a coffee shop and drink coffee? They walked over to the nearest coffee shop and sipped their coffee.

Igor, told Roger that his team now had no work as the RFID successfully completed its manufacturing. Can you give me some suggestions on what they could be doing at the present time.

Roger said, sure. They can be putting the RFID project to use in various other industries, such as sticking RFID modules on containers for the container industry, so that their containers can be traced anywhere in the world allowing missing or stolen containers to be traced or tracked down. Each RFID active tag would contain the container number, the consignee, the ship's name and the type of product that the container held, etc. If this is of interest, I suggest that you and your team visit the container companies in Cuba with the view of securing a contract with them.

The various Cuban manufacturing companies, for example, sugar cane candies, that export their products internationally and who pack their product into cartons, similarly can be approached.

Roger said, try these for a start, then put your question to your team members to see what they come up with. Remember your team members come from the other nearby countries to Cuba, and they may have special needs that Cuba doesn't have.

Igor said to Roger, now that your Telecom project is complete, and whilst you are thinking about how to present it to the world, why don't you return to Havana and get something moving there for all of us? You will be given the identical salary, per diem and leave entitlements as you enjoyed on your previous contract and even the same hotel room.

Your contract can be terminated by you at any time with one day's notice, and you can employ one other person to assist you, who would be on the same benefits and conditions as you, said Igor, having Vivian in mind.

Roger said, let me think about it overnight, and then I will give you my answer before you return to Havana.

The next morning, Roger went over to the dean's office with Igor and arranged with the university for Roger's hire for an indefinite period, to commence from tomorrow. It was nothing new to his dean now as he had been down this road a couple of times before with Roger and Igor.

That night, Igor, Neville and Roger caroused until closing time.

The next day, on his arrival at the Hotel Cococabana, Roger registered with Igor's assistance, then settled into his previous hotel room. Igor arranged for him to meet his team at two in the afternoon. He went to breakfast with Igor and had his usual morning meal of bacon, eggs, tomato on toast with sausage. Even though it must have been close to a year since Igor took over, nothing had changed.

At two in the afternoon, Igor and Roger met the assembled team. After the usual social formalities, Igor explained that Dr. Redman had returned to work with you on new RFID projects in the same capacity as he worked with you previously. Nothing had changed, only the project.

Roger noticed the happy smiles on all of their faces, without exception. Igor then handed over the floor to Roger.

Roger asked his team if they had any ideas about a new project. There was no response as they had never thought about anything other than the Cigar tracking RFID. Roger said, not having any thoughts on the subject at the moment is not a problem as he had a couple of ideas that he would present to them, to determine which one they should like to commence with first.

Roger said, your RFID project can be used in various other industries, such as attaching RFID modules on containers for the container industry, so that their containers can be traced anywhere in the world allowing missing or stolen containers to be traced or tracked down. Each RFID active tag would contain, as a suggestion; the container number, the consignee, the ship's name and the type of product that the container held, etc. This list would be added to and modified by the container company. I suggest that we visit the container companies in Cuba with the view of securing a contract with them.

Another suggestion made to his team was, the various Cuban manufacturing companies, for example, sugar cane candies, that export their products internationally and who pack their product into cartons, similarly can be approached.

Roger asked his team for comments and any other suggestions. They commented that they wished to visit the container owners in the first instance and once that one gets going, then approaching other Cuban manufacturers and perhaps, even employing more engineers.

Roger asked his team to set up meetings with the container people with a view to providing them with a service, along the lines already described.

Roger said that if the container people expressed an interest, they could employ us through the US military and this is why he needed Igor in on these meetings, so he could provide details of the US military's interest and involvement.

Initial meetings with the main container company were arranged, and Igor, Roger and one team member attended. Roger explained what technically he could do for them, and Igor explained how they were structured and the team member explained the time frame for their development and implementation process. The container people expressed a strong interest in their technology and asked for a second meeting to be scheduled in a week's time, giving them time to formulate some sensible questions and provide them with a list of what should be contained in each active tag and where their control panel was to be placed, that showed on a world map where each container was located.

As the number of meetings increased as time passed, so did the project details become more defined, and the contract details clearer. All parties; US military, Roger's team and the container company were all satisfied. Roger's team member was changed at each meeting, so that the team remained actively involved without being too large a number at each meeting.

The team members were most enthusiastic as they had a hand in defining this project. They worked on their project in their laboratories, together with a container company employee who was there to check that what was being designed was what was required.

They worked well and after three months, Roger was due for leave. Igor arranged for him, the commercial private jet back to Rochester and a car to take him to and from each airport. Igor said he would go on leave when Roger returned.

Chapter 17

Surprise!

After a heavy night with Neville, Roger awoke, and he was very hungry and looked forward to a bacon, egg and toast breakfast with fruit juice and coffee. After showering and changing his clothes he walked downstairs and noticed his car was still parked in its usual place. All is in order, he thought. He started walking to his usual cafe thinking about how he was going to enjoy eating heartily in a few minutes when he noticed an apparition running towards him. Was this somebody who looked very much like Ming? He thought.

When she was about twenty yards away, she yelled at the top of her voice, "Where have you been for the last year and a half? I thought you had run off from me."

Roger thought; so she didn't die in the prototype bomb explosion. He yelled back, "What have you been doing?"

They walked towards Roger's cafe, and Roger had to answer Ming's questions before he could get a word in. When he had answered all of her questions, except his success with the prototype tests, and orders for breakfast had been placed, she was of the mind to answer his questions. Not that he was really interested in anything she would have to say as he knew it would all be lies and then more lies. Entertainment value only and he didn't need to laugh right now as he was trying to concentrate on eating his breakfast.

Ming continued, "Did you know those foreign agents who stole your prototype blew themselves up? You are a naughty boy planting a bomb in your prototype so that it would explode if it was not handled properly." They blamed me, you know. Roger asked, "How do you know that?"

She replied, "Two of them tried to kill me after the bomb went off. They came to my safe house and crept up the stairs, but I killed them once they had entered my front door. After that, I killed the other three living in a motel after they returned to their motel by taxi."

Roger knew better than to follow this line of questioning as she did not want to disclose to him any of her covert operations and would start making up stories as she was not as open as Vivian.

Roger said to her, in earnest, "Why don't you get back to Physics and stop playing secret agent?" She replied, "I would do anything you asked of me if you marry me."

Roger was truly touched by her frankness, and by the love that she felt for him at that moment.

Roger replied, "I would marry you if I could trust you, but you cannot control your mouth and many times that has caused me considerable grief." Roger continued, "If I married you, how long do you think it would last? I wouldn't give it three months. It is better to continue the way we are."

Ming started crying and then broke into her inconsolable sobbing. "You are my life." She said between her sobs. "I love you so deeply that you are on my mind more than anything in this world."

Roger said, "OK, I will marry you, but no more spying on me and reporting my activities to the government." She reddened, forgetting that he already knew, "How do you know that?"

After a few moments she added, "I promise as we will be one."

Roger said, I have a new contract in Havana. You can return with me and be paid the same salary as, I, if you wish. It is on the design of Radio-Frequency IDentification (RFID) circuits for tracking lost or stolen containers and the US military is assisting by paying our salary and that of the team as well as our component costs as a part of the indirect support to the Cubans. It will continue for some months more, then this project will flow on and adapt to other industries.

Ming burst crying out loud again, this time because she was so happy. When will we get married? She asked.

Roger answered, after we return from leave from Havana, that is after four months henceforth.

As if it was like an afterthought Roger asked, "Can I leave all the wedding arrangements for you and your girlfriends?"

Ming replied, "Yes. I will happily relieve you of this task, but you must advise me when I ask."

Do you need to inform your control that you are going to Cuba after one month, for a year?

Yes, but I will inform her after you make your arrangements. Roger rang Igor and informed him that he would be bringing Ming with him as his employee, when he returned. Igor said, I will arrange with my people here and when I return, I will arrange there, as we will have a week during which we both overlap.

The next month was wedding preparation time for Ming, and all the details were taken care of by herself and her friends. The wedding invitations were prepared but not yet posted.

When Igor came out on leave, he arranged for Roger to be Ming's sponsor and booked the jet to take them back to Havana. He had already normalized her immigration in Havana. They arrived in Havana and were picked up at the airport and taken to the hotel where they both registered and each given a room key to Roger's room. They relaxed that afternoon with Ming adjusting to her surroundings by walking the hotel grounds. She said to Roger, "This must have been a top hotel in its day."

Roger said, "Yes, and they still play music in the afternoon, evening and night in the lobby and in the bar area."

She was most happy to see the all-night pizza place in the hotel.

That evening, Roger showed her old Havana where they enjoyed themselves until they were exhausted.

The next morning he took her down to the laboratories and introduced her as Dr. Lovelace. He told the team that she would be working with us on the present project and on the new project. Each team member introduced himself to her and briefly explained his part in the project and his area of expertise.

Roger explained the purpose of the present project and how far they had advanced. He explained how his team operated by uploading to their own name, found on his server, their days work just before closing time.

He then spent the next week explaining all the detailed design, testing and circuit schematics and how the circuit schematics were outsourced for turning into occupied printed circuit boards, returned ready for testing. By the time they were due to take their leave, she was very familiar with all aspects of the project. Igor had returned from leave, and was soon to go again. Roger said to him, Ming and the team would be approaching the candy industry for contracts with them on their return from their leave. Igor said he would enjoy joining them in their meetings in the days to come.

Roger and Ming returned to Rochester. Ming was highly excited as her wedding Day was approaching.

Roger said to Ming, "As part of our marriage. I will not keep any secrets from you, unless I have your permission."

Ming asked him if he was going to tell her that he was gay and already was married. No, he replied, you should know that I am not of that persuasion. Yes, what is it? Are you marrying me for my money? Because, if that is the case, you're committing a major screw-up, I gave it all to the Blind Cat's Association last week. Roger said, "No!"

She was starting to get bored with her own jokes and said, "What is it then?"

Roger said, "It is to do with my project."

She bleated, "Did somebody steal it again for the fortieth time?"

Roger answered patiently, "No, nothing like that."

Ming by now most exasperated, said, "Well, what is it? I know . . ." she interrupted herself. "It was all a big mistake and really was a failed ice-cream making machine?"

Roger said, "No."

Ming screeched at him, "Why don't you tell me before I punch your stupid head."

Roger answered, "Later, when you have calmed down."

She bellowed at him, "I am calm, look at me!"

Roger laughed at her and said, "Why are you trembling so?"

She started crying, "You are going to tell me that you have canceled the wedding?"

Roger said, "No, I have successfully finished my Telecom project."

Roger went and lay down on his bed to have a short nap. Before five minutes had passed, he was snoring. Ming came into the bedroom and demanded to know, "What do you mean you have successfully finished your Telecom Project?"

Roger was roused back to consciousness and answered, "What do you mean you have successfully finished your Telecom Project?"

She slapped him until he was fully awake. Say it again, she said. Roger answered, "I have successfully finished my Telecom project, and I can talk to people the other side of the Universe."

She hugged and kissed him over and anew, saying congratulations my clever husband.

Ming gurgled, "Show me darling."

Roger replied, "Wait here and I will go and fetch it."

Roger went to his commercial safe storage place and took the two units out and brought them back to the apartment to show Ming. When he returned he gave her one after activating it. He activated the second unit and walked into the bedroom. Everything was crystal clear. She says, it's beautiful.

Roger said, if I call Peter, we can have it in conference mode. Peter came on line noticing that he was being called, and Roger placed his unit into the conference mode. The three of them discussed Ming's wedding, and she described the preparations that were being made. After the conversation concluded, Roger closed the units down at his end and packed them into their boxes and took them back to his commercial storage place, again securing them under lock and key.

Ming asked Roger if she could tell her control. Roger said please do not breathe a word of it to anyone because it will cost us our lives and don't think you're stronger and faster than the rest of the world. You made me a marriage pledge, so don't break it, because if you do blab, and you are not dead I will have the marriage annulled. That I promise!

OK, she said I will not say anything to anyone, I promise.

Roger held her tight and told her that he loved her very, very, much.

Whilst Ming is making her wedding arrangements, Roger is making arrangements to get the prototype out of his commercial storage place again so that this time Igor, who has returned to Rochester on leave, can complete some final adjustments. Lina tries to snoop on Roger's offices, but Igor sends her packing, stating that he will make a report to the University Administration on her behavior.

Peter sends a Stegan coded email to Roger informing him of the number of toasts made to Roger last night by Peter's co-workers on his pending marriage to Ming. Once back in his offices Roger informs Igor of the latest news from Peter and hands to him one of the prototypes.

Roger asks Igor to peak up the PCM (Pulse-Code Modulation) unit on the Prototype Transmitter used for coding the message prior to coding the entangled pair generator. Whilst this is happening, Roger tunes up the entangled pair receptor bringing in the distant, half of the pair sent from afar more clearly. When finished, both men pack the prototype into an especially made wooden box Igor previously had made, ready for sending to Roger's commercial safe place. The finalized design plans are sent back to a secret storage location on the Internet and Roger's work laptop is turned off. The office looks like it had never been occupied. A van pulls up outside, and three agents jump out waving their guns. Igor says to Roger these are not members of the Russian faction, and they want to kill Ming for putting down two of their men a year or more ago.

Igor fires and kills one of the agents. Realizing there are other agents, he then calls for other security guards to come to their aid. Two more shots are fired, killing the second and third of the three foreign agents and after that, Ming suddenly appears unfazed. She calls her control and explains to her what happened and asks her to send a cleanup squad to take the dead agents from Roger's offices and clean up.

Roger says to himself, quoting Neville: she eats people like you for breakfast. He took the two fine tuned units back to his commercial storage place and put them both under lock and key. Roger returned to his offices to rejoin Ming.

During the walk back to Roger's apartment Ming asks Roger if he is going to give the prototype and design details of his invention to the Government.

Roger answers, "I don't think that is a clever thing to do, because it will cause our country to become more arrogant and controlling of other countries than it is already." Roger continued, "Better to call a World Conference on New Technologies and demonstrate the prototype's capabilities and the far-reaching implications of this newly applied Physics. Then, everyone has a chance."

Ming looked worried and said, "Our Government will not let you have that freedom. If anyone hears you express this view, we will be dead within hours of them reporting it." She continued, "Roger, as soon as the wedding is over, we should go elsewhere for a while and let things settle down."

Roger replied, "Yes, let's do that and tour France. We should go as soon as the wedding has finished and not attend the reception."

Ming asked, "Have you got another feeling?"

Roger replied, "This feeling is very strong."

They felt happier as they had come to a common agreement. Ming held Roger's arm tightly as they walked the remaining distance to the apartment.

CHAPTER 18

CONCLUSION

The next morning, Ide comes with Government agents to Roger's offices demanding to know where the prototype, and its designs are being kept. Igor states that if they do not desist in their harassment, a foreign country will be given the prototype and design details. Igor firmly asks them to leave. Ide shouts at Igor that he hasn't seen the last of him and then leaves with his agents.

Roger dresses for the wedding. Ming goes to her dressmaker and has her wedding dress put on. They both leave for the church in different cars. Peter, who is the best man, rides with Roger.

Once the marriage ceremony has completed, they and their entourage leave for the reception, but Roger and Ming with Peter and Igor's knowledge leave for Paris. Roger and Ming return to Havana at the end of their leave to complete their present candy project and commence new ones.

The food is excellent; the drink is flowing, and the wedding guests are beginning to become inebriated. The people sitting in the seats meant for the bride and groom are very happy, and they are the picture of newlyweds.

Two shots ring out and the unsuspecting proxy bride, and her groom are dead.

They are assassinated by the driver assassin, the one who was not killed by Ming's mobile bomb placed in the Avensis glove box by her a couple of years ago. This driver assassin falsely blamed Ming for the Prototype explosion that killed Ming's group, because she was the only one not killed in her group.

Every Government has a vested interest in not letting any other government get the prototype and its design, so the guilty government will never be known.

Once Roger hears about what happened, he made the decision not to open Pandora's box and just leave things as they are.

Roger's design is lost to the world. The prototype is with a secure commercial storage place that will not release it to anyone. Even if it was seized, it would self destruct if the correct activation codes were not entered after three tries. The final design is in some secret place on the Internet, known only to Roger.

Nobody wins!